Praise for Peter Handke and *Repetition*

"Peter Handke was and is one of the most eminent narrative and dramatic writers of postwar Europe."   —*Boston Globe*

"Every word Peter Handke speaks has consequences."
                                                       —*The New Republic*

"Peter Handke can write with an intensity that scalds the reader....A dense, complex examination of the limits of language and the limits of the world."   —*San Francisco Chronicle*

"What distinguishes Handke's cerebral fiction is that he both feels and thinks passionately. Whether he's dissecting an emotion or propounding a character's thoughts, he can write with an intensity that makes many of his contemporaries look anemic by comparison....A writer whose own rangy trip through literature has rarely been less than fascinating."   —*The Village Voice*

"*Repetition* is a complex, thoughtful, and poignant book. A personal story of a particular individual struggling to come to terms with his particular life, of one storyteller struggling to find his voice, it is also an expansive and joyous meditation on storytelling itself."
                                                 —*The Christian Science Monitor*

"A beautiful and evocative novel...some of the most glorious lyrical prose to be found anywhere in recent years....In lyric power, in execution and, best of all, in use of the bewitching fabric of memory, Handke has written a work unexcelled in years."
                                                       —Newark *Star-Ledger*

"*Repetition* is a moving hymn to the art of storytelling."
                                                       —*The Buffalo News*

"Handke fans will be rewarded again by a radiant, at times hallucinatory narrative that seeks our spiritual freedom as it invents its own form."   —*The Boston Herald*

REPETITION

PETER HANDKE

Collier Books

Macmillan Publishing Company

New York

REPETITION

Translated

by

Ralph Manheim

Translation copyright © 1988 by Farrar, Straus and Giroux, Inc.

Originally published in German under the title *Die Wiederholung*, © Suhrkamp Verlag 1986

Published by arrangement with Farrar, Straus and Giroux, Inc.

Collier Books
Macmillan Publishing Company
866 Third Avenue, New York, NY 10022
Collier Macmillan Canada, Inc.

A portion of this book originally appeared in somewhat different form, in *The New Yorker*

Library of Congress Cataloging-in-Publication Data
Handke, Peter.
    [Wiederholung. English]
    Repetition / Peter Handke : translated by Ralph Manheim. —
1st
Collier Books ed.
        p.   cm.
        Translation of: Die Wiederholung.
        ISBN 0-02-020762-X
        I. Title.
PT2668.A5W4713   1989
833'.914—dc19   89-532   CIP

Cover art by David Monteil
Cover design by Lee Wade

First Collier Books Edition 1989

10 9 8 7 6 5 4 3 2 1

Printed in the United States of America

CONTENTS

"The kings of old died;
they could not find their food."

ZOHAR

"I stayed with this one and that one."

EPICHARMUS

"... *laboraverimus* ..."

COLUMELLA

One | THE BLIND WINDOW

A QUARTER OF A CENTURY, or a day, has passed since I arrived in Jesenice on the trail of my missing brother. I was not yet twenty and I had just taken my final school examination. I ought to have felt free, for after weeks of study the summer months lay open before me. But I had set out with mixed feelings, what with my old father, my ailing mother, and my confused sister at home in Rinkenberg. Besides, after being released from the seminary, I had got used, during the past year, to my class in the state school in Klagenfurt, where girls were in the majority, and now I suddenly found myself alone. While my classmates piled into the bus together and set out for Greece, I played the loner who preferred to go to Yugoslavia by himself. (The truth was that I simply didn't have the money for the group trip.) Another reason for my unease was that I had never been outside of Austria and knew very little Slovene, though it was hardly a foreign language for an inhabitant of a village in southern Carinthia.

After a glance at my newly issued Austrian passport, the border guard in Jesenice spoke to me in his language. When I failed to understand, he told me in German that Kobal was a Slavic name, that the word meant the span between parted legs, a "step," and consequently a person standing with legs outspread, so that my name would have been better suited to him, the border guard. The elderly official beside him, in civilian clothes, white-haired, with the round, rimless glasses of a scholar, explained with a smile that the related verb meant "to climb" or "to ride"; thus, my given name, Filip, "lover of horses," fitted in with Kobal, and he felt sure I would someday do honor to my full name. (Since then, I have often found the civil servants of this so-called progressive country, which was once part of an empire, surprisingly well educated.) Suddenly he grew grave, came a step closer, and looked me solemnly in the eye. I should know, he said, that two and a half centuries ago there had been a Slovene hero named Kobal. In the year 1713 Gregor Kobal, from near Tolmin on the headwaters of the river which in Italy farther down was known as the Isonzo, had been one of the leaders of the great Tolmin peasant revolt, and in 1714 he had been executed along with his comrades. It was he who had said—and his words were still renowned in the Republic of Slovenia—that the Emperor was a mere servant and that the people had better take matters into their own hands. Thus informed—of something I already knew—I, with my sea bag over my shoulder, was permitted to step out of the dark frontier station without showing any cash, and to set foot in the north Yugoslavian town, which in those days our school maps still identified by its old Austrian name of Assling (in parentheses), side by side with the Slovene Jesenice.

For a long while I stood outside the station, with the Karawanken Mountains, which I had seen in the distance all my life, close at my back. The city begins at the exit from the tunnel and winds down the narrow river valley, surmounted by a tenuous strip of sky, which broadens to the south and is immediately veiled by the smoke of the iron foundries. Jesenice is a long village with one exceedingly noisy street, the side streets being little more than steep paths. It was a warm evening at the end of June 1960, and the surface of the street gave off a dazzling brightness. It came to me that what made the station so dark were the buses which stopped outside the big swinging door in quick succession and drove on. Strange how soothing the overall grayness—the gray of the houses, the street, the cars, so very different from the bright colors of the cities of Carinthia, "Carinthia the beautiful" according to a nineteenth-century Slovene song—was to my eyes in the evening light. The short Austrian train that had brought me and that would soon go back through the tunnel seemed as clean and bright as a toy train beside the massive, dusty Yugoslavian trains, and the blue uniforms of its crew, who were talking loudly on the platform, provided a dash of exotic color amid the prevailing gray. It also struck me that the swarms of people in the streets of this smallish town, quite unlike the inhabitants of the small towns in my own country, took notice of me now and then but never stared at me. And the longer I stood there, the more certain I became that this was a great country.

Now, only a few hours later, how far behind me seemed my afternoon in Villach, where I had visited my history and geography teacher. We had talked about my plans for the fall: Should I do my military service at once, or get a deferment and study? But study what? And then, in one of the parks, the teacher had read me a fairy tale that he himself had written, asked me for my opinion, and listened to it with an expression of total seriousness. He was a bachelor and lived alone with his mother, who, while I was there, kept asking through the closed door whether her son was all right and whether he wanted anything. He had accompanied me to the station and there, as secretively as if he felt someone was watching, he had slipped me a bank note. I was very grateful, but I hadn't been able to show it, and now too, when I tried to visualize the man across the border, all I could see was a wart on his pale forehead. The face that went with it was that of the border guard, who was hardly older than myself and yet, to judge by his bearing, his voice, and the look in his eyes, had evidently found his place in life. Of the teacher, his apartment, and the whole of Villach I had preserved no image apart from two pensioners playing chess at a table and the glitter of the halo over the statue of the Virgin Mary on the main square.

Fully present to my mind, however—and still fully present today, twenty-five years later—was the morning of the same day, when I took leave of my father on the wooded hill from which the village of Rinkenberg took its name. With sagging knees, dangling arms, and gout-gnarled fingers, which at that moment impersonated furious clenched fists, the frail, aging man, much smaller than I, stood by the wayside Cross and shouted at me: "All right, go to the dogs like your brother, like our whole family! None of us has ever amounted to anything, and you won't either. You won't even get to be a good gambler like me." Yet, just then, he had embraced me for the first time in my life, and I had looked over his shoulder at the dewy wetness on the bottom of his trousers, with the feeling that in me he was actually embracing himself. But then in memory my father's embrace held me, not only that evening outside the Jesenice station, but down through the years, and I heard his curse as a blessing. In reality he had been deadly serious, but in my thoughts I saw him grinning. May his embrace carry me through this story.

Standing in the twilight, in the roar of the through traffic, which seemed positively soothing, I reflected that up until then I had never felt held in a woman's embrace. I had no girlfriend. When the one girl whom I knew, so to speak, embraced me, her embrace struck me as mischievous or defiant. Yet how proud I was when we walked down the street together, keeping our distance, but obviously belonging to each other in the eyes of the people coming in the opposite direction. Once somebody called from a group of strolling little-more-than-children: "Have *you* got a beautiful girl!" And another time an old woman stopped, looked from the girl to me, and said literally: "Lucky fellow!" Such moments seemed a fulfillment of longing. And then the joy, in the changing light of the movie house, of seeing the shimmering profile beside me, the mouth, the cheek, the eye. The ultimate was the sense of bodily closeness, which sometimes came unsought; even a purely accidental contact would have seemed an infringement. So perhaps I had a girlfriend after all. For to me the thought of a woman meant, not desire or lust, but the wishful image of a beautiful companion—yes, my companion would have to be beautiful!—whom I would at last be able to tell . . . Tell what? Just tell. At the age of twenty I conceived falling-into-one-another's-arms, loving, being fond of one another, as a constant, forbearing yet unreserved, calm yet exclamatory, clarifying and illuminating telling, and in that connection I thought of my mother, who, whenever I had been out of the house for any length of time, in town or alone in the woods or out in the fields, assailed me with her "Tell me." Despite frequent rehearsals, I had never, at least before her illness, succeeded in telling her anything. As a rule, I could only tell unasked—though, once launched, I needed the right questions to keep me going.

And now, outside the station, I discovered that since my arrival in Jesenice I had been silently telling my girlfriend about my day. And what was I telling her? Neither incidents nor events, but mere impressions, a sight, a sound, a smell. The jet of the little fountain across the street, the red of the newspaper kiosk, the exhaust fumes of the heavy trucks—once I told her about them, they ceased to exist in themselves and merged with one another. And the teller was not I, it was the experience itself. This silent telling deep inside me was something greater than myself. And, without growing older, the girl to whom it was addressed was transformed into a young woman, just as the boy of twenty, in growing aware of the teller inside him, became an ageless adult. We stood facing each other, exactly at eye level. This eye level was the measure of the telling. I sensed the tenderest of strengths within me. And it said to me: "Jump!"

A star appeared, a constellation in itself, in the yellowish factory sky over Jesenice, and a glowworm flew through the smoke of the street down below. Two railroad cars bumped together. In the supermarket, the checkout girls were relieved by cleaning women. At a window in a high-rise building, a man stood smoking in his undershirt.

* * *

Exhausted as after strenuous exercise, I sat in the station restaurant until almost midnight, over a bottle of the dark, sweet drink which at that time substituted for Coca-Cola in Yugoslavia. Yet I was wide awake, quite otherwise than in the evening at home—whether in the village, at the seminary, or in the city—when I was always too tired to be good company. At the only dance I was taken to, I fell asleep with my eyes open, and in the last hours of the year my father tried in vain to keep me from my bed by playing cards with me. I think that what kept me awake was not so much the strange country as being in a restaurant; in a waiting room, most likely I would soon have felt tired.

I was sitting in one of the brown wooden booths, rather like a choir stall. In front of me, the bright tiers of station platforms, and behind me, the equally bright highway with its illuminated apartment houses. Behind me, full buses were still running this way and that; in front of me, full trains. Of the travelers, I saw no faces, only silhouettes; but I saw the silhouettes through a face reflected in plate glass—my own. With the help of this reflection, which did not portray me as an individual but showed only a forehead, eye sockets, and lips, I was able to dream the silhouettes not only of the passengers but also of the apartment-house dwellers as they moved through their rooms or, occasionally, sat on the balconies. It was an airy, luminous, sharp dream in which I had friendly thoughts about all the dark figures. None of them was evil. The old people were old, the couples were couples, the families were families, the children were children, the lonely were lonely, the dogs and cats were dogs and cats, each individual was part of a whole, and I with my reflection belonged to this nation, which

I envisaged on an unceasing, peaceful, adventurous, serene journey through the night, a journey in which the sleeping, the sick, the dying, even the dead were included. I sat up straight to get a better view of my dream. The one thing that troubled me was the larger-than-life portrait of the President, hanging in the exact center of the room, over the bar. Marshal Tito was unmistakably there in his heavily braided uniform with all its decorations. Leaning forward over a table on which his clenched fist rested, he looked down at me with bright, fixed eyes. I could almost hear him say: "I know you," and I wanted to answer: "But I don't know myself."

My dream went no further until the waitress appeared in the dingy light behind the bar; in her shadowy face, nothing was distinct but her eyelids, which almost hid her eyes even when she was looking straight ahead. Suddenly, while contemplating those eyelids, I saw my mother, ghostlike but very real. She put the glasses in the sink, skewered a receipt on a spike, ran a cloth over the brass. Nameless horror when for a moment her eyes, mocking, impenetrable, met mine; horror that was more like a jolt, a shift into a larger dream. In this dream the sick woman had recovered. Thoroughly alive, she bustled, disguised as a waitress, from room to room of the restaurant. Her heels peered out of her slingback shoes. What sturdy legs my mother had now, what swinging hips, what a tower of hair. And though, unlike most of the women in the village, she knew only a few words of Slovene, here, in conversation with an invisible group of men in a neighboring booth, she spoke it with ease and self-assurance. So she wasn't the foundling, the fugitive, the German, the foreigner she had always pretended to be. For a moment, I felt ashamed that this person with the brisk movements, the singsong speech, the loud laugh, the quick furtive glances, should be my mother, and then, through this strange woman, I saw her as precisely as never before. Yes, until recently, my mother had spoken in such a singsong, and whenever she had actually started to sing, her son had wanted to stop his ears. In any choir, however large, I could instantly pick out my mother's voice: a quavering, a trembling, a fervid outpouring, which totally captivated the singer, but not the listener. And her laughter had been not only loud but positively wild, a scream, an outburst of joy, of anger, of bitterness, of contempt, of condemnation. When she cried out with pain at the beginning of her illness, her screams had still sounded like the surprised, half-amused, half-indignant laughter which she tried, more and more feebly as time went on, to cover up by singing trills. I conjured up the various voices in our household and heard my father swearing, my sister giggling and weeping in the course of muttered conversations with herself, and my mother laughing from end to end of the village—and Rinkenberg is a long village. (I saw myself as mute.) Then I realized that my mother was not merely self-assured like the waitress but positively imperious. She had always wanted to run a big hotel, with the staff as her subjects. Our farm was small and her demands were great. In her stories about my brother, he was always represented as a king cheated out of his throne.

And she saw me as the rightful heir to the throne yet doubted from the start that I would ever reign. Sometimes, in looking at me, her face froze into an expression of pity without a glimmer of compassion. I had often been characterized by someone—a priest, a teacher, a girl, a classmate; but in that silent look of my mother's I felt not only characterized but seen through and condemned. And I am sure that it wasn't after a certain lapse of time, for any specific reason, that she started looking at me like that, but that she had done so ever since I was born. She lifted me, held me up to the light, laughed inwardly, and condemned me. And later on, when I was a baby thrashing about in the grass, screaming with the love of life, she would hold me up to the sun to make sure, laugh at me, and again condemn me. I tried to think it had been the same with my brother and sister before me, but I couldn't. I was the only one who elicited the exclamation which commonly followed that merciless look: "Aren't we a pair!" which she sometimes addressed to a farmyard animal about to be slaughtered. True, at an early age I felt the need to be seen, perceived, described, known, but not like that. For instance, I had felt known on one occasion when, not my mother, but my girlfriend, had said: "Aren't we a pair!" And when for the first time, after all the years at the seminary, where no one called us by anything but our family names, I heard the girl next to me at the state school address me quite casually by my first name, I took it as a characterization that exonerated me, almost as a caress. I had a feeling of relief and I can still see the sparkle of the girl's hair. And so, once I learned to decipher my mother's looks, I knew: This is no place for me.

Yet twice in those twenty years she literally saved me. When I was transferred to the seminary from the

Gymnasium in Bleiburg, it wasn't because my parents wanted to make something better of me. (I believe my father as well as my mother were convinced that I would either amount to nothing at all or become "something out of the ordinary," by which they understood something ghoulish.) The reason for the change of schools was that at the age of twelve I acquired my first, and from the start deadly, enemy.

There had always been enmities among the village children. We were all neighbors, and proximity often made a neighbor's idiosyncrasies unbearable. It was the same among grownups, even old people. For a while two neighbors would pass each other without a greeting; one would pretend to be busy in his house or yard, and the other, within plain sight, would also be busy in his own way. All at once, even without fences, there would be an inviolable boundary between properties. Even in his own home a child who felt he had been unjustly treated by a member of the family would stand silent in a remote corner of the living room with his face to the wall, as though in observance of an old custom. In my imagination, all the living rooms of the village are joined into a single room of many corners, all of which are occupied by quarrelsome, sulking village children, until at length one of them, or all at once (as always happened in reality), breaks the spell with a word or a laugh. It's true that no one in the village referred to anyone as a friend—they spoke instead of "good neighbors"; but it is equally true that at least among the children there were no quarrels leading to lasting hostility.

Even before I came up against my first enemy, I had suffered persecution, an experience that had its

effect on my later life. But there was nothing personal
about this persecution; it was simply a child from
Rinkenberg being persecuted by children from another
village. The children from that other village had a
longer, harder way to school than we did; they had to
cross a deep ditch and, if only for that reason, were
thought to be stronger than we were. On the way home,
which as far as the fork was the same for both groups,
we Rinkenbergers were regularly chased by the Humt-
schachers. (Though they were no older than ourselves,
I couldn't see them as children. Now for the first time,
as I look at pictures on the tombstones of those killed
in early accidents, I am struck by how youthful, not to
say childlike, they all were even as young men.) For an
eternity we ran along a road (there were never any cars
at that time of day), pursued by the menacing roar of
the faceless, heavy-legged, clumsy-footed horde, brandishing gorilla-length arms like cudgels, wearing their
schoolbags on their backs like combat gear. There were
days when, hungry as I was, I would dawdle in the
safety of Bleiburg until the jungle menace had passed;
at such times the town was dear to me, though as a rule
I longed to go home. But then came a sudden change.
Once again, starting at the edge of the town, I was
pursued by the howling, so terrifying precisely because
it was incomprehensible. But this time I let my fellow
villagers run and sat down in the grass triangle enclosed
by the road and the forked path running into it. In this
moment, with the enemy bearing down on me, I was
confident that nothing would happen. I stretched out
my legs in the grass, looked southward at Mount Petzen,
which forms the Yugoslavian border, and knew that I
was safe. I felt shielded by the fact that I thought and

saw the same thing at the same time. True enough, nothing happened to me. As they came closer, my persecutors slowed down, and one or two of them followed my eyes. "It's beautiful up there," I heard. "I went up there with my father one time." I looked at them and saw that the horde had broken down into a few individuals. They smiled at me as they sauntered by, as though relieved that I had seen through their game. No words were exchanged, yet it was clear that from then on there would be no more persecution. Looking after them, I noticed their sagging knees and dragging steps. How far they still had to go in comparison with me! And I began to feel a bond with them— at a distance—as I had never done with the children next door in my own village. And with the passage of time, the chaotic, dust-raising plunging and lunging, the terrifying guttural shouts of the Humtschach horde became a dancing, skipping procession, which to this day is gamboling down that childhood road like a festive tribe, for no other purpose than to live on in this image. (It's true that when they were gone I was trembling all over and was unable to leave my grass triangle for quite some time. I leaned against a wooden milkstand and silently counted out numbers.)

But with my first enemy, nothing helped. He was the son of our next-door neighbor; his mother beat him all day long, and his father all evening. (I was never beaten at home; when my father was angry with me, he slapped his own chest or face before my eyes; most of all, he pounded his forehead with his fist, so violently that he staggered backward or fell to his knees. On the other hand, my brother, though blind in one eye, was not only beaten but locked up in the potato cellar dug into the slope behind the house, where he could certainly see more when he closed his one eye than when he kept it open.) My "little enemy"—as I call him now, in contrast to the "big enemy" I had later—never assaulted me. Yet he was instantly my enemy, at first glance, which for a long time nothing followed, not even another glance. None of the usual sticking out of tongues, spitting, tripping up. My childhood enemy did not declare himself; he was simply there with his enmity. And then his enmity erupted in aggression.

One day in church, when the Gospel was being read and we were all standing, I felt a light blow in the hollow of my knee, little more than a poke, but enough to make my knee buckle. I turned around and saw him gazing into space. From that moment on, he left me no peace. He didn't hit me, he didn't throw stones, he didn't insult me—he only blocked my way at every turn. Whenever I stepped out of the house, there he was beside me. He even came into my house—in the villages it was usual for children to go in and out of their neighbors' houses—and attacked me, so inconspicuously that no one else noticed. He never used his hands; all he ever did was push me lightly with his shoulder (you couldn't even have called it shoving as in soccer); it looked as if he was trying in a friendly way to call my attention to something, but in reality he was forcing me into a corner.

Yet as a rule he didn't even touch me, he mimicked me. I'd be walking along. He'd jump out of a bush and walk behind me, imitating my way of walking, putting his feet down at the same time as I did and swinging his arms in the same rhythm. If I broke into a run, so would he; if I stopped, so would he; if I blinked, so would he. And he never looked me in the eye; he merely studied my eyes, as he did every other part of my body, so as to detect every movement when it had hardly begun and to copy it. I often tried to mislead him about my next move, I'd feint in a wrong direction, then suddenly run away. But he never let himself be outwitted. His imitating was more like shadowing; I became a prisoner of my shadow.

Perhaps, all in all, he was just annoying. But in time this annoyance became an enmity that got under my skin. He became ubiquitous, even when he was not actually with me. When I was happy for a change, my happiness soon vanished, because in my thoughts I saw it aped by my enemy and thus called into question. And the same with all my feelings—pride, grief, anger, affection. Confronted with their shadow, they ceased to be real. And where I felt most alive, tucked away in some hiding place, I had only to make the slightest move toward something, whether it was a book, a pond, a hut in the fields, or an eye, and he would come between us and cut me off from the world. No hatred could have expressed itself more murderously than in this aping pursuit; it was as though he were driven by silent whiplashes. Since being hated to such a degree was beyond my understanding, I attempted a reconciliation. But he was not to be appeased. Not for a moment did he hesitate. Quick as a guillotine blade, he mimicked my gesture of reconciliation. Not a single day, not even a dream passed without my shadow. When I screamed at him for the first time, he didn't recoil; he pricked up his ears. My scream was the sign he had been waiting for. And in the end it was I who became violent. In fighting him at the age of twelve, I no longer knew who

I was; in other words, I ceased to be anything; in other words, I became evil. My childhood enemy showed me (and I'm sure this was just what he had planned) that I was evil, more evil than he, an evil person.

At first I only thrashed about, rather like a swimmer in fear of drowning. My enemy didn't get out of the way; on the contrary, he held out his face in a gesture of defiance. His mask was as close to me as the sidewalk might be in a dream of falling. My grabbing at it was not a defensive reflex; it was the statement, the admission, the confession the world had been waiting for: I was no better than he; at last, by my act of violence, I had admitted that I was my enemy's still more evil enemy. And true enough, at the touch of his saliva and nasal mucus, I had a twofold feeling of violence and injustice, an experience I never want to repeat. Before my eyes a mask of triumph: "You've passed the point of no return!" Then I kicked him in the behind, I put my whole heart into it. He didn't defend himself but stood his ground with an indelible grin. He had attained his aim: from that day on, I was "his aggressor," so to speak, in the eyes of all. Now he had every reason and right to hound me. Our hitherto secret enmity had blossomed into a war, which had to be fought openly and could only end in the damnation of us both. One day his father saw me beating his son. He came running, separated us, threw me to the ground, and trampled me with his stable boots (subjecting me to a long, high-pitched litany of names such as escaped my own father only when he felt the need of warding off landslides, lightning, hail, or household and garden pests).

This beating was a lucky thing for me, the only good luck, I might say, that came my way for the next

ten years. It loosed my tongue; I managed to tell my
mother (yes, my mother) about my enemy. My story
began with the command: "Listen!" and ended with
another command: "Do something!" As usual in our
family, it was my mother who did something. Her action
consisted in taking her twelve-year-old son, under the
pretext that the priest and the teacher had won her
over, to be examined for admission to the seminary.

In Klagenfurt, on the way back from the examination,
we missed the last train to Bleiburg. We walked out of
town and stood on the road in the rain and darkness,
though I have no recollection of getting wet. After a
while, the driver of a small truck on his way to Maribor
on the lower Drava in Yugoslavia, stopped and picked
us up. There were no seats in the back, and we sat on
the floor. As my mother had told the man in Slovene
where we were going, he tried at first to chat with her.
But when it became apparent that her Slovene amounted
only to formulas of greeting and snatches of a few folk
songs, he fell silent. From this silent ride through the
night on the metal floor of the truck, I preserved a
feeling of oneness with my mother which remained in
force at least throughout my ensuing seminary years.
My mother had got a permanent for the trip; for once
she wasn't wearing her head scarf, and despite the
heaviness of her fifty-year-old body, her face, touched
now and then by a beam of light, looked youthful to
me. She sat there hugging her knees, with her handbag
beside her. On the outside, the raindrops ran obliquely
down the windowpanes, and inside, tools, packages of
nails, and empty jerricans collided with us. For the first
time in my life, I felt a kind of release, of impetuous

joy within me—something on the order of confidence. With my mother's help, I had been put on the path that was right for me. This woman was a stranger to me, I had often literally denied her and have often denied her since—the word "mother" had seldom crossed my lips—but on that summer evening in 1952 it struck me for once as self-evident that I had a mother and was her son. That evening she was not the peasant woman, the farm worker, the stable maid, the church-goer she often impersonated in the village, but revealed what was behind all this: manager rather than house-wife, traveler rather than stay-at-home, woman of action rather than onlooker.

Where the road turned off to Rinkenberg, the driver let us out. I didn't even notice that my mother had taken my arm until she turned around. The rain had stopped, and at the edge of the plain Mount Petzen rose in the moonlight, every detail as sharp as a hiero-glyphic: the ravines, the cliffs, the tree line, the cirques, the line of peaks: "Our mountain!" My mother told me that down there along the mountainside, my brother, long before the war, had traveled in the same direction as "our driver," southwest across the border, on his way to agricultural school in Maribor.

My five years at the seminary are not worth the telling. The words "homesickness," "oppression," "cold," and "collective confinement" suffice. Never for one moment had the priesthood, at which we were all ostensibly aiming, appealed to me as a calling, and few of the children seemed to have the vocation; here at the seminary the mystery which in the village church had still emanated from the Sacrament was dispelled from morning to night. None of the priests at the school

impressed me as a shepherd of souls; either they sat
withdrawn in their warm private rooms—and if they
sent for one of us, it was at the most to warn, to threaten,
or to pump—or else they would move about the buildings, always in their black, floor-length cassock-uni-
forms, acting as wardens and prefects. Even at the altar,
celebrating the daily Mass, far from being transformed
into the priests they had once been consecrated as, they
executed every detail of the ceremony in the role of
policemen: when they stood silently with their backs
turned and their arms raised heavenward, they seemed
to be listening to what was going on behind their backs,
and when they turned around, supposedly to bless us
all, their true purpose was to catch me red-handed.
How different it had been with the village priest: before
my eyes he had just carried crates full of apples down
to the cellar, listened to the news on the radio, cut hairs
out of his ears; and now in the house of God he stood
in his vestments, never mind his creaking joints, before
the Holy of Holies—removed from the rest of us, who
thus became a congregation.

The only good company I had at the seminary I
enjoyed alone, when studying. In my solitary study,
every word I remembered, every formula I applied
correctly, every watercourse I learned to draw from
memory, anticipated my one overriding desire: to be
out in the open. If asked what the word "kingdom"
meant to me, I would not have named any particular
country but only the "kingdom of freedom."

And to my mind the man who in my last year at
the seminary became my great friend was the embodiment of this "kingdom" which thus far I had glimpsed
only in study. He was not a contemporary but an adult,

and he was not a priest but a man from outside, from the world, a lay teacher. He was still very young; having just completed his studies, he lived in the so-called teachers' house, which, apart from the seminary building and the bishops' tomb embedded in the hillside, was the only structure on the secluded, treeless knoll. Inconspicuous as I was to everyone else (years later, when I ran into former classmates, I always heard the same description: "quiet, aloof, self-absorbed," in which I did not recognize myself), he noticed me at once. Everything he said in class was addressed to me, as though he were giving me a private lesson; and his tone was not that of a teacher; rather, he seemed in every sentence to be asking me if I agreed with his way of organizing his subject matter. He spoke as if I had long been familiar with the material and he was only waiting for me to assure him with a nod that he was not misleading the others. Once, when I went so far as to correct him, he did not look the other way but expressed his delight that a pupil should know better than his teacher; that, he said, was what he had always wished for. Not for one moment did I feel flattered. This was something very different: I felt recognized. I had been overlooked for years, and now at last someone had taken notice of me. In so doing, he had awakened me, and I awoke with exuberance. For a time all went well with me, my classmates, and above all the young teacher. Every day in my thoughts I went over to the teachers' house after class; I passed from the stuffy religious dungeon into the airy realm of study, research, and contemplation of the world, into a solitude which struck me as glorious at the time. When he went away on weekends, my thoughts were with him in the city, where he did nothing but compose himself for his schooldays; and when he stayed at the seminary, the one lighted window in the teachers' house was for me an eternal light very different from the trembling little flame beside the altar of the dark seminary chapel.

In those days I never thought of becoming a teacher myself—I wanted to remain a pupil forever, the pupil, for instance, of such a teacher, who was at the same time his pupil's pupil. Of course this was possible only while distance was kept, and we forfeited this necessary distance, I perhaps in the exuberance of waking, he perhaps in the exuberance of a discovery which up until then he had only let himself dream of. Or perhaps the trouble was that I couldn't bear for long to think of myself as chosen. Something drove me to shatter the image he had formed of me, much as it resembled my own. I wanted to remove myself from his field of vision. I longed to live in obscurity as I had for the last sixteen years, hidden in the big blue cavern that was my desk, where no one could have any opinion, high or low, of me—yes, after becoming even better known to someone than to the Doppelgänger who had often haunted me in the past, I really and truly longed for obscurity. To be regarded for any length of time as a model, if not a marvel, was intolerable, not because of what my classmates might think, but in my own eyes, and I longed to vanish behind a wall of contradictions. So it came about that after asking a question proving that my thought had kept pace with his, and being buffeted by a look expressing an emotion deeper than joy, I made a hideous face, which was intended only to divert attention from myself but which—I could feel it the moment he did—wounded the young teacher to the quick. He went rigid, left the room, and stayed away till the end of that period. No one else knew what was wrong with him. He thought he had seen my true face in that moment; he thought my earnestness, my love of the subjects studied, my affection for him, who put his whole self into his teaching, was a pretense; he thought I was a cheat, a hypocrite, and a traitor. While the other students talked excitedly, I looked calmly out of the window. The teacher was standing in the yard with his back to the building. When he turned around, I saw not his eyes but his pursed lips, as hard as a bird's beak. That hurt me, but I didn't mind. I was actually glad that at last I had no one but myself.

In the days that followed, the beak became even sharper. This, however, was not an enemy who hated me but a cold judge whose verdict, once arrived at, was irrevocable. And the cavern of my desk did not prove to be the refuge I had imagined. It was all up with my studying. Every day, the teacher proved to me that I knew nothing, or that what I knew was not what was "wanted." My so-called knowledge was some sort of foolishness; it had nothing to do with the subject but was entirely my invention, and in this form, without a certified formula, was no good to anybody. I stared at the cavern where once, as I warmed my forehead, the luminous world of signs, distinctions, transitions, connections, and common denominators had dawned for me, and I was alone with the black cloud inside me. Unthinkable that it would ever break up; it grew thicker, it spread, rose to my mouth, my eyes, took away my voice, my eyesight. This of course no one noticed. During common prayer in church, I had only moved my lips, and in school, since this was our principal teacher, it wasn't long before I ceased to be questioned or even taken notice of. It was then that I discovered what it is to lose one's voice—not only to fall silent in the presence of others but to be incapable of saying a word to oneself, or of making a sound or a gesture when alone. Such muteness cried out for violence; acquiescence was inconceivable. And this violence could not, as with my little enemy, be directed outward; my big enemy was a weight inside me, on my abdomen, my diaphragm, my lungs, my windpipe, my larynx, my palate, blocking my nostrils and ears, and the heart at the center of all that ceased to beat, pound, throb, spurt, and bleed, and just ticked sharply, angrily.

And then one morning someone came into the classroom and summoned me to the rector's office. The rector called me by my first name and told me my mother would be phoning any minute (he had always called me Filip in her presence, though otherwise I was invariably addressed as Kobal). I had never before heard my mother's voice on the phone, and today, though I've forgotten almost all her modes of expression, her speaking and singing, her laughing and moaning, I can still hear her voice of that morning—muffled, as one might expect of a voice from a post-office phone booth, monotonous and clear. She said my father and she had agreed to transfer me from the "boys' seminary" to a secular school, and this without delay. I had already been registered at the Gymnasium in Klagenfurt and in two hours they would pick me up at the entrance in a neighbor's car. "Starting tomorrow, you'll attend your new class. You'll be sitting beside a girl. You'll take the train every day. You'll have your own room at home, we don't need the storeroom anymore; your father is making you a chair and a table." I started to protest, but I soon stopped. My mother spoke with the voice of a judge. She knew me inside and out; she had jurisdiction over me. The decision rested with her, and she decreed that I should be set free immediately. Just this once, her voice rose up from deep within her, from a silence she had stored up all her life, stored up perhaps for the very purpose of enabling her, in a single moment, on the right occasion, to make a powerful statement, after which she would fall back into the silence where her people had their throne and kingdom; a light, wingèd, dancing, chanting voice. I reported my mother's decision to the rector, he accepted it without a word, and before I knew it, a happy little group was sailing across the open plain, the reprieved prisoner and his suitcase on the back seat, under a towering sky, in a world as bright as if the car top had been taken down. Whenever the road ahead of us was empty, our neighbor at the wheel would drive in wide zigzags, singing partisan songs at the top of his voice. My mother, who didn't know the words, hummed the tune and from time to time, in a voice that grew more and more festive, shouted the names of the villages bordering my homeward road on the left and right. Seized with dizziness, I held fast to my suitcase. If I had had to give my feeling a name, it would not have been "relief" or "joy" or "bliss," but "light," almost too much of it.

Nevertheless, I never really returned home after that. During my years at the seminary, every trip home had been bathed in the atmosphere of a great festive journey, and not only because, apart from the summer vacation, we were allowed to go home only on the major feast days. Before Christmas, we released prisoners stormed down the hill in the pitch darkness, left the winding road at the first opportunity, climbed over the fence with our bags, cut across the steep, deserted, frozen pasture, plodded on over the water meadows and the brooks steaming with frost to the railroad station. In the train I stood out on the platform, jostled my schoolmates, whose shouts of joy rang in my ears. It was still night, an invigorating darkness encompassed heaven and earth, the stars overhead and, down below, the sparks rising from the engine, and I am still able to think of the wind blowing through this black force field as something sacred. My whole body up to my nose was so filled with the air of that journey that I felt as if I had no need to breathe for myself. I heard the jubilation, which those around me shouted, but which I myself only had silent within me, expressed not by my own voice but by the things of the outside world: the pounding of the wheels, the rattling of the rails, the clicking of the switches; the signals that opened the way, the gates that guarded it; the crackling of the whole speeding, roaring train.

Each of us left the group with the certainty that he still had the best part of his journey ahead of him, the adventurous footpath ending in a home unknown to his fellow convicts. And once, indeed, when on such a day I left the station and cut across the fields to the village, I was accompanied by something in which I saw the Child Saviour announced by the religious calendar. True, nothing more happened than that the spaces between the shriveled cornstalks by the wayside flared up as I passed. These spaces appeared to move, step by step, identical from row to row, empty, white and windy, and I had the impression that it was always the same small space that not only accompanied me but flew fitfully ahead, a puff of wind that flushed like a bird in the corner of my eye, waited for me, and then flew on ahead. A handful of corn chaff rose from a furrow in a fallow field; pale yellow leaves hovered motionless for a time, then in the form of a column moved slowly over the fields, while in the background a train, almost hidden by the fog, seemed now to stop, now to shoot ahead, as fitfully as the airy something beside me. I ran homeward, burning to tell them something which, as I already knew in the doorway, could not be told just then, and not in words. Once the door opened, nothing existed but the house, warm, smelling of scrubbed wood, inhabited by people who, unlike those at the seminary, belonged to me. My face, covered with soot from the early-morning train trip, told them all they needed to know.

The seminary had been so foreign a place that from there, regardless of whether to the south, west, north, or east, the only direction was homeward. At night, as I lay in the dormitory listening to the trains rolling across the plain below, I could conceive only of passengers on their way home. An airplane on its transcontinental route passed directly over the village. And that, too, was where the clouds were heading. The path leading to the steep descending cattle track showed the way; on the deserted, grass-overgrown paths, I was so near the goal that I seemed to hear someone say: "Warm," as in a game of hide-the-thimble. The bread truck that came once a week drove on to a place about which I knew nothing but its name, but where the light was the same as at home. Objects in the distance—a mountain, the moon, a navigational light—seemed to be bridges through the air to the place where, as it says in my birth certificate, my parents "resided." My daily thoughts of flight were never directed toward the city, let alone toward any foreign country, but always toward my native place: a barn, a certain hut, the chapel in the forest, the reed shelter by the lake. Nearly all the boys at the seminary came from villages, and if one of them actually ran away, he was soon found somewhere near his village or making a beeline in that direction.

But now that I was free and traveled back and forth day after day between my remote village and the city school, I discovered that I no longer had a fixed place. In my eyes the village of Rinkenberg—which had hardly changed during my years at the seminary, not the church, not the low Slovenian farmhouses, not the unfenced orchards—had ceased to be a coherent unit and was only a sprinkling of houses in the countryside. The village square, the roads leading up to the barns, the bowling alley, the beehives, the meadows, the bomb craters, the wayside shrine, the clearing in the woods were still there, but they did not form the fabric in which I had previously moved as a native among natives, a Rinkenberger. It was as though a protective roof had flown away and the harsh, cold light no longer revealed meeting places, festive scenes, nooks and crannies, points of view, benches to rest on—in short, the landmarks that coalesce to form a whole village. At first I put the blame on the village, where in many instances hand tools had been replaced by machines, but I soon realized that I was the disrupter, I was out of tune. Wherever I went, I stumbled, collided, missed my aim. If someone was headed my way, I evaded his eyes, though we may have known each other since childhood.

Because I had been away for so long, because I had not stayed home, because I had left my proper place, I felt guilty; I had forfeited the right to be here. Once a boy of my own age, with whom I had attended grade school in my village days, started telling me bits of local news, but broke off in the middle, saying: "You look like you don't know what I'm talking about."

I was unable to get back in with my age group. For one thing, none of the others was still going to school; some had taken over their fathers' farms, others were plying a trade, but all were working. Though legally minors, they struck me as adults. Whenever I saw them, they were either at work or on their way to work. In their farm clothes or aprons, with their faces set straight ahead, their always alert eyes, their ready fingers, they had acquired a military quality, and similarly the babbling voices of the schoolroom had given way to monosyllabic utterances, to curt nods or vacant stares as they passed on their mopeds (with, at the most, a laconic wave of the hand). Their pleasures as well were those of adults; and I as a matter of course was left out of them. With a shudder of wonderment, almost of awe, as though worshipping a mystery, I contemplated the so serious, attentive, sure-footed couples on the dance floor. This young woman with the dignified movements was the little girl who had once hopped over the chalk lines of hopscotch squares. And not so long ago the young lady who now picks up her skirt as she steps daintily onto the dance floor was showing us her hairless pubis in the cow pasture. How quickly they had all outgrown such childish pursuits! And now they were literally looking down on me. Every one of the boys had already suffered a serious accident; one had lost a

finger, another an arm or an ear; one at least had been
killed. Some were fathers; several of the girls were
mothers. One of the boys had been in jail. And what
about me? It came to me that during my years at the
seminary my youth had passed but I had never for one
moment known the experience of youth. I saw youth
as a river, a free confluence and flow from which I was
excluded when I entered the seminary. My years at the
seminary were lost time that could never be retrieved.
In me something was missing, and would always be
missing. Like many young men in the village, I had lost
a part of my body; it had not been cut off like a hand
or a foot; no, it had never had a chance to grow; and
it was no mere extremity, so to speak, but an irreplace-
able organ. My trouble was that I couldn't go along
with the others; I couldn't join in their activities or talk
with them. I was a stranded cripple, and the current,
which alone could have sustained me, had passed me
by forever. I knew that without youth I could do
nothing. I had missed it once and for all, and that made
me incapable of movement; especially in the only company that would have been right for me, that of my
contemporaries, it gave me a feeling of painful inner
paralysis, and I swore that I would never forgive the
people I held responsible for this paralysis—and those
people existed.

Though I was often glad to stand apart, in the long
run I couldn't reconcile myself to being alone. At first
I associated with my juniors, with children. They were
glad to have me, as a referee in their games, as a helper,
as a storyteller. In the hour between the onset of dusk
and nightfall, the open space in front of the church

became a kind of children's forum. They would sit on window ledges or on their bicycles, and as often as not they had to be called several times before they would go home to bed. They didn't talk much, they just sat there together while the bats circled around them, growing almost invisible to one another as the time passed. With the help of certain paraphernalia, I would try my hand as a storyteller. From time to time, I would strike a match, tap two stones together, blow into my cupped hands. Actually, I never did more than evoke sounds and sights: clubfeet walking, a stream swelling, a will-o'-the-wisp coming closer. And my listeners were not eager for a story, they were satisfied with my evocations. But not content with such marginal participation, I would sit in the midst of the children, as though I were one of them. They took me for granted, but my former playmates, who had become "big" boys and girls in the meantime, made fun of me. Once when I ran a race across the square with some children, hardly any of whom came up to my shoulders, a girl whom in my seminary nights I had often seen swathed in blue veils—I was never able to conjure up a naked woman— passed on stiletto heels. Though she hadn't even looked at me—a glance out of the corner of her eye had told her all she wanted to know about me; namely, the worst—her lip curled almost imperceptibly.

At one stroke, not only the children's company but the square itself was closed to me. Something drove me to the strip of land on the edge of the village, known locally as "behind the gardens." This area, though inhabited, was not really part of the village. Unmarried persons lived there—the roadmender, for example. He occupied a one-room house with thick dark-yellow walls, suggesting the porter's lodge of a nonexistent manor house (there had never been such a manor in or near any of the villages). I never once set foot in the house and altogether kept my distance from the man. He was the only person in the village with a secret, which, however, he displayed freely and had no need to hide. Maintaining the village streets and pathways was only his everyday occupation. But there were days when he abandoned the gravel box out on the desolate highway and metamorphosed into a sign painter, stood, for instance, on a ladder over the entrance to the inn at the center of the village. As I watched him adding a shadowy line to a finished letter with a strikingly slow brushstroke, aerating, as it were, a thick letter with a few hair-thin lines, and then conjuring up the next letter from the blank surface, as though it had been there all along and he was only retracing it, I saw in this nascent script the emblem of a hidden, nameless, all the more magnificent and above all unbounded kingdom, in the presence of which the village did not disappear but emerged from its insignificance as the innermost circle of this kingdom, irradiated by the shapes and colors of the sign at its center. At such moments, even the painter's ladder took on a special quality. It didn't lean, it towered. The curbstone at its feet gleamed. A haywagon passed, its strands of hay plaited into garlands. The hooks on the shutters did not just hang down, they pointed in definite directions. The door of the inn became a portal, and those who entered looked up at the sign and bared their heads in obeisance. The foot of a chicken scratching about in the background became the yellow claw of a heraldic animal. The road where the sign painter was standing led, not to the small town nearby, but out into the country and at the same time straight toward the tip of his brush. On certain other days, amid the blowing leaves of autumn, the driving snows of winter, the flowery clouds of spring, the heat lightning of summer nights, I had perceived the wide world as a pure Now; but on signposting days there was something more: an exalted Now, an Era.

And I saw the roadmender in still another avatar, touching up the paint on the wayside shrines. One of these was shaped like a chapel, with an inner room, but this room was so small it would have been impossible to take a single step in it. Time and again I found him at work, squeezed into this little box at a remote crossroads, visible only from his head to one elbow, which he rested on the frame of the little window that opened outward. The shrine made me think of a hollow tree trunk, an engineer's cab, a sentry box; and I had the impression that the man had carried it into the wilderness on his shoulders. The painter didn't even have room enough to take a step backward and examine his work. But his serenity, as he stood there with his hat on his head, not for one moment put off by my presence, showed that he had no need of more room. The mural he was retouching was invisible from outside; to see what it represented, a passerby would have to lean over the window ledge. Only the dominant color was suffused in the little house, a luminous blue, in which, if I kept looking, every one of the painter's movements struck me as exemplary. I resolved that at some future date I, too, would do my work so slowly, so thoughtfully, so silently, uninfluenced by anyone who happened to be present, in perfect independence, without encouragement, without praise, expecting nothing, demanding nothing, without ulterior motive of any kind. Whatever this future work might be, it would have to be comparable to this painting, which ennobled the painter and with him the chance witness.

It was during those years—when it was brought home to me day after day that since the premature, abrupt breaking off of my childhood there could be no renewed contact, no continuation, no permanence for me in the village—that my confused sister came closer to me for the first time. The odd part of it is that since earliest childhood I had felt drawn to all the idiots in the vicinity, and they to me. In their perpetual wanderings, they often came to the window and pressed their noses and lips to the pane. And during my schooldays in Bleiburg, the one place to which I was drawn time and again was the mental home. After school, I would regularly make the detour that took me there. The idiots would greet me through the fence by screaming and waving their arms—I also remember their hugging the air—whereupon I, intermittently screaming and waving my arms on the deserted highway, would go happily home. In a sense, the mentally deranged and feebleminded were my guardian angels, and when I hadn't seen any of them in a long time, the sight of an idiot gave me a sudden burst of health and strength.

However, I didn't regard my sister as one of the happy band of the feebleminded or insane. She had always been solitary and gloomy, and as long as I can remember I had feared her and avoided her. The look in her eyes did not seem confused to me, as I had been told, but fixed; not empty, but clear; not lost, but always alert. Those eyes were constantly appraising me, and not at all favorably. And the gauge (for I regarded that fixed stare as a gauge) did not register my mistakes or misdeeds, but my basic failing: falsehood; I was not what I purported to be, I wasn't authentic, I wasn't anything, I was only pretending. And indeed, it was impossible to be friends with her; whatever I did—even if I was only looking into space—I had the feeling that I was trying to put something over on her or myself, and making a bad job of it at that. For a while at least, she had mocked me now and then with her almost pitying giggle; later she would keep a malicious silence after those crushing moments of appraisal. Consequently, I kept out of her way when possible (but then I might suddenly discover her on the balcony, where she had set her appraisal trap).

Another thing that may have put me off was that she was so much older than I. Between her and my brother there was only a year's difference; but between her and me it was two decades. When I was very little, I actually took her for a stranger in the house, a mysterious intruder, who would someday pull a pin out of her hair and stick it into me. And then, when I got back from the seminary, she did indeed take the pins out of her hair, by which I mean that she let her hair down and opened up to me. She developed a feeling for me, a kind of enthusiasm. With enthusiasm she crossed the fields to meet me when I came from the train; with enthusiasm she carried my bag; with enthusiasm she handed me a bird's feather, brought me an apple, served me a glass of cider. I had denied it all the while, and now at last I was what I was: at last she wasn't the only confused one who didn't belong anywhere;

now I, too, was just that. At last she had an accomplice, an ally, and it was possible for her to be with me. Instead of blasting me, her eyes rested on me, and while hitherto they had foreseen nothing but calamity for me, they now proclaimed pure joy in my, her, our presence; but they were never obtrusive; when I needed it, they merely gave me a look that escaped everyone else, a mere hint, a sign.

To my mind, the right posture for my sister is sitting, a tranquil, erect sitting, with her hands beside her on the bench. Though every house had a bench in front of it, it was usually the men, especially the old ones, who sat there. I remember my father only as old, but I have no recollection of him seated. As for the women of the village, I saw them "always on their feet," as housekeepers were said to be: walking in the street, bending over in the garden, and indoors actually running. It may have been my imagination, but it seemed to me that no Slovene woman could move from one place to another without running. Short as the distance might be, a Slovene woman ran from table to stove, from stove to sideboard, from sideboard to table. This running in small spaces was a quick sequence of skipping, flitting on tiptoes, running in place, changing feet, turning, and skipping some more; seen as a whole, it was a kind of clumsy dancing, the dancing of women who had been servants for many years. The young girls as well, no sooner back home from school, took to running; vying with their elders, they galloped like servants around their kitchen-living rooms. Even my mother, who was not a Slovene, had acquired the native custom; just to bring me a cup of tea, she would hop with downcast eyes and bated breath, as though I were an unexpected noble guest. Yet I can't remember any such guest ever coming to our house, not even the parish priest. But my sister, alone among the village women, appears to me seated. She sat on the bench in front of the house; there she sat for all to see, and all she did was sit. I regarded her, just as I did the roadmender, as a model. Sitting there, playing with her fingers, without the usual rosary, she transformed herself into a phantom, seen only by him whom she herself chose to see; that is, by me. Excluded like the sign painter from the dance, she, too, in her fool's freedom, embodied the center of the village. And it seemed to me that the age-old little stone statue, which dwelt, ignored by all, in a dark niche in the church wall, might have sat there as she did. Now it was reduced to a torso, a hand, and a head, and the only protuberances on the weather-beaten face were the eyes and the broadly smiling mouth, both closed. Here in the open, eyelids, lips, and the hand with the stone ball reflected the sunlight, and the whole image receded into the shimmering wall, its pedestal.

Yes, there was the moment with the children in the dusk, the moment of the painter working without witnesses, the moments when my sister and fellow conspirator was sitting in the sun. Yet all these moments could not in the long run take the place of the village I had lost.

The dream was over. Other dreams had to help out, big ones and little ones, by day and by night. But in those years I failed to make a place for myself in the city. Though I no longer felt at home in the village and instead of coming straight home after school I often took the last train, I remained in every respect an outsider in the city. I went neither to cafés nor to the movies and killed time drifting or sitting on park benches. It may have been partly due to the geography of Klagenfurt that I had nowhere to go. The lake was too far for walking, and this city, which seemed enormous to me, the capital of a whole province, had no river running through it, with banks to stroll along or bridges to stand on. Apart from the railroad station, the only building that offered me any kind of shelter was the school. I spent whole afternoons alone in my classroom or, when it was being cleaned, in a side room off the lobby, where unused tables and benches were stored. Sometimes there were other out-of-town students, and there, as the enormous deserted building grew steadily darker and quieter, we formed a little class of our own, sitting on the windowsills and standing in the corners. It was there that I met the girl with whom I once went to the movies, after all; she lived as far away as I did, in the opposite direction, in a village which, quite otherwise than in my days at the seminary, I conceived to be infinitely more alluring than my own. Her face glowed in the failing light of the corridor, and I fancied that she could only be the daughter of a noble house, living on a magnificent street.

With my classmates, on the other hand, it was only during our lessons together that I felt an affinity. In the schoolroom I spoke up (sometimes I was actually the spokesman for the class or the one who was consulted in doubtful cases). But after school I was left alone. The others all lived in town, with their parents or with local families. And they were all the children of lawyers, doctors, manufacturers, or businessmen. I was the only

one who could not have said what his father did for a
living. Was I the son of a "carpenter," a "farmer," a
"flood-control worker" (over the years, my father had
been all of these); or would it suffice for me to answer
evasively that my father was "retired"? Regardless of
how I concealed my origins, of how I might ennoble or
debase them or pass them over, as though—and that is
what I should have preferred—I had no origins at all,
I nevertheless recognized what I had long dimly felt in
my dealings with the children of the teacher, the policeman, the postmaster, the bank clerk in Bleiburg;
namely, that I was not one of them, that we really had
nothing in common, that we were not of the same world.
They had social grace, I had none. I found their parties,
to which they politely invited me at first, not only odd
but positively repellent. Standing at the door of the
dancing school, listening to the teacher counting out
the time in a voice of command, I'd have said that the
people in there were convicts who had actually chosen
a life term in this place, and when I touched the door
handle, it had the feel of a handcuff. Once at a garden
party someone threw a hammock over my head, and
there I sat with my knees drawn up, as in a net from
which there was no escaping, surrounded by Chinese
and storm lanterns, under the spell of soft music and
splashing fountains, encircled by dancing or chatting
couples.

Outside the classroom, I was always out of place. Wherever I turned, I was in the way; by stumbling before
every sentence, I brought lively, witty conversations to
a halt. While the others walked in the middle of the
sidewalk with head high, I slunk bent forward along

walls and fences, and when, no matter where, they stopped in the doorway to let themselves be seen, I took advantage of that moment to slip in unnoticed beside them (a stratagem which sometimes, as the laughter in the room indicated, really succeeded in calling attention to me). Altogether, though I alone was aware of it, the time I spent out of school with my fellow students was poisoned by my obtuseness. Years later a man seen in a streetcar recalled to me the picture I had of myself in those days: he was sitting with a group of friends who were telling jokes. He regularly joined in their laughter, but always just a little too late; then suddenly he would stop laughing, freeze, and, much too loudly, rejoin the chorus of laughers. None of the others noticed what was instantly obvious to me, the outsider. He seemed to get the gist of the jokes, but without understanding what was funny about them. Missing the double meanings and allusions, he took everything he heard seriously. During moments of silence I saw by his dismayed look that he took every detail of their stories for literal truth. And that day in the streetcar I said to myself: That is exactly the way I behaved with my schoolmates, and only an outsider such as I am now could have noticed that one of us was not really a member of the group.

Once several of us were sitting at a table, talking. At first I joined in, but then, suddenly, it was all over between me and the others, the group on one side, myself on the other. I could hear them talking, but I couldn't see them; at the most, a limb or two flashed across the corner of my eye. But that made my hearing all the sharper; I could have reproduced the intonation as well as the words of every sentence with terrifying accuracy and more realistically than the best tape recorder. They were only saying the usual things, amusing themselves. But the mere fact of their saying such things and their way of saying them infuriated me. Hadn't I just been trying to join in? Yes, but now I was sitting deathly still on the fringe, wanting them to question me about my silence. And they, it seemed to me, were talking all the more glibly past me, over my head, as though their only purpose were to show me that they were something special and that I didn't exist for them. Yes, by talking and talking without the slightest pause while I sat there reduced to silence, these sons and daughters of the bourgeoisie meant to rebuff me and my class. And even if an unfriendly word was never dropped, their way of speaking, their flat, glib singsong, was directed against me. I felt the energy that had accumulated inside me before this get-together—the urge to say something for once—reverse itself behind my forehead and strike back at me, benumbing my whole brain. That was my first experience of "loneliness," which up until then had been a mere word to me. Then and there I resolved that I would never go in for this sort of society; and wasn't it a silent triumph to be unable to join in such talk, to be different? I left the table without saying goodbye, and the talk didn't subside for so much as a moment. Later, when the story got around, it came to my ears that I hadn't had a good upbringing, as they put it, "a proper nursery," and it occurred to me that, sure enough, there hadn't been a separate room for the children in our house. These incidents left me with a habit that I had to break myself of later; when I got into an argument, I invariably addressed my adversary, however singular, by the second person plural.

I came to feel at home while on the move, riding in trains, waiting at railroad stations and bus stops. My daily ninety kilometers, or, counting distances covered on foot, three hours back and forth between village and city, gave me the time and space I needed to live in. I heaved a sigh of relief every time I was restored to the society of my mostly unknown fellow travelers, whom I had no need to classify and who did not classify me. During the trip we were neither rich nor poor, neither better nor worse than anyone else, neither German nor Slovene; if anything, we were young and old—and on the return journey in the evening it seemed to me that even age had ceased to count. What were we, then? In the classless local train we were simply passengers, and the same was true of the bus. Sometimes, for various reasons, I preferred the bus; for one thing, the trip took longer; moreover, it was dark; and lastly, in the bus even people I knew only too well seemed transformed. In the village or in Bleiburg I identified these people by their voices, their way of walking, the look in their eyes, their way of leaning their elbows on the windowsill, of turning their heads to look at a passerby, or by what I knew of their families or past history, but once they boarded the bus, they became indefinable. And being indefinable, they were something more in my eyes than they would otherwise have been; shorn of their particularities, they appeared at last alone and unique in the here and now; in the roaring, lurching bus, ennobled as it were by the journey together, they seemed more in their place than in the pews they maintained in church at home. Grown indefinable, they revealed themselves. They hinted at something that I could not interpret, and this was their reality; their greetings from passenger to passenger were true greeting, their questions were a real wanting to know, and though I could not hold on to these things, I ought to have! How sheltered, as though among my own kind, I felt with these people, consisting almost always of persons alone or of a child with adults, being conveyed by a reliable driver (who at home may have been a morose neighbor) over roads and city streets, all bound together, not by some excursion or pleasure trip, but by a necessity which carried them away from house and garden to the doctor, to school, to market, or to some administrative office. And this feeling did not always need the protection of darkness. One bright morning I sat behind some women who were carrying on a conversation from side to side of the bus about the relatives they were all on their way to visit in the hospital. Their talk of illness, a distinct sequence of voices, one loud, one soft, one plaintive, one calm, each in turn setting the tone, transformed the moving bus into a stage belonging exclusively to these women, a glass cage in which the light of a whole country had accumulated, and this light, the light of another country which was nevertheless present and traveling along with the bus, dispersed and spiritualized everything that was heavy and corporeal. The women's head scarves shimmered, and bunches of garden flowers peered out of their handbags.

In very much the same way, I kept seeing the passengers who got out at the bus stops and hurried away into the darkness. These stops were also stages;

the scenes enacted on them consisted solely of people coming, going, and waiting. Some, before turning away, lingered a while in the circle of light, as though in no hurry to go home (I was one of these); the others had barely got out of the bus when (like children sometimes in a dream) they vanished as though for all time. And the emptiness they left behind was marked by a warm seat beside me, condensed breath on the windowpane, fingerprints and hair smudges.

At that time, my favorite stage was the area around the municipal bus station and a side street parallel to the railroad line, with its ticket office and a long row of ports from which buses left for different parts of the country and on certain days even for Yugoslavia and Italy. Here I had the impression of being at the center of action. This action, to be sure, was only the smell of the glossy-black wooden ticket office floor, the roaring of the cast-iron stoves, the banging of doors, the flapping of posters against the busports outside, the trembling of a starting bus, the crackling and banging of another that was parking, the blowing of dust, leaves, snow, and newspapers through the windy street. And what these things were doing, or the mere fact that they were there, the faint yellow streetlights high up in the trees, the cracked supports of the ports, the rusting sheet-metal signs indicating destinations—that was enough action for me, no need for anything more to happen, that was plenty. If a face emerged from the darkness and became personally recognizable, it was too much. It was worse than a nuisance, it destroyed the magic. I couldn't help making up stories about this, and the hero was always someone who claimed to be God, or an idiot who, ridiculed by all when he got in, avenged himself during the night ride by steering the bus off a precipice. Even my girlfriend merely cut off my view when she turned toward me as her bus was pulling out on the other side of the street. I couldn't respond to her wave until she was out of the picture and the square was empty again. Then, to be sure, the whole country was full of her; I accompanied her on her trip and she me on mine.

Yes, trains and buses, railroad stations and bus stops were my home in my days as a commuting student. The homesickness of my years at the seminary was a thing of the past; on days when there was no school, something drew me to the road with its bus shelters, which, unlike the village, deserved to be called "places." I longed to be always on the move, a vagrant, without fixed abode. My old homesickness, the most painful of all the sufferings I had thus far experienced, a torment which unlike other torments fell from a clear sky on me alone, while the whole world around me remained bright, and which, also unlike other torments, was irremediable, had given way to a carefreeness which, as long as it had no goal, I identified with boredom, but once it had a goal, with wanderlust: pleasure in place of torment.

During my commuting days, it came to me that my parents were also strangers in the village. They were so regarded not by other villagers but by themselves. Outside the house, they were respected. My father was given honorific positions (in Rinkenberg, these were almost always connected with the church). My mother was regarded as an expert in dealings with the author- ities and with the outside world in general; she was a kind of village scribe, who wrote letters and petitions for neighbors. But at home, once they were alone and especially when neither was working, they would grow restless, or sit and brood, as though they were there against their will, prisoners or exiles.

The memory of my father pacing the floor, rushing over to the little radio, scowling as he turned the tuning knob, makes me think of a soldier given up for lost in an advance post, trying desperately to pick up a signal telling him to come in. At first I thought this was brought on by the silence of the stable, which had emptied over the years, and of the barn, where the old farm implements had ceased to be anything more than souvenirs or junk. But then I saw that what drove him to keep on making strictly rectilinear chairs and tables, without a trace of ornament, in his old workshop behind the house, though he had no orders, was incurable rage and indignation provoked by an injustice. I'd sometimes look in through the windows and see how he worked without a glance at what he was making. Either he'd be staring into space, or he'd raise his head abruptly, and for a moment there'd be defiance in his eyes, followed by a look of prolonged resignation. When he was working, his bursts of temper, which had become legendary in the region, gave way to a sustained rage that made him trace thick, heavy lines, hammer nails ferociously, and make his corners as sharp as possible. Later on, I thought it was because, twenty years after my brother's disappearance, our house was still a house of mourning; because a disappearance, unlike an unquestionable death, leaves a family no peace; every day he died again for them, and there was nothing whatever they could do about it.

But that wasn't it, either; at any rate, not that alone.

Their feeling, deforming, as it were, every corner of the farm, that this was not their home, that this village had been inflicted on them as a punishment, was much older. It was a—our only—family tradition, handed down from father to son, perhaps most clearly exemplified in a saying that had been passed from generation to generation: "No, I won't go in, because if I do, there won't be anyone there."

Our family legend was rooted in a historical event. It seems that we really were descended from Gregor Kobal, the instigator of the Tolmin peasant revolt. The story is that after his execution his descendants were driven out of the Isonzo Valley, and that one of them crossed the Karawanken Mountains to Carinthia. Henceforward, every firstborn male was baptized with the name of Gregor. The part of this story that counted for my father was not that his ancestor had been a rebel and guerrilla leader, but that he had been executed and that his family had been banished. Since then, we had been a family of hirelings, of itinerant workers, homeless and condemned to remain so. The only right we retained, in which we could find brief moments of peace, was the right to gamble. And when my father gambled, even as an old man, he hadn't his equal in the village. As he saw it, another aspect of the sentence of banishment was that in his home he was obliged not only to give another language precedence over Slovene, which had after all been the language of his ancestors, but to ban the use of Slovene altogether. As he regularly showed when talking to himself, often very loudly, in his workshop, he himself spoke it in his innermost consciousness, but he felt forbidden to let it out or pass it on to his children. Thus, it had been no more than justice when he married a woman of the hostile, German-speaking nation. He behaved as if a supreme will, more powerful than that of the Emperor who many years ago had ordered the execution of our ancestor Gregor Kobal, decreed that after the disappearance of his eldest son, the last of that name, he must suppress any Slovene sound in his house. Thus, when others were present, his language escaped him only in curses or in moments of overpowering emotion. He spoke it freely only when gambling, when drawing a card, when bowling, when imploring a curling stone to slide straight to its goal. At such times he felt entitled to speak Slovene as much as he pleased, and then he, who otherwise never opened his mouth, spoke more than anyone else. Otherwise, when he was not totally silent, he spoke German, a German free from the slightest tinge of dialect, which he passed on to everyone else in the family and for which, in every part of the country, I was later upbraided, as if I were speaking a forbidden foreign language. (I must own that my father's way of speaking German, serious, graphic, laboriously pondering every word as though intimidated by the presence of foreigners, still sounds in my ears as the clearest, purest, least garbled, and most human-sounding voice I have ever heard in Austria.)

It should not be thought that my father accepted the condemnation of the Kobals, their exile, their servitude, and the suppression of their language with resignation; to him it was an outrage. But he did not seek redemption in insubordination, let alone resistance; he sought it in his variety of violent, scornful, contemptuous obedience to the unjust commandment, which, he hoped, would bring it to the attention of the one competent authority, who would then at last intervene. With all his strength, especially the strength of his obstinacy, he was intent on redemption for himself and his family. As his outbursts of temper and his cruelty to animals showed, he was determined to win it by the force of his impatience—and this seemed implicit in his yearning; he had no hope, no dream, no idea, and never uttered any proposal to us concerning the form the redemption of his family here on earth might take. For this he blamed the two World Wars, the first of which he spent exclusively on the banks of our legendary home-country river, the Isonzo, while the second, as the father of a deserter, he had waited out in Rinkenberg, his place of banishment.

My mother, however, the Slovene by marriage, the foreigner, took an entirely different view of the clan tradition. To her, it was not a sad story of unsuccessful struggle and banishment but, in a manner of speaking, an attestation of the family's aim and aspiration, a promise. And, unlike my father, she did not expect salvation from any outside agency. She demanded it of ourselves. Whereas my father, always in vain, put his trust in God and in blind acceptance of fate, she was resolutely godless and wherever possible lived by her own law (which she, too, derived from her experience of the two World Wars). And this law decreed that her family, by which she meant her children, had for centuries had their home on the other side of the Karawanken Mountains, and would someday, by their own efforts, make good their claim to it. There they must go, to the southwest, to take back their land, whatever it might amount to. And that would wipe out the disgrace that had once been inflicted on "us" through the murder of our ancestor by the authorities. (My mother, the foundling, the foreigner, used the most imperious "we" for the family that had given her asylum.) And she epitomized the revenge we would take on the Emperor, on the counts, the powers that be, in short, the "Austrians"—for this Austrian woman an expression of supreme contempt—in a pun on the name of the village in the Isonzo Valley, where we were supposed to have originated. After our return home, our resurrection from a thousand years of servitude, this village, called Karfreit in German but properly, that is, in Slovene, Kobarid,* would be renamed Kobalid, to which my father replied scornfully that this name could also be translated "To clear out on horseback," and she should kindly, as befitted the likes of us, let it go at Karfreit, or at least at Kobarid, which can be interpreted to mean an aggregation of crystals or a cluster of hazelnuts, and my mother would counter by asking whether he, who seemed to have degenerated once and for all into a subject, had forgotten that the last news of his son, the resistance fighter, had come from the celebrated "Kobarid Republic," where in the midst of the war a single village had proclaimed itself an anti-Fascist republic and for a time had remained one; to which, in turn, my father replied only that he knew nothing of any such news or any such resistance.

The two of them, it is true, would meet time and again in front of the only picture we had (except for the enlarged photograph of my brother in the crucifix-and-radio corner): it hung in the entrance and was a map of Slovenia. But here, too, my parents usually

* The Italian Caporetto. [Trans.]

stood and argued. My mother, ordinarly so godless and
blasphemous, would lift up her voice and chant names
from the map, syllable after syllable, on a hovering,
tremulous high note, while my father shook his head
at her pronunciation of the foreign words when he
didn't curtly and gruffly correct her. Though her lips
twitched like a rabbit's and her tongue froze, she
persisted in her Slavic litany, chanted Ljubljana instead
of Laibach, Ptuj instead of Pettau, Kranj instead of
Krainburg, Gorica* instead of Görz, Bistrica instead of
Feistritz, Postojna instead of Adelsberg, Ajdovščina (the
sound of which I awaited with special eagerness) instead
of Haidenschaft. Unlike her other singing, strangely
enough, my mother's litany of place names, however
faulty her pronunciation, sounded beautiful to me. Each
of these names struck me as an invocation, as all seemed
to merge in a single, tender, high-pitched entreaty,
which my father, as far as I can remember, did not
contradict, but responded to in the role of the people—
the common people; and the entrance hall, with its
wooden floor, its banister-framed wooden stairway leading to the cellar, and its door opening out on the
wooden balcony, became a nave, more imposing than
the nave of the village church had ever been.

Yet my mother had never been across the border.
The Yugoslavian towns were known to her chiefly from
her husband's stories, and to him these names still
embodied nothing but the war. Actually, he spoke much
less of towns and villages than of one and the same
rocky hill that kept being stormed, lost, retaken, and so
on, over the years. According to him, the World War

---

* The Italian Gorizia. [Trans.]

had taken place on just such a bare, chalk-white mountain ridge, with a front line that moved a stone's throw forward or backward from battle to battle, and if other veterans in the village were to be believed, that was how they had all seen it. My father was always shivering, but he seemed to shiver still more when he spoke of the deep clefts in the mountain, which even in the summer were full of snow. He had known many kinds of fear, but his overriding fear had been and still was that he might have killed a man. He showed his numerous wounds, in the shin, the thigh, the shoulder, with indifference; it was only when the conversation turned to the Italian at whom he had leveled his gun when ordered to do so that he lost his composure. "I aimed over his head," my father said. "But after my shot went off he jumped up in the air like this, with his arms outstretched. And then I didn't see him anymore." Wide-eyed, he came back time and again to this one moment; for even after thirty, forty, fifty years, the man kept jumping up in the air, and it would never be known for sure whether he had let himself drop back into the trench or had toppled into it. "Stinking mess," my father cried and repeated the sentiment in Slovene— "*Svinjerija*"—as though that language were better able to express his hatred of history, the world, and all earthly existence. Be that as it may, he had seldom seen a town or village during the war; at the most he had been "near" or "on the road to" one. Only Gorica meant something more to my father than a battlefield. "Now that's a city," he said. "Compared with it, our Klagenfurt is nothing." But if questions were asked, his only answer would be: "There are palm trees in the parks and there's a king buried in the monastery crypt."

What in my father's stories was no more than the heartbreaking and infuriating names of battlefields stimulated my mother's inventiveness. What with him was a curse—"damned Ternovan Forest!"—she transformed into a place of promise. From mere place names she created, for my benefit (my sister wouldn't do), a country that had nothing in common with the reality of Slovenia; it was built up exclusively from the names of the battles or scenes of misery mentioned casually or with horror by my father. This country, which consisted entirely of towns with magical names such as Lipica, Temnica, Vipava, Doberdob, Tomaj, Tabor, Kopriva, became in her mouth a land of peace where we, the Kobal family, would at last recapture our true selves. Yet this transfiguration may have resulted not so much from the sound of words or the family legend as from the few letters received from my brother when he was in Yugoslavia during the years between the wars. Often he would prefix with a word of praise the very place names through which his father had cursed the world as a whole: "The holy [Mount] Nanos," "the holy [River] Timavo." From the start my mother's fantasies, remote as they may have been from experience, made a stronger impression on me, the second, late-born son, than did my father's war stories. When I think back on the two of them, I see one weeping and one laughing storyteller, one standing aside, the other center stage, asserting our rights.

The household's present, however, its daily life, was dominated by my father's prisoner mentality. His being a stranger in the village made him a domestic tyrant. Because he was nowhere at home, he bullied the rest of us; he drove us from our places or at least poisoned them for us. When my father entered the living room, the atmosphere became unpleasant. He had only to stand at the window for the rest of us to be seized with a nervousness that made our movements spasmodic. At such times, even my seated sister could not assert her power; peace of mind gave way to a breathless rigidity. And his uneasiness was contagious: a small man walking in circles in the big room; around him, more and more eyes, heads, limbs began to twitch. Often this twitching would infect us if he merely opened the door, let his look of injured hopelessness rest on the members of his family, and disappeared, or if we sensed that he was standing motionless in the hall, as though waiting at once for his savior and for the landslide that would bury him along with his house and garden. Once he was back in his workshop, we breathed easy, but even then we could hear his cries of rage, and though we had got used to them over the years, they still gave us a start; not even in his place of work, where he might have felt independent and free, did my father feel at home.

Even on Sunday, apart from the afternoon card game, the peace associated with the day visited our house only on our return from Mass, when he put on his glasses and opened the weekly Slovenian church gazette, the only newspaper he read. He moved his lips soundlessly at every word, as though not only reading but studying the lines, and in the course of time his slowness engendered a calm that surrounded him and filled the house. During this reading period, my father at last found his place—in sunny weather on the bench in the yard; otherwise, on the backless stool by the east window, where with a childlike, scholarly look he studied letter after letter. As often as I evoke that image, I feel that I'm still sitting there with him.

To tell the truth, we didn't even eat together at that time. As though my father were still working outside, his food was brought to him in a tightly closed mess kit, either at the house of the mountain peasants or at his place beside one of the mountain torrents; my mother ate at the stove while cooking; my sister, as befitted a confused person, spooned her food out of a bowl on the doorstep; and I ate wherever I happened to be. We all longed for the arrival of the card players, and not only because my father regularly won: his calm as he sat there, carrying off one daring coup after another, gave rise to a merriment which encompassed the losers as well as the winner. Whenever the so uncommon, neither malicious nor commiserating but simply triumphal laughter of the player whose daring had brought him success erupted, all were glad to join in. And the others were my father's friends, underlings like himself, village notables, natives, who all became equal at the card table, talkers, storytellers, with no one over them. But friendship lasted only as long as the game; when the game was over, they broke up without delay, and all went home, as isolated as ever, mere neighbors, acquaintances, villagers known to one another chiefly by their weaknesses and oddities—the skirtchaser, the skinflint, the sleepwalker. And my father, though he stayed at the table holding a deck of cards in one hand and counting his winnings with the other, had again lost his place. When the lamp over the card table was turned off, the light in the house seemed to flicker and threaten to go out at any moment, for in those days before the whole country was electrified, our region was supplied with a feeble, uneven current by a small power plant on the Drava that wasn't even as big as a water mill.

Though my father—mason, carpenter, and cabinetmaker in one—had built the house with his own hands, he was not its master. Because this self-driven laborer was incapable of stepping back from his work and contemplating it for so much as a moment, he could not regard himself as its creator. Though he took a certain pride in other construction he'd had a hand in—the roof of the church tower, for instance—he never so much as glanced at anything he had made in his own home; while putting up a wall with the utmost care, he would stare blindly into space; and instead of stopping to look at a stool he had just finished, he would busy himself with wood for the next one. Still a young man, my father slaved for years, building, almost unaided, the first house the Kobal family had owned in more than two centuries. And yet I cannot conceive of his climbing to the edge of the forest and looking proudly down on the village of Rinkenberg with the house he had built for himself and his family in its midst; I cannot even conceive of a housewarming with Kobal, the proud owner, lifting a mug of cider.

More than anything else, it was this incapacity of my father's for living in his house that spoiled my homecomings in my last years at school. Even if my walk from the railroad station or bus stop had gone well, even if, still full of my journey in the midst of unknown, warmth-giving shadows, I had overcome the obstacle that was the village, I was seized with a malaise on entering our property: my scalp itched, my arms stiffened, my feet felt bulbous—and there was nothing I could do about it. Not that I had conjured up some image on my way, not that I had been daydreaming, drunk as it were with self-absorption; well, to tell the truth, I had been daydreaming, but only about the things around me, the night, the falling snow, the rustling in the corn, the wind in my eye hollows, and all this, because my journey was still going on in my mind, more clearly than usual, paradigmatically, symbolically. The milk can on the stand became a sign; the successive puddles gleaming in the darkness joined to form a line. But near the house the signs lost their force, objects their singularity. Often I stood for a long while at the door, trying in vain to catch my breath. What had been so clear became confused. No longer able to dream, I could no longer see. The elder bush, which on the path rose from limb to limb like a Jacob's ladder, disappeared in the garden, becoming a mere part of a hedge; the constellations overhead, each decipherable only a moment before, were now a meaningless glow. With the help of my sister, who had come to meet me, I might possibly cross the threshold safely; she distracted me like a dog or cat; like a dog or cat, she fitted into my dreamlike sequence of signs. But, in the hall at the very latest, I seemed to hear my father's morose pottering in every room, a mood which instantly spread to me, not so much sobering me as infecting me with such gloom that my only desire was to go to bed then and there.

It was only when my mother fell sick that my father learned to live in the house. In the course of those months, the house became a home for the rest of us as well. They kept her in the hospital after her operation, and it was then that he moved, as it were, from his workshop to the house. He no longer worked in wordless fury for himself alone—every gesture an expression of despair that no one understood him and no one could help him anyway. Now he would pause for a time, say what was on his mind, and even ask for help in his distress. Throwing off the clumsiness which, because of his impatience, had always overcome me when asked to help him, I worked beside him with as sure a hand as if I had been alone. And my sister, overlooked and shrugged off until then, but now suddenly treated as an equal by her father, proved to be the soul of reason; all she had needed was to be spoken to and taken seriously. Just as a word can suffice to make a person stricken with paralysis for some unfathomable reason jump up and run, our father's "Do this, do that" transformed my confused sister from one minute to the next into a young woman who was far from stupid. She understood him without his having to explain, she was transformed from a bothersome bystander into an active human being who didn't see through me and look on the dark side of everything but rather foresaw what would be needed and did what had to be done. She still sat most of the time, but now she sat by the stove, over the cabbage pot, at the bread oven, next to the currant bush, and our father would sit beside her, often doing nothing. Even when working, he didn't seem solitary or possessed; his work was done with the same thoughtful deliberation as his reading, in harmony with something which as I saw it was the light shining into the house, the luminous brown of the windowsill, or the color of his own eyes, which only then became clear to me, a deep blue suggesting the backgrounds of wayside shrines.

Though my father was strictly orthodox in his religious beliefs, there was something superstitious, as I see it now, in the almost grim deliberation with which he performed certain routine actions, as though each one were calculated to combat my mother's illness—the tying of a knot to strangle it, the driving of a nail to stop it from spreading, the plugging of a barrel to shut up the pain, the propping of a branch to give her strength; when he dragged a sack through a doorway, it was to bring her out of the hospital; when he cut a rotten spot out of an apple, it was . . . and so on.

Once my father "made himself at home," life in the house became natural for the first time. Every time I returned from school, I slipped easily into our family life, while my sister, who for years had been immured in her love story, the collapse of which, attributed to my father, had supposedly been responsible for her confused condition, forgot all about it and became a social animal, even when she was not working. She challenged the champion card player to game after game, lost every time, and invariably grew as angry as only a person of sound mind can. Biting her lips, even bursting into tears in her anger—her grief was forgotten—she appeared perfectly sane, and to me, the adolescent boy, it seemed that we—the young woman sweeping the cards off the table, my triumphantly laughing father, and myself—were all the same age.

Of course this daily life of ours was marginal. We were like stand-ins, who in all their activities never cease to wait for the regulars to come back and take things in hand. The house regained its center only when my mother was brought back from the hospital. After that, the regular workers were not some mere strangers but our very own selves; the stand-ins gave themselves a jolt and became, each in his accustomed place, regulars. We had been told that the patient hadn't long to live, but how were we to know? She was free from pain and lay or sat up in her bed, hardly noticeable, quite unlike the healthy woman who, while doing certain kinds of work, had moaned and groaned for no reason. It never occurred to me that she was going to die. Nor, apparently, to my father and sister. My father, who since retiring some years past had scarcely stirred from the farm, now took to going farther and farther afield, first walking to the neighboring villages of Rinkolach and Dob, which for a man of his stamp amounted to crossing a border, then actually to the north, across the Drava "to the Germans," where to his mind the innermost circle of "foreign parts" began. My sister dressed with care, kept herself and the house neat and clean, and most of all functioned as the experienced cook who conjured up still nameless dishes that had never been seen in our house before. And this, too, seemed to suit the bedridden woman in the center. She let my father tell her—it was late spring—about the progress of the fruit blossoms, and the grain, the level of the Drava, the thaw on Mount Petzen; let my sister, who was at last good for something, wait on her, as though this were what she had been longing for all her life, and devoured the ceremoniously served dishes with shining eyes (for a brief moment the smell of the cooking made us forget the smell of my mother's medicines). And what about me? I, too, had my role in the ceremony— and God help anyone who muffed his part—the role of storyteller. At last I was able, without being questioned, to sit down beside her bed—at the middle, because, as the superstition had it, the angels of death stood at the head and foot—and tell stories to drive them out of the house. And what did I tell my mother? My wishes. And when her eyes mocked them, that only made me start over again, start further back, circle around them in other words. And when word and wish became one, a warmth invaded my whole body and suddenly something akin to belief would appear in the eyes of the incredulous listener—a quieter, purer color, a glimmer of thoughtfulness.

But the leading role in this ceremony was played by the house. Every hitherto sullen, uncomfortable corner of it now proved to be livable, the right place for such thoughtfulness. The wood and the walls had a tone; the space between bed and table, window and door, fireplace and water tap widened. My father had built a house where, whatever part of it one moved or sat still in, it was good to be, a house where hitherto inconceivable things became possible. He himself proved it, for instance by playing us a concert of classical music on the radio, and calling each instrument by name as it emerged from the farthermost corner of the room, in such a way that I distinguished their different sounds as I would later in a concert hall. And then he surprised us by doing something in the daylight that he normally did only in church by candlelight. Coming home from one of his forays, he threw himself on his knees, both knees at once, and for a long time touched his forehead to my mother's. Often in later years I saw this grouping of man and wife in two mountains of the Karawanken range, the pointed Hochobir and the broad Koschuta.

It was only at night that the ark which sheltered us during those months broke apart. Especially in the hours before dawn, I would start up, awakened by a soundless bursting, and lie awake with the others, who, I knew as though there had been no walls, were also lying awake. My mother hadn't moaned. No mirror had shattered—there were no mirrors in our house; no owl had hooted in the woods behind the house. No clock was ticking—there were no clocks in the house; and no train was rumbling across the Jaunfeld Plain. Nor was it my own breathing that I heard, but only a whispering, arising, it seemed to me, from the troughlike valley deep down in the plain where the Drava flowed. My sister lay downstairs in the former dairy, where the drain still gave off a sour smell; my father, with wide-open eyes and toothless mouth, lay beside my mother, who alone was asleep or at least had not been awakened, and the slightest creaking resounded through the house like the crack of a whip, to which other sounds, which unlike the strokes of the church clock could not be counted, responded echolike from indeterminate directions. And when my father, before the first birdsong, went out on one of his rambles, I felt that he was running away from his dying wife and leaving us alone in his nightmare house.

During one such night I dreamed that we were all walking back and forth in the dark, deserted living room, and that my brother was standing in the middle, shedding tears of gratitude because we loved him. Looking around, I saw the others weeping, too, and my father in a corner weeping because he had finally been found out, exposed as someone who loved his family and no one else. And it was only thus, weeping, moving back and forth with dangling arms in the deserted room, forbidden to approach one another, forbidden to touch one another, that we Kobals could be a family, and that only in a dream. But what did I mean by "only in a dream"?

Because the day before I left for Yugoslavia I saw with waking eyes the truth of my dream vision. I should already have boarded the train; I had an unsuccessful, distraught, unfeeling leave-taking behind me, but after an hour alone at the Mittlern station I decided to go back and spend one more night at home. I left my sea bag with the men at the ticket office and turned back eastward, first along the railroad line, then through the sparse Dobrawa pine woods, the largest coppice in the country. It was an early-summer afternoon, and the sun was behind me. In the woods, where I knew the places to look, I found the first mushrooms of the year: small, firm chanterelles, almost white in the gravelly Dobrawa soil; then boletes, each a perceptible weight in my hand, more and more of which beckoned to me as, while walking, I, ordinarily none too sure of my sense of color, began to distinguish the colors more clearly; and finally, at the edge of the woods, jutting out from the grass, its tall, thin, hollow stalk swaying in the wind, a single parasol mushroom, visible from far off. I ran to it as though I had to be first to reach this king. Its cap, as large as a shield and domed in the middle, extended beyond the palms of both my hands but weighed less than the thinnest wafer.

After wrapping my mushrooms in my brother's enormous handkerchief, which like various articles of his clothing had been forced upon me for my journey,

I approached Rinkenberg and the house, where I was sure of finding my mother lying with her face to the wall, my sister on all fours about to relapse into her confusion, and my father sitting down among the ashes like Job.

Not at all. The house stood open and empty, my mother's bedclothes hung out of the window, airing. I found the three of them on the grassplot behind the house, with a fourth person, a neighbor, who had helped my father carry my mother out of the house in an armchair. She was sitting there barefoot, in a long white nightgown, an old horse blanket over her knees, and the others were sitting around her on the grassy bench provided by a slight hollow in the plot. At first it seemed to me that I had surprised my family in some secret, as if they were glad at last to be among themselves without me, able at last to let themselves go. For, though quiet, they seemed exuberant; my sister was amusing herself making faces in all directions, imitating the expressions of various people, challenging the others to guess who; one of these various people, the most laughed at—by my father as well, whose hat was on crooked—I recognized as myself. (I had many times felt myself to be unwanted, an intruder, a spoilsport, and often enough I really was.) But when they noticed me, the grassplot was suffused with a radiance which now, a quarter of a century later, brightens this deserted place for me. My ailing mother gave me a smile of infinite kindness, a smile such as I had never known, and it lifted me off the ground.

I sat down with them, the family was complete. My sister quickly prepared the mushrooms, and even I enjoyed them, though as a rule I was keener on gath-

ering than on eating them. Though no table was set up,
no cloth laid, it was a banquet, and our neighbor, who
had just been leaving to answer the call of work, took
time out for it. From then on, all I remember is sitting
there for hours without anyone saying a word. Long,
narrow eyes, bent at the corners like boat keels. From
that unaccustomed vantage point—we seldom sat on
this grassplot, ordinarily our washing was spread out
there to bleach—my father's house seemed to stand
alone, not in the village named Rinkenberg, but in an
unknown and nameless part of the earth, under a
strange sky. In the rooms, a breeze that could be felt
out here in the soft meadow grass. A pear on the
espalier wobbled and fell. The boards of the long-
abandoned apiary showed their colors, which taken
together disclosed a face, and that face was repeated in
the white of the cat half hidden under the dark green
box tree. The barouche in the shed, superannuated like
the farm implements, stood out from the other vehicles
and parts of vehicles with its festive unweathered gloss;
one last time it drove out of the shed and over the
countryside alone, followed by a flock of birds which
proceeded to dive through the air like dolphins. But
we were not in an enterprising mood; we had been
seized with a kind of timidity, along with a confidence
that was all the stronger because there was no reason
for it. Only my sister disturbed the order of things with
her activity, coming and going, talking, combing my
mother's hair, washing her feet. True, in disturbing the
order she also reinforced it; her activity was needed to
make the order cogent and enduring; and whenever
she touched the woman in the armchair, took hold of
her, turned her around, she did so officially, so to speak,

as our representative. In my recollection, it is not a group of people sitting there in the sun, but only the usual dazzlingly white sheets, spread out on the grass. Someone is sprinkling them from a watering can, the sound of water is a sharp crackling, the little puddles on the sheets evaporate quickly, and the grassplot is an inclined plane from which everything else, including myself, has vanished, slid away.

That is the story of those hours. But what of the event that made me turn back? Was it just a momentary impulse? Why, to begin with, had I gone to the Mittlern rather than the Bleiburg station? I had missed the midday train and had so long to wait until the afternoon train that I decided to kill time by walking two stations and ten kilometers westward. But incapable as I was of dawdling, of walking slowly, of making a detour, I was still much too early. The Mittlern station, built of undressed gray stone, lies outside the village, at the edge of the Dobrawa Forest, and is a massive, imposing edifice for the Jaunfeld Plain, where almost everything—the houses, the trees, even the churches—and the people tend to be rather small. For an hour I walked back and forth outside it. Not a sound but for the crunching of the black gravel under my feet and, on the other side of the single-track rails gleaming in the sun, the occasional sighing of the wind in the pines, which with their thin trunks and small dark cones I now regard as the emblem of that whole countryside, along with the whiteness of the isolated birches (even the surface roots are white) which fringed the forest and at that time had not yet been moved into parks as ornamental plants. The stationmaster lived on the second floor; the window curtains were torn and in the window boxes grew the inevitable gleaming-red geraniums, the smell of which had always repelled me at home. Behind the windows, no sign of life. At intervals, petals shot downward, somehow reminding me of insect wings. I sat down on a bench in the shade, facing one end of the station. The bench stood beside a bush on which hung, instead of the present scraps of white paper, greenish condoms. At my feet, almost submerged in grass, a circular stone. An old foundation? I raised my head and saw in the end wall of the station a rectangle—a blind window the same whitish-gray color as the wall, but set in from it. Though no longer in the sun, this window shimmered with reflected light from somewhere. In Rinkenberg there was only one such window, and it happened to be in the smallest house, the roadmender's, the one that looked like the porter's lodge of a nonexistent manor. It, too, was the color of the wall—yellow in that case—but was bordered with white. Whenever I passed, it caught my eye, but when I stopped to look, it always fooled me. Nevertheless, it never lost a certain undefined significance for me, and I felt that such a window was lacking in my father's house. Now, at the sight of the Mittlern blind window, I remembered: one night in January 1920, forty years ago, my father carried my brother, a child barely able to walk at the time, here in a wheelbarrow. The child was suffering from "ophthalmic fever" and my father was taking him to Klagenfurt to see the doctor. His nocturnal effort was in vain, the eye was lost; in the picture in the radio-and-crucifix corner there was nothing in its place but a milky whiteness. But this memory explained nothing. The significance of the blind window remained undefined, but suddenly that window became a sign, and in that same moment I decided to turn back. My turning back—and here again the sign was at work—was not definitive; it applied only to the hours until the following morning, when I would really start out, really begin my journey, with successive blind windows as my objects of research, my traveling companions, my signposts. And when later, on the evening of the following day, at the station restaurant in Jesenice, I thought about the shimmering of the blind window, it still imparted a clear message—to me it meant: "Friend, you have time."

Two | THE
EMPTY
COW PATHS

WHAT I HAVE WRITTEN thus far about my father's house, about the village of Rinkenberg and the Jaunfeld Plain, must have been clearly present to my mind a quarter of a century ago in the Jesenice station, but I couldn't have told it to anyone. What I felt within me were mere impulses without sound, rhythms without tone, short and long rises and falls without the corresponding syllables, a mighty reverberation of periods without the requisite words, the slow, sweeping, stirring, steady flow of a poetic meter without lines to go with it, a general surge that found no beginning, jolts in the void, a confused epic without a name, without the innermost voice, without the coherence of script. What I had experienced at the age of twenty was not yet a memory. And memory meant not that what-had-been recurred but that what-had-been situated itself by recurring. If I remembered, I knew that an experience was thus and so, exactly thus; in being remembered, it first became known to me, nameable, voiced, speakable; accordingly, I look on memory as more than a haphazard thinking back—as work; the work of memory situates experience in a sequence that keeps it alive, a story which can open out into free storytelling, greater life, invention.

It is strange that even then, as often as I in my booth looked toward the bar, the waitress looked back, as though my way of looking, sitting, moving, tapping my fingers on the table, told her the whole story for which I have only now found the words, as though there were no need for me to tell her anything more. For hours, wordlessly busy with my story, I had been fiddling with my empty bottle and the woman at the bar had been twirling an empty ashtray to the same rhythm. Unlike my enemy's aping, this parallel twisting and turning invigorated me. And another reason why I felt no pressure to get up and go was that some men were still playing dice in the next booth; as long as they were playing, I could sit there. It pleased me that I could not understand the language the invisible men were speaking and that I, a foreigner, was able now and then to pick up a die that had fallen on the floor and hand it to these men, who almost certainly were no more at home in Jesenice than I was (Serbs, Croats, or Macedonians, no doubt; wouldn't they, otherwise, have gone home long ago?), fancying as I did so that I was someone from a neighboring village showing a group of real foreigners, who had drifted in from the ends of the earth, the way. And it gave me special pleasure that by looking at the waitress I would for a while be seeing a recovered, vivacious, healthy version of my mother. Of course I must have been tired, but the sight of her kept me awake, so I can't remember any tiredness. It was only when the dice players had gone that the actress playing the part of my mother broke the spell by reverting to waitress and coming from behind the bar. Her movements now running counter to mine, she asked me to leave: "It's almost midnight."

My fatigue didn't hit me until I was out on the street. It wasn't the different place but the transition. I had gone through it without stopping, as though there were nothing there, and after a few steps the surroundings of the last few hours had disappeared. I was no longer anywhere, and what now stopped was my breath.

I couldn't go back to the station and I didn't know where else to go. I stood still. This was not a contemplative standing-there as when I arrived, but a blind loitering in no way connected with my first day in another country. How often in my life before and since I've stood around like that! Where would I go next? What was the solution? There was one and it had to be found. Distraught, I turned this way and that, describing a pattern of aimlessness. How often in my life I've wandered like that, even in my own house, my own room, with my eyes in a clothes cupboard, my hand in a tool drawer.

By then there were no buses running, only a file of Yugoslavian army trucks, one after another, all headed for the border. The tarps were open and in the caves thus created I saw soldiers sitting back to back on both lengthwise benches. The two in the foreground at the edge of the platform were resting their arms on the cross strap barring the exit from the cave. Even in this detail, each truck was a repeat of the one preceding it. The straps were narrow and sagged, and yet the soldiers' arms resting on them were as inert, as motionless as if they had been tied fast, not by cords, but by fatigue. I followed the column out of town northward, in the direction from which I had just come. A smaller patrol car rolled slowly past me. The occupants looked at me but didn't stop. Remembering my Humtschach persecutors, I raised my hand in a quick salute, which was actually returned; a fugitive from the army wouldn't have looked like me. Then more covered wagons with their pyramids of backs, their rigid double heads, their arms supported by straps, their dangling hands; this caravan would never end. And then, almost disappointingly, there came a last truck, open at the back like the rest, but empty, and this empty cave reminded me of a particular tunnel through the Karawanken Mountains, the exit of which, as I looked back from the last car of a train a few hours ago—seen through the Jesenice night, that moment was already part of a meaningless past—had been as far away from me as the black semicircle was now. No more army trucks. The road was deserted. But a trail of fatigue and exhaustion seemed to cover the whole width of the valley, a cloud of smoke—incomparably more stifling than that of the big iron foundries in the south—which blotted out the last patch of sky and, like the legendary army of the air, attacked me momentarily from above, applying screws to my temples and straps to my forehead, and pushed me past the last houses of the town, into no-man's-land.

This first night in a foreign country might perhaps be told briefly, but in my memory it has become the longest in my life, decades long. At the age of twenty I wouldn't have dreamed of stopping at a hotel—and not only because I wanted to save money. Yet my only thought was sleep, and the tunnel did not strike me as an insane idea. I would go in where my train had just carried me out. All that mattered was a niche to sleep in.

Unseeing, I found the path alongside the tracks; unseeing, I found the hole in the fence, as though it were bound to be there. Already I was in the tunnel, as though in a house, and there, as I had foreseen, I found a niche, a recess in the rock, screened off from the tracks by a concrete parapet. "My stall," I thought. With the flashlight I had brought with me to search for some trace of my brother in a cave farther south (that at least was my youthful fancy), I lit up the clay floor, which looked rather like a brook with glittering mica along its banks. The concrete wall revealed nothing but a bit of hair clinging to it, an eyelash, which made me think of my history teacher in Villach at the Austrian end of the tunnel. Only that afternoon he had told me that the vehicular tunnel running parallel to mine had been built by prisoners during the last World War, and that many had died, some of them murdered; he had even advised me, though only in jest, to spend the night there if I found no other place. The sleep of one "still innocent," he said, "would help to purify the place of injustice, to banish the evil spirits, to blow away the horror"; he was writing just such a fairy tale, he told me. Since the last war, he said, he had seen something sinister in all tunnels, even the innocent Jesenice tunnel built under the Empire.

I began, in the darkness, by eating a piece of bread and an apple, the smell of which dispelled my initial queasiness, as though the fruit gave off a breath of fresh air. Then I lay down and curled up. But I could not sleep, or if I did, it was only to have instantaneous and interminable nightmares. My father's house lay empty, a ruin. The Drava rose from its deep valley and overflowed the whole plain. The sun shone on the Dobrawa heather and war had been declared. But I also woke up drenched in sweat because I had lost one of my shoes, because all of a sudden the part in my hair was on the left side instead of the right, because the soil in all our flowerpots at home had cracked and the flowers had dried out. Once, what made me start up was no dream but a night train, which sped by with an enormous din, scarcely a step from the parapet. It could only be an international express on its way to Belgrade, Istanbul, or Athens, and I thought of my schoolmates bound for Greece, who would be sleeping out of doors in their tents or sleeping bags, a good deal farther south no doubt. Excited by their evening expedition through a foreign town, by the warm night, and by the unaccustomed company of the boy or girl who sat beside them in class, they would talk and talk, and those who had already dozed off would be slumbering peacefully, free from nightmares, under the protection of their comrades. And I cursed myself for not being with them.

What tormented me most was not this place I had got myself into, this dark, supposedly haunted tunnel, but a sense of guilt. Not because I had left my family in the lurch, but because I was alone. That night, I discovered that even if I had done no particular wrong, it was a crime to be alone of my own free will. I had known that before and would learn it again in the future. A crime against whom? Against myself. Even the company of enemies would now have been a lesser evil. And hadn't my girlfriend, who unlike myself was fluent in Slovene, offered any number of times to guide Filip Kobal through his legendary homeland? Could I conceive of anything better at this moment than our two bodies breathing together? Than to lie beside her all night and wake up in the morning with my hand on her belly?

* * *

But the real nightmares were still to come. The story interrupted when I left the station restaurant went on in my sleep, but now it was different from what it was in my waking state—it was violent, abrupt, incoherent. It no longer poured out of me with an "and," a "then," and a "when," but chased me, harried me, drove me, sat on my chest, choked me until the only words I could get out consisted entirely of consonants. Worst of all, no sentence was ever completed, all my sentences broke off in the middle, rejected, maimed, garbled, disqualified, while at the same time I was forbidden to stop talking and, without pausing for breath, I had to keep starting all over, trying again, as though chained for life to a verbose, senseless rhythm which brought forth no meaning but with its retrograde movement destroyed and devalued what meaning I had arrived at during the day. Dragged into a dream light, the storyteller in me, only a short time before seen as the secret king, had become a forced laborer. Caught in the embrace, which would end only with death, of a story that had struck me when awake as the soul of gentleness but had now become a cruel monster, I was powerless to frame a single serviceable sentence. How malignant the spirit of storytelling could be!

And then, after a long onslaught, I suddenly succeeded in turning out two clear sentences, the one following naturally from the other, and in the same moment the pressure on me was relieved, I had a companion again. In my dream, this companion was a child; true, the child corrected me, improved on my story, but in so doing commended the teller. After that a tree, laden branch after branch not with fruit but with stones, which if not for the child would have signified "disaster," proved to be a miracle tree; a number of confident swimmers including myself disported themselves in the raging flood, and the sleeper felt the ground under his cheek to be a book.

Thus, my longest night included an enjoyable hour of half sleep, during which I was able to stretch out. Part of my pleasure consisted in lying on my back with my hands clasped under my neck, listening to the dripping from the ceiling of the tunnel. For a change, I didn't have to lie on my left side to feel at peace with myself. I had crept into the tunnel as a refuge, and now I made myself at home, using my brother's overcoat as a blanket. The darkness around me was a good deal lighter than long ago in the potato cellar. From the nearby exit, gray on gray, glowworms kept flying in and out. Holding one in the palm of my hand, I lit up an astonishingly large circle around me. I always associate the sleep of the exhausted Odysseus on reaching the isle of the Phaeacians with this sort of sheltered feeling.

But when the hour was over, my sleep suddenly fell away from me, and it was then that I began to feel alone for good. Half sleep had been, as it were, my last companion in solitude, my guide and protector. And now from one minute to the next it proved to be a delusion. My word-mangling dream had been a whirligig of ghosts, and now my waking seemed to be the punishment it threatened. And this punishment consisted not in being exposed to the elements in an undoubtedly inhospitable place, but in being stricken dumb. Here, far from human society, objects ceased to have a language and became enemies, executioners in fact. Yet what was destroying me was not that the iron bar protruding from the tunnel wall reminded me of torture or execution—but that, though sound of body, I was without company and, stricken mute, no longer company to myself. True, I saw the bar bent in the shape of the letter *S*, of the figure 8, of a treble-clef sign, but that was once upon a time; the fairy tale of the *S*, the 8, and the treble-clef sign had lost its symbolic meaning.

So I fled. Not from dread of the tunnel's history, not from the silence or the stifling air, or for fear of a cave-in or a lineman—I'd have been only too glad if the lineman had grabbed me by the scruff of the neck and cursed me in every known and unknown language— but in a single impulse of horror at the otherworldly speechlessness that was pressing in on me, for over and above bodily death it meant destruction of the soul, which, now that I am trying to speak of it, is recurring more violently, more devastatingly than ever. Then I had only to run a few steps to be out in the open, whereas today I am confined to the tunnel; there is no escape, no niche, no parapet, and my only way to humankind is to equip the objects of a mute planet, whose prisoner I have become through wishing (*mea culpa*) to be a storyteller, with eyes that look at me forgivingly. And that is why I now see the little knot of glowworms in the grass outside the tunnel blown up into a fire-spewing dragon guarding the entrance to the underworld—whether to defend a treasure there or for my protection, I do not know.

But what the upper world, or just the world, can be, I learned on the way back. Though it was still a long time till morning and there was no moon, I could see the contours of the valley clearly. The river that

went with it, the Sava Dolinka (or, as my father would
have said in German, *"die Wurzener Save"*), was a dull
glow moving between the sparsely wooded banks. On a
sloping meadow leading down to the water, a horse was
standing beside a tree; though it was too early for flies,
the horse was swishing its tail. The sound it made in
pulling up grass was the dominant sound of the countryside, accompanied by the faint murmur of the river
and the rumbling in the distant freight yards. Between
the railroad line and the bottom of the valley, the
meadow merged into a cluster of small gardens, which
in my memory have remained "the hanging gardens of
Jesenice." They formed a pattern of vegetable patches
and fruit trees, surrounded by low fences; in the center
of each one, there was a wooden hut with a bench in
front of it. This pattern, partly sloping, partly terraced,
continued down to the river, from which the gardens
seemed to draw their water. Their color, already growing visible, was a yellowish white: in the trees, early
apples, and in the gardens, beans. The path beside the
tracks where I was walking was soft—the dust was so
deep, so dense and yielding, that it didn't even retain
my shoe prints; and the dew didn't moisten it but
collected in little balls that stayed on the surface. With
my first step out of the tunnel, a stone weight had fallen
from my shoulders and the taste of metal was gone
from my teeth; my eyes were washed, not by the dew,
but by the strange sight of it. The previous night, I had
taken in the details of the valley, but now I saw them
as letters, as a series of signs, beginning with the grass-
pulling horse and combining to form a coherent script.
I now interpreted this land before my eyes, with the
objects, whether lying, standing, or leaning, which rose

up from it, this describable earth, as "the world"; and I was able to address this land, without special reference to the valley of the Sava or to Yugoslavia, as "my country." And at the same time this manifestation of the world was the only conception of a God that I have managed over the years to arrive at.

And so my further progress in that predawn hour became a deciphering, a continued reading, a transcribing, a silent taking of notes. (But hadn't I as a child, to the ridicule of my family, been in the habit of writing in the air?) And I then distinguished two bearers of the world: on the one hand, the earth's surface that supported the horse, the hanging gardens, and the wooden huts; and on the other hand, the decipherer, who had shouldered these things in the form of their hallmarks and signs. And I literally felt my shoulders broaden in my brother's too-spacious coat and—because the perception and combination of signs operated as a counterweight to the burden of material things—straighten up as though my deciphering transformed the weight of the earth into a single freely flying word, consisting entirely of vowels, such a word as the Latin *Eoae*, translatable as "At the time of Eos," "At dawn," or simply, "In the morning."

Long before sunrise, I saw the valley plunged into another sun, the sun of letters, which receded into the tunnel of night and there provided a kind of expiation by joining the cracks in the clay of my sleeping place— suffused with a bronze glow—into a regular script of polygons, a memorial tablet befitting the place. Since then, whenever I've taken the train through the Karawanken Mountains, I've stood by the window, waiting in the darkness for the first glimmer of daylight from the Yugoslavian end. And quickly as the train leaves the tunnel, I always have time to glimpse the clay niche, usually strewn with leaves that have blown in, and in it the curled-up twenty-year-old with his cylindrical sea bag, an air sculpture. To me the place is then not so much the scene of war crime or the cave of speechlessness that it was that night, as my shelter. *"Eoae!"* Wherever I chance to be in the morning, when I first look out of any window, that has become a rousing cry—aloud or only in thought—whereby the vowels that pour from me are translated back into the things outside me, this tree, the neighbor's house over there, the road between them, the airfield in the distance, the line of the horizon, thus opening up my senses to the new, literal, and describable day.

E-O-A-E: I made my way in darkness over a strip of land between the railroad line and the river. Though I didn't see a living soul, the country seemed alive and inhabited, because what spoke to my senses was all man-made and, as it were, ready for action. Near the station, work had actually begun in a few warehouses and workshops. A switchboard was lit up, while the rest of the room was still in darkness; the needles of gauges trembled and advanced; a regular thumping in every corner. A big steel wheel was set in motion and turned faster and faster, until the spokes disappeared and the whole wheel became a solid circle on the back wall. A lamp on a table in a dark office lit up a telephone, a slide rule, an alarm clock. The door of a loading ramp stood half open; the ramp opened out on a railroad yard with signals that changed colors. One nighttime image after another, it seemed to me, of unremitting activity. There was no one to be seen, though I assumed the presence of workers. Only once was the "work" series broken—by a cloth lampshade, a yellow dome behind a single curtain, it, too, untended by any human being—but resumed at once with the clatter of a warehouse ventilator, a fast-moving belt sliding back and forth on its slippery bed, and the shadows cast by puffs of chimney smoke on the road—on which I was now walking, because there was no other way of getting ahead.

I had seen similar things at home on the other side of the border, especially on the periphery of the few cities I knew, and I wondered why there I had always felt excluded, whereas here I had no difficulty in sensing the vibration from these enclosed shops; and the one room with the dome-shaped lampshade, very differently from anything I ever experienced at home, caught my imagination as an embodiment of ease and comfort, as the luminous center of the series, a temple of safety and warmth. I was reminded of a conversation heard the day before among a group of workers who had been sitting on a bench at the Austrian frontier station in Rosenbach, waiting for their bus. It went roughly as follows: "Another day."—"Thursday already."—"But then it'll start all over."—"It'll soon be fall."—"And then it won't be long till winter."—"At least it's not Monday."—"When I get up, it's dark; when I come home, it's dark again. I haven't seen my house yet this year."

Why did this at first sight so inhospitable predawn industrial zone here in Yugoslavia, kept in motion by invisible hands as though for all time, give me an entirely different impression of workers, in fact of human beings in general, from anything I had ever known in my own country? No, it was not, as we had been taught, the "fundamentally different economic and social system" (though I'd gladly have been faceless, with a number instead of a name, and even given up my supposed freedom); nor was it only that this was a foreign country (though, on my very first day there, many of the usual sights had struck me as stimulating novelties): it was something more than a mere thought or feeling—it was the certainty that at last, after almost twenty years in a non-place, in a frosty, unfriendly, cannibalistic village, I was standing on the threshold of a country which, unlike my so-called native land, did not lay claim to me in the name of compulsory education or compulsory military service, but to which, on the contrary, I could lay claim as the land of my forefathers, which thus, however strange, was at least my own country! At last I was stateless; at last, instead of being always present, I could be lightheartedly absent; at last, though there wasn't a soul in sight, I felt that I was among my people. Hadn't a child pointed at me on the platform in Rosenbach and shouted at the top of his lungs: "Look, somebody from down there!" ("Down there" meant Yugoslavia, while Germany or Vienna was "out there.") The free world, it was generally agreed, was the world from which I had come—for me at the moment, it was the world that I had so literally before me.

That this was a delusion I knew even then. But I didn't want that kind of knowledge, or rather: I wanted to get rid of it; I recognized this wanting-to-get-rid-of-it as my life-feeling; and the inspiration I gained from that delusion is still with me.

When I think back on that hour, it was not the machines, whether operating or standing in readiness, which deluded me into thinking that there, unseen, my people were indefatigably at work, but, most of all, the lights, that of the shaded lamp in the one dwelling, that of the office lamp on the desk, and especially the white, dusty, floury, fluorescent light, reproduced from workshop to workshop as from room to room in a flour mill. Into harness! Shoulder a wheel! Join in! Most surprising was this urge to be active in someone who otherwise, according to my father, was "just about useless for any kind of work." And it wasn't because there was no one around who might have watched me (for as a rule, again according to my father, being watched "made me all thumbs"); no, here, I was sure, it wasn't at all like at home; anyone who wanted to could watch me and I wouldn't feel observed. Every one of my movements would be "right."

But was it this empty vision of light that attracted me to those workshops, to those invisibly at work there? Was I not in reality drawn to a very different kind of working together which expressed itself most clearly in my silhouette entering the picture from outside, from the edge, from the road, and being fleetingly sketched into it as I passed? No, my father's leather strap, his travel amulet, was not tied around my wrist to give me a better grip but, if for any purpose, for warmth; my sense of oneness with the workers came less from any desire to work with them than from pleasurable, unburdened passing-by.

Thus I learned the differences between conformity, consonance, and congruence. Conformity: I have always found it intolerable to keep in step with others, even with one person; if I found myself in step with someone, I had to stop instantly or quicken my pace, or move to one side; even when my girlfriend and I chanced to fall into step, I saw us as two soulless marchers-against-the-world. And consonance, too, was impossible for me: if anyone else, and not only in singing, gave me the keynote, I was incapable of taking it up and sustaining it; or conversely, if someone else took up my intonation, I was immediately thrown off; only the dissonance of the quarrel to which this prompted me saved me from falling silent (such quarrels were often brought on by my girlfriend speaking of us as "we," a word I could never bring myself to utter).

Congruence was a different matter, a powerful experience; I felt this, for instance, one morning when I turned the window handle and simultaneously heard in the distance the closing of a car door, the scraping of a snow shovel, and a train whistle screeching at the horizon; or another time, when a bowl was put down on the stove just as I was opening a letter; or when I now look up from my writing and, as often happens at this time of day, a sunbeam strikes the darkened painting on the opposite wall and moves from left to right like a spotlight, making every tree, every sparkle on the water, every fork in the road, every fringe of cloud stand out from the somber surface. And I had the same experience that day, when before daybreak, carrying my sea bag with my brother's two books, a welcome burden, I passed the pounding, whistling, or just silently bright industrial installations of Jesenice. I even strode more firmly in order to set this congruence in motion—no, I wasn't going to let any big or little enemy kick me in the legs from behind—and then, just as I had caught sight of the empty workshops, I glimpsed the first human being of the day, the outline of a bus driver in a dark, otherwise empty bus, moving at high speed, as though it were already expected at every bus stop in the valley, and then the first couple, a man and a woman at the window of a tall building, she standing in a housecoat, he sitting in his undershirt. What has remained most clearly in my memory over the years is the mist on the windowpane, which made me guess that the man up there was not about to set out for work but had just come home from his job, sweating, breathing heavily after a night of labor, which transferred itself to me as though it were my own.

A single unset table and an oilcloth-covered kitchen chair were standing in front of a restaurant, diagonally across from the station. I sat down in the chair and let the day break. My seat was slightly below the level of the tracks and of the street and sidewalk, from which a few steps led down to a small, polygonal concrete surface which was bordered on the other side by a semicircle of houses, each wall of which formed a different angle with the next, thus giving the impression of a bay sheltered on all sides and offering a protected vantage point from which one looked not down as usual but upward from below and instead of a panorama saw a proximate but all the more impressive view, as though from the bottom of a hollow. The houses were low and old, but each dated from a different period. Just behind them began the sloping valley with its mass of dark foliage, above which the tips of the spruces were gradually coming into sight.

In my hollow, it would long be night. Was I dreaming that tiny bird, a motionless silhouette up on the edge of the sidewalk? I had never seen a day bird at night. The street looked like a wall with this wren sitting on it. The restaurant opened early; the first customers were railroad workers; they drank their coffee or schnapps—I could see them over my shoulder—in one gulp and were gone. The sky, which had looked rainy in the first light, was cloudless and radiant. An aged waitress with the furrowed face of a man brought me a pot of coffee with milk and a plate piled with thick slices of white bread. The skin on the coffee reminded me of my brother, who, so I was told, had always detested those rubbery blobs. When, on his first leave from the front, my mother, supposing the war had cured him of his fussiness, served him the usual coffee, he had pushed the cup away, saying: "Don't bother me." I saw the milk welling up and forming a skin that broke into islets on the dark surface, which then grew lighter. The mound of white bread beside it didn't last long. Fresh as it was, it took in air after being compressed in cutting, and swelled up under my hungry eyes. I ate it, razed and demolished it in one go. That white bread has meant "Yugoslavia" to me ever since.

When I looked up after eating, droves of people were passing on the sidewalk up above; the street had become a dike. Summer vacation couldn't have begun yet, there were too many schoolchildren among the passersby, leaning into the wind. It was indeed windy, and the tall meadow grass at the edge of the dike sighed like dune grass. Though I have never been at the seashore, I couldn't help thinking that the Atlantic dunes must begin right after the railroad tracks.

An old man came out of the restaurant with a second kitchen chair and sat down at some distance from me; to enjoy the view, he had no need of a table. Without exchanging so much as a word, we watched developments together; we both looked at the same thing, we studied it for the same length of time, then, simultaneously, passed on to something else. I have never known such a view as on that morning after my longest night, never beheld such space and such a horizon as in that seeing, which I knew to be one with that of the man beside me. We immersed ourselves in the glow on the throat of a pigeon which was crossing the concrete bay above us, or turned our heads back to the dike, where clouds of smoke from the steel mill were drifting up the valley in the direction of the tunnel, as though to smoke out the whole length of it.

When at home, before my trip, I had looked southward in clear weather, it seemed certain that, under the bluing sky beyond the mountains, there could only be cities resplendent with color, spreading out over a wide plain, unobstructed by any chain of hills, the one merging with the next all the way to the sea. And yet the industrial city of Jesenice now, gray on gray, squeezed into a narrow valley, shut in between two shade-casting mountains, fully confirmed my anticipation. Looking up at the dike, I saw a man with a gleaming red saw in each hand, followed by two children eating ice cream and a woman in an advanced state of pregnancy, wearing an airy dress and clogs. The perpetual clatter of the long-distance trucks on the single strip of unasphalted cobblestones reminded me again of my brother, who in his prewar letters spoke of a similar stretch of road between Maribor and Trieste. On every one of his excursions to the Adriatic, the car (the school principal's) had been "thoroughly shaken for a short while," and after that he had felt "bathed in salt air."

In Yugoslavia, time as well as space seems to be measured differently than it is beyond the northern mountains. Comparable to sedimentary rock, the buildings before my eyes pointed to strata of the architectural past, from the foundations of Imperial Austria to the bay windows of the kingdom of the south Slavs and the smooth, unornamented upper stories of the present People's Republic of Slovenia, not omitting holes for flagpoles just below the attic windows. While looking at one of these façades, I suddenly wished with all my might that my missing brother would push open the decrepit terrace door, with its opaque grooved glass, and show himself. I even thought in words: "Forefather, show thyself," and saw the head of the old man beside me turn toward the bay window. And for a moment, as though my call were its own fulfillment, I caught sight of my brother, full-grown (as I had never known him), broad-shouldered, brown-skinned, his thick, dark, curly hair combed straight back, his imposing forehead and his eyes so deep in their sockets that his white blindness remained hidden. A shudder ran through me, as though I were seeing my king, a shudder of awe, but even more of terror, which made me leave my place in the hollow without delay and slip into the torrent of passersby on the street above.

It received me at once. My impression from below was false; it was not a torrent at all but an astonishingly leisurely flow in which my excitement over my successful evocation of an ancestor was appeased by an unhurried present.

To walk in such a flow was something new to me at the age of twenty. The village knew nothing of the kind—

the best it could do was a struggling step-by-step or the marking time of holiday processions and funerals; at the seminary, one walked either alone or in a compulsory group (even our Sunday walks had to be taken in a group, in columns of two, with those behind treading on the heels of those in front of them, and anyone who thought of drifting away was instantly detected and whistled back); and in the small towns of Austria—those were the only ones I knew, for Vienna, the capital, when we went there on a school excursion, was hidden from me by the shoulders of my schoolmates and the index fingers of the teachers—I could only trot along on the fringe with my eyes to the ground. On those streets, I immediately grew skittish (perhaps a more concrete word than the usual "shy"); that is, I didn't know which way to look, or else I looked in all directions, anything but straight ahead. In the small towns—not at all as in the village of Rinkenberg—my gaze was either distracted at every step by shop windows, advertising posters, and, above all, newspaper headlines, or, as happened once when I directed it toward the vanishing point of the street, it fell, or so I imagined, straight into the eye trap of someone coming in the opposite direction. The trap was not just a look; it was a stare, or rather an eyeless, faceless blank, with no organ attached to it but a monstrous trunklike mouth which with a single word, always monosyllabic, always inaudible, that I could always lip-read even in its typical dialect form, sucked me in and snapped shut over me. Yes, in the towns of my native land it was not possible, when one stepped out into the street, to merge with a flow of people; one was immediately, so it seemed to me, hemmed in and pocketed by people who had been trudging in a vicious circle with their dogs since the world began, who, as usual with people condemned to move in such circles, unfailingly felt themselves to be in the right and in their proper place. Is it mere imagination that, to this day, certain *"Grüss Gott"*'s fired at me in my native land strike me more as threats than as greetings ("Out with the password, or else!"), and that especially when they are bellowed by children, I often involuntarily fling both my hands into the air? Whether walking on the side or in the middle of the street, I always felt myself appraised, judged, found guilty by the Austrian crowd, the Austrian majority, and time and again I accepted their verdict, though with no idea of what I was guilty of. What a relief to be walking down a street, convinced that some member of the eye-trapper gang must be studying me from the side, and then to look up and see nothing but the vacant eyes of a doll in a shop window.

On this Yugoslavian street there was no majority, and accordingly no minority, but only a varied and yet harmonious bustle such as, apart from the small town of Jesenice, I have known only in big cities. And here, for the present, I was the foreigner, to whom, in the streets of Carinthia beyond the mountains, I have always been grateful, because he distracts attention from me, but who here had his place in the crowd, among the people of the street. While back there I would be constantly changing place, getting clumsily out of the way, bumping into people, here I just walked along, and each one of my steps, unaccustomed as I was to the crowding, found room on the pavement. At last I didn't trot or shuffle (as all of us did in the corridors of the seminary), but found my natural gait; I felt my feet rolling from the toes over the balls to the heels; now and then, in passing, I kicked some little thing aside with a feeling of quiet impudence which, as I discovered only after I had done it a few times, harked back to my childhood long ago. And what delighted me most about this crowd, when I compared it to other crowds I knew, was what it lacked, the things that were missing: the chamois beards, the hartshorn buttons, the loden suits, the lederhosen; in short, no one in it wore a costume. These people in the street were free not only from costume but also from insignia, from marks of caste; even the uniforms of the policemen did not stand out, but rather, as was only fitting, suggested public service. It was a blessing to be relieved of my skittishness, to be able to raise my eyes and look straight ahead, at eyes which, instead of appraising me, merely showed their colors, and these colors, black with brown with gray, revealed "the world." Another thing that contributed to my newfound pride—and in this I was no longer a foreigner—was that I recognized my inner and outer resemblance, something no mirror could have shown me, to the other people in the crowd. Like them, I was gaunt, bony, awkward, with rough-hewn features and arms that dangled inelegantly, and my nature like theirs was compliant, willing, undemanding, the nature of a people who had been kingless and stateless down through the centuries, a people of journeymen and hired hands (not a noble, not a master among them)—and yet we children of darkness were radiant with beauty, self-reliant, bold, rebellious, independent, each man of us the next man's hero.

The passersby were the consonants that went with the vowels which things awakened in me, though no words sprang from their union; I was merely seized by a second wind, independent of my own lungs, a wind of enthusiasm which suddenly enabled me to read the sober headings of a Slovenian paper being carried past me, no screaming headlines as in my German paper, but just news, as refreshing as the absence of costumes. And all at once I began to understand much of what was being said in the crowd. Was it because here in the street no one spoke to me? Did it mean that since my days at elementary school, where I had been obliged to speak the foreign language with my teacher, I had not become forgetful—but only obstinate? *Jutro* was still morning, *danes* today, *delo* work, *cesta* road, *predor* tunnel. I was also able to read the names of the shops; they were all so simple. Unlike the shops in the north, with their loud, pretentious signs, the dairy was identified simply by the word for milk, the bakery by the word for bread, and I didn't translate the words *mleko* and *kruh* into a different language, but back into images, into the childhood of words, my first images of milk and bread. The bank, *banka*, that followed was the same old word, but it, too, took on an original character because its windows were not showcases, there were no displays; the space which in my native land might contain a pyramid of bright-colored strongboxes was empty—with an emptiness that stood open to me, and to which I could address myself as I could to the empty faces of the passersby. Among them I had no need, as at home, to look for a relative or a fellow villager to deliver me with a smile of recognition from that file of mere masks. The emptiness of the faces here meant they were not wearing masks. I have before me a picture of some young fellows squeezed into a tractor trailer, swathed from top to toe in fur disguises. They are on their way to an Alpine city to take part in the traditional hunt. Before entering the city, they are not yet holding the necessary rods and chains, and the enormous terror-instilling masks they will pull over their heads are still at their feet. Protruding from their fur ruffs, the faces of these young fellows, peasants no doubt, seem thin, soft, approachable! In much the same way, I was able to look into the procession of faces in Jesenice as into a single face, and it gave me the dignity I had never experienced at home, either in myself or in anyone else—well yes, in my father, during the Easter vigil in the Rinkenberg church, when, clad in a floor-length purple robe, he, along with a few other villagers, knelt beside the hollow that was supposed to represent the tomb of the resurrected Christ, then in one movement threw himself down in front of it and, covered by his candlewax-spotted robe, lay unrecognizably still on his belly. And just as my father named the instruments in the radio concert, I was now able, through the roar of the traffic and factories, to distinguish clearly the sound of colliding buffers in the railroad yards, the rattling of carts in the supermarket, the hissing of steam from an escape valve, the scraping of a stiletto heel, the pounding of a hammer, and the sound of myself inhaling and exhaling. And strangely enough, it occurred to me, this, too, this surprisingly acute hearing resulted from something that was not here, something that was absent in this Slovenian factory town. It was the absence of the usual striking church clocks that sharpened my hearing of the things around me. So it was not just any country, but this particular one, this country of deficiencies, which could be compared to and distinguished from my usual country and thus deciphered as "world."

But the kingdom of the world that I perceived in

this way exceeded the limits of present-day Yugoslavia
and all the kingdoms and empires of olden times, and
gradually its signs lost their definition. The Cyrillic
letters on the newspapers of certain passersby were still
clear, the vestiges of an old Austrian inscription on a
public building were legible, as was the ancient Greek
χαῖρε—Greetings—on the tympanum of a villa; but, on
the other hand, the word PETROL on a gas station, which,
seen through the branches of a tree, reminded me of a
China known to me only from dreams, was ambiguous,
and an equally exotic Sinai Desert opened up to me
behind the high-rise buildings at the sight of a dusty
long-distance bus, on the front of which the roller
indicating its destination had stopped exactly in the
middle between two illegible place names. As it passed,
a fragment of a Hebrew scroll struck my eyes—yes,
struck my eyes, for the landscape that opened up around
the script was fraught with terror.

The vagueness was underlined by a blind window,
to which my gaze was now drawn as to the center of
the world. It was fairly high up the slope on the sunny
side of a large house, which I fancied to be the manor
belonging to the porter's lodge across the border. It
stood by itself; in front of it there was only a single
spruce, whose fur-brown bark brought out the massive-
ness of the yellow façade. A steep stone stairway led
across a strip of meadow to the entrance. A child was
on the stairway with his back to me; one foot a step
lower than the other, he seemed hesitant; the steps were
too big for a child. The slope was hatched, so to speak,
with strange oblique grooves, small terraces overgrown
with grass, whose fine shadow pattern was repeated in
the oblique grooves of the façade. This made the house

behind the spruce look more like a yellow rock than like a building. It seemed uninhabited. The child on the steps was in the entrance not to a house but to a playground.

The blind window was, far and wide, the only one of its kind. It owed its effect to the absence of something ordinarily present: to its opacity. Thanks to its extreme vagueness, it reflected my gaze; and the muddle of languages, the confusion of voices within me fell silent: my whole being fell silent, and read.

I had never thought it possible that I would lose this blind window; I had felt it to be an unalterable sign. Yet one side glance sufficed: the light emanating from it was gone. The window next to it—a "sighted" window, as it were—was pushed open and closed again, by hands belonging to two different people, a very old woman, then a young one. The old woman—as I recognized in the same moment—was more than old, she was dying; with a last burst of revolt she had tried to get out of the room where she was being held fast, to escape through the window grating from death; a face convulsed with horror, with sucked-in lower lip and wide-open eyes, which would never again close unaided.

The window remained empty, the morning sun was reflected in it, but the light which had been bright only a moment before had not just gone out, it had been swallowed up. The child had vanished, too, as if he had been a phantom, and the oblique grooves on the house and the hillside now appeared to be shadows. "Filip Kobal has a thing about appearances." My history teacher had often said that—a mixture of praise and blame. Today, once again, the "appearance" had been dispelled. Already the grimace of a little girl crying with all her might came my way, and after that there was nothing female, male, or childlike about the crowd. On the sidewalk there was nothing but a huge, hard, bony mass of repulsive yokels, pushing, shoving, getting in one another's way, under the vigilant eye, peering from every possible angle, of the Chief of State, who, whether as a young partisan leader in an automobile factory, as a white-clad admiral, as an imposing dinner-jacket-wearer on the arm of his equally imposing wife in the lobby of a movie theater, as an imperator's head cast in concrete in the courtyard of a school, was now the sole ruler over us all. A last searching glance up at the blind window merely reinforced the authority of the state, for, as though I had attracted suspicion with that glance, a policeman beckoned me with a slow movement of his curved forefinger to the other side of the street, where he asked for my papers. Later, it occurred to me that this policeman was the same young man, about my age, who had examined my passport on my arrival the day before. But in that hour of solar eclipse no one seemed to recognize anyone else; it was as though we had all lost our memories.

Counting my steps, I entered the station. A damp stairway led down to the toilets as to a bunker. The usual bunker woman was sitting there; nothing was missing but the bunch of keys at her waist. In the lockless cubicle, I looked in vain for the usual graffiti and drawings; they would have helped me on. There was no faucet over the washbasin, only a hole in the wall. The waiting room upstairs was dark and stank. The first thing I noticed about the other people sitting

The Empty Cow Paths   101

there was the whiteness of a striking number of bound
or plastered limbs. The light didn't come from the
station platform but from the dark corridor in between.
Later, I distinguished, here and there, a leather cot
over an injured thumb, and the man sitting next to me
had a scab in his hair. (I'm not exaggerating, such things
caught my eye.) In myself as well, I noticed only what
was repellent: the caked clay on my shoes, the black
rings under my fingernails. Anyone would have known
that I had spent the night in my clothes and hadn't
washed. My scalp itched, and so, though it was midsummer, did the seminary chilblains on my toes. I tried in
vain to decipher my next destination on the map; the
light that fell was barely enough for the white of the
lowlands and the pale blue of the glaciers.

I went out on the platform, where a worker was
cracking open the concrete with a pneumatic drill. The
morning train to Austria was on the opposite track,
ready to leave. The compartments were bright, clean,
and almost empty (this train was not yet used, as in
later years, by many Yugoslavs for shopping trips to
Villach). Again, blue-uniformed train men were standing by the locomotive, along with Austrian border
guards, not recognizable as such because they were out
of uniform; in their shirtsleeves, with their jackets slung
over their shoulders, they all seemed to be waiting for
a tardy passenger. All at once, though I didn't stir from
the spot, I was in a hurry. Make up your mind! I felt
an almost irresistible urge to return across the border,
to go home to my village, my room, my bed, and get
my sleep out. But my most immediate refuge was the
language, my familiar native German on the side of the
locomotive. *Heimatbahnhof* (home station) would do—

for it wasn't the meaning that mattered but the look of the word—or the legend *Arbeitsrichtung* (working direction) over the arrow.

Undecided as I was, I felt utterly confused. The pneumatic drill was making star-shaped cracks, as when one walks on the surface of a frozen puddle. One of the cracks reached almost to the soles of my shoes. Shaken by the sound of the drill, I looked down and found the blind window in the gray of the concrete. Again it was a friendly sign meaning "to have time." Hadn't I wanted too much with my "kingdom of the world"? Who was I, actually? Looking at the pavement, I saw once and for all who I was: a foreigner, someone who might have some business here but who had no say. I had no claim to so-called human dignity as I did at home in my own country. This realization brought me something more than relief—it brought me serenity.

The Austrian train pulled out. Hadn't the conductor given me a questioning look? The station became large and luminous. The sparrows, which landed abruptly on the pavement at my feet and were already off again, had sat on the bushes of Rinkenberg only a moment before, and the oval plantain leaf in the roadbed also came from there, a so-called garden escape. With long strides, like decision incarnate, I went into the station and bought a ticket; with long strides, like a man who knows at last that what he is doing is not for himself alone, I took the underpass to the far platform and, after a quick wash at the pump, leapt resolutely into the southwest-bound train as though my jaunt across the border was over and I was now starting on my real journey. I had no sooner settled in my window seat than I fell asleep. If I still preserve an image of the adolescent I was then, with the torn-up pavement under my feet, it is perhaps because the pavement just then was threatening to keel over, just as certain objects impress themselves on our minds only when at the last moment we save them from falling and they rest in our trembling hands, available for examination.

I spent the next few days in the Bohinj region, studying my brother's two books. Whenever I opened my eyes in the train for fear of missing my stop, I saw in the meadows those long, narrow wooden frames known as "hay harps": two wooden posts (perhaps made of concrete today) rammed into the ground, and embedded in them a number of parallel bars, on which, under a shingle roof, the first hay of the year was drying. This first crop was full of spring flowers, and the gray mass of hay was shot through with color. The bars extended beyond the posts and suggested bundles of road signs, all pointing in the same direction. The train seemed to be following these closely spaced arrows, which from valley to valley inclined farther westward, and in my sleep the harps on both sides of the tracks took on the shape of an enormous chariot which carries the passengers to their destination without passage of time.

I no longer spent the night in the open, but stayed at a hotel in Bohinjska Bistrica, the biggest village of the region. This I decided to do after seeing the low prices and counting my money. It occurred to me later that, thanks to my teacher's gift, to some tutoring I had done, and to a story I had sold to a newspaper ("Did you write that yourself?" asked a classmate, shaking his head), I might perfectly well have gone to Greece with the others.

Actually, it was this story I had published, far more than any shortage of money, that had kept me out of the group trip. It was about a young fellow repairing a bicycle in a courtyard. The setting was described in detail, the light, the wind, the rustling of the trees, the rain that was beginning to fall. In the end the hero hears a cry and rushes into the house, where, on the floor of an empty room, he finds his father or his mother—I don't remember which—dying, his or her eyes reflecting the outside world for the last time. It wasn't the content that mattered; what alienated my classmates was the mere fact of my writing. Some of them, it's true, belonged to a drama group, but that I should write and publish my writing struck them all as strange, to say the least. My girlfriend, too. Before even reading my story—she had barely had time to see the page with the title and my name on it—she gave me a strange, disapproving look, which, after she read it, turned to a complex expression compounded of incomprehension, pity, surprise, and, above all, reserve. Later on, I kept remembering that her neck stiffened when I tried to draw her close to me.

But hadn't I myself provoked this general revulsion? Hadn't I, on the day when the newspaper appeared, eyed everyone who opened it as someone who would immediately learn of my crime and disgrace me by telling others about it? Much as I had looked forward to publishing this story—a project instigated by my fairy-tale-writing history teacher and promoted by a reporter who wrote local notes—to how at last they'd all see who I was, it struck me afterward as a stigma, and luckily the one place where it did not follow me was the village where in those days—today an adver-

tisement at the entrance to the village announces "Rinkenberg reads *The* . . ."—I never saw a newspaper even
at the presbytery. But in the places where up until then
I had felt most at home, as a commuter in trains and
buses, I had disgraced myself forever in my own eyes.
Where I had managed to be inconspicuous even to
myself, a Nobody, I was now on display as "a certain"
So-and-so. In emerging from obscurity I had forfeited
my element. The sense of well-being I had known in
crowded places, especially while standing in the corridor
of a railroad car or in the center aisle of a bus, gave
way to a feeling of intense discomfort; I had become
identifiable, exposed to a spotlight that singled me out,
thus condemning me—and this is what shamed me most
of all—to intrude on the privacy of my fellow passengers.
Was that why in the last few weeks I had gone to school
on my bicycle, a trip which, there and back, had taken
me half a day? There were many motives that may have
impelled me to take this solitary journey; but one of
them was certain: to make people forget that, whether
in reality or only in my imagination, I had betrayed
myself by becoming a public figure. And now, with
every hour in which I was privileged to be unknown, I
felt oblivion spreading around me, a feeling that became
more salutary with every passing mile. Immediately
after my arrival in the Bohinj, I was drawn to a hamlet,
marked on the map as Pozabljeno, meaning roughly
"the forgotten place" or "forgetfulness." And in whatever strange places I walked, stood, sat, lay, or ran in
the days that followed, people left me alone as though
that were the natural thing to do.

Only the teacher in Villach still haunted this no-
man's-landscape, repeating over and over what, when

he first saw my story in print, he had cried out with a gesture as though giving a musician his entrance: "Filip Kobal!"—just my name, the first time I ever heard it in that form, Christian name before family name, for up until then I had been addressed exclusively as "Kobal, Filip"; at my recent army medical, for instance. "Forget it" was my silent answer. Yes, I was resolved never to appear in the paper again; never again to expose myself, my family, and my fellow villagers to such disgrace. My dream of fame was a thing of the past. Hadn't I always known, especially when surrounded by people in the train or bus, even when I myself was reading a book, fascinated by a report of a new invention, enjoying a piece of music, that I would never amount to anything, that sooner or later I was bound to fail, that, as a fortuneteller at a fair, undoubtedly convinced that she was flattering this countrywoman and her son who was patently unfit for farm work, had told my mother, with luck I'd get to be a bookkeeper or some sort of clerk who wouldn't have to deal with anything but numbers. So wasn't it part of my destiny to be counting money in a Slovenian hotel room?

The Bohinj is a broad valley surrounded on all sides by mountain ranges, once the base of a glacier, which on its western edge left the large, tranquil, and almost always deserted Bohinj Lake behind it. From its northern bank rises the massif of the Julian Alps, culminating in the still glacier-covered Triglav, or three-headed mountain, a model of which on the lakeshore is used by vacationing children to play on. The mountain range in the south is the last barrier of any size between there and the sea; there the Isonzo (the Slovenian Soča) has its source, and the slopes between which it flows from then on show no tree line. Difficult of access, the Bohinj basin has been remote from the world down through the ages; mule tracks were its only link with the Isonzo Valley and the Friulian Plain, and the eastern route by which I had come had been opened up only when the railroad was built.

Because I grew up on the great Jaunfeld Plain at some distance from the mountains, I have always found it surprising that Austria should be regarded as an Alpine country and dubbed the "Alpine Republic." (Hardly anyone in our village owned skis, and there was only one sled track, from the edge of the forest down to the road, so gently sloping that you'd hardly got started when you came to a stop.) But in the Bohinj I found myself really surrounded by mountains and felt that I was in an Alpine country, which, to be sure, did not mean chasms, ravines, a sunny and a shady slope, and a narrow sky; despite the dip in the ground, I was on a high plateau with a wide view. If I now close my eyes, what opens up before me is a valley centered on the empty fjord-blue lake, sheltered by the mountains, subdivided by moraine waves.

And yet the Bohinj, at least as seen from the slightly raised railway station, is a busy region. When I first got out of the train, I saw and smelled hardly anything but wood. On the freight siding I saw piles of whole tree trunks, of beams, boards, and laths, and in among the houses I heard power saws. In all the days I spent there, I never saw an idle person; anyone who appeared at first sight to be doing nothing proved to be waiting for a bus at one of the unmarked bus stops (a board fence, a weighbridge), waiting for a sawed pine tree to fall, for fine weather in which to turn the hay, or merely, like the old cook at the inn, for milk to come to a boil or whatever she was cooking to be done. The soldier I saw one day standing quietly by the side of the road proved, when I came closer, to be holding a radio to his ear, and the children who seemed to be tearing leaves off the bushes for no apparent purpose turned out to be scouts learning to follow a trail. The church was in the middle of a meadow and was big enough to be a cathedral. On Sunday, a long line formed outside the confessional. If anyone left the church after unloading his sins, he took barely time enough for a breather before going back to his prie-dieu to say his penance. The people in this valley did not emanate the tranquil assurance of old settlers; theirs was the impatience, the alertness, the constant guardedness of newcomers, which often, in the light of its geographical situation, made me look upon the Bohinj as a separate European country. I almost deplored the lack of an idiot or a drunkard, who might for a moment, in moving about this industrious community, have distracted these people from their hardworking seriousness. But then one day, while looking for places in which to study my two books, while pausing, looking back, turning off the path, feeling the grass here and there (was it soft enough to sit on?), leaning against a tree, tearing myself loose from the resin and staggering on, I realized that I myself might have been mistaken for just such a one.

The hotel where I was staying was called the Black Earth after a peak in the mountain range to the south, a big house, dating from before the World Wars, in which I began at once to look for the blind window. As the only guests apart from myself were a few mountain climbers, I had a room with four beds, enough for a whole family, to myself. It was on the second floor, above the entrance; from one window I looked out on a row of spruces, perhaps what was left of a forest, which ran straight through the village, and from the other side on a torrent which passed right next to the house, with a wild roar that drowned out all the trucks and power saws. The only sound that came through was an occasional train whistle or the sudden boom of a military plane. I could see the spruces (but not the water) sitting down, so I moved the little wooden table to the window on that side, and tried the different chairs. As I couldn't make up my mind in favor of any of them, I lined them up at the table and switched from time to time.

The first day, I unpacked the two books but didn't open them. I left my room door open, because, what with the roaring of the brook, a closed room would have made me feel cut off from the world; as it was, a clatter or some shrill sound rose up to me now and then from the kitchen or dining room. On the wall of the corridor, just across from my door, hung a black-and-brown stuffed grouse in an attitude of courtship—outstretched neck, swollen from screeching, eyes closed—just as it had been shot. The keyboard next to it, bearing keys of every imaginable shape behind a glass pane, looked something like an almost complete butterfly collection. At the very first moment, I had the impression that I had seen all this before, or better still, that I had returned here not to an earlier life but to one dimly foreseen, though more real, more palpable than anything I could have imagined. Was it because of the table, chairs, and bedsteads, which reminded me of my father as carpenter, because of the spray outside the windows, which reminded me of my father as flood-control worker? Or because of my brother's letter, in which he had used the odd expression "ancestral country" in speaking of the Bohinj? For it wasn't just my room and the house that I seemed to have rediscovered so palpably, but also the town of Bistrica, the "transparent," the "clear," the "brook village," and the whole valley: a child marvels at it, a man of twenty contemplates it, a man of forty-five surveys it, and in this moment all three are one and ageless. And Bistrica was very different from the usual village; it was more like the suburb of a city, which would grow as a number of such suburbs coalesced; a development that seemed foreshadowed by the few big buildings, the self-service store on the periphery, and the cathedral in the meadow.

It seemed so inappropriate for the son of a poor countryman to sit down at a table in a restaurant and expect the waiter to serve him that at first, apart from crackers and cookies from the self-service store, my daily fare consisted of the bread and apples my sister had put into my sea bag. They were the last apples of the year before, so old that I had only to pick one up and the seeds would rattle. I didn't eat bread and apples because I had to but because they were, and remained for many years, my favorite food; the word "delicious," I felt, applied to nothing so much as to the tart sweetness of apples eaten along with caraway-seasoned, barely salted rye bread. Bread, the apples, and my clasp knife were lined up on my windowsill. Looking at the floured loaf, I thought of the far side of the moon, though of course it waned more in a week than the planet in a month, and soon the lesser moons would be gone, too; the last slices were so thin that, held up to the light, they suggested a network of transparent snow crystals, and before long they, too, had melted away.

But my story became a real fairy tale only when I opened the books and found a bank note inserted in each of them like an endpaper. It was then that I remembered my sister saying that on my travels I should "eat one hot meal every day"; then at least my stomach "won't feel that it's away from home." As in the dream of finding money, which I often had in those days, I began to see bank notes everywhere, and regretted that my sister hadn't baked one into the bread or pushed one under the skin of an apple. Folding the bank notes and sticking them into my back trouser pocket—no one in the family possessed a billfold—I noticed that I was repeating the gesture with which my father, after every game, casting a long look of triumph and vengeance around him, would pocket his winnings. This enabled me to regard the money his daughter had filched from him as my winnings and to change it into dinars. That same evening, I ordered a hot meal with an unwavering voice and, as I thought, no accent. In the waiter's face I detected an attentive look, which today I interpret as a smile.

The first of the two books was a copybook with hard covers in which my brother had made notes during his studies at the agricultural school in Maribor. Because it was thick and with its hard cover smelled like a genuine book, I had always regarded it as one. Along with the other tome, a big Slovenian–German dictionary pub-

lished in the nineteenth century, a packet of letters, a
uniform cap from the Second World War (son), a
bayonet and a gas mask from the First World War
(father), it had ordinarily been kept in the chest that
stood on the wooden balcony under the eaves of our
house. Until I began to read, these were the only books
in the house, and they were always kept in the blue
chest, half out of doors. When I looked at them, I never
took them into the living room, but sat on the chest, as
though exposure to the weather were inseparable from
such reading—the wind on the pages, the changing
light, and getting spattered now and then by the rain
blowing under the overhang of the roof. Where these
books had their place was also my place, for my father,
normal as he found it to study the Sunday paper by the
living-room window, wanted no books in the house; he
muttered angrily whenever he caught me indoors with
a book, and a moment later my page would be streaked
with whitish trails.

How, over the years, I searched for places in which
to read books! I would sit behind the milk stand at the
roadside, on the bench by the distant wayside shrine,
on a spit of land above the sluice in the Drava, at my
feet the dammed-up river, so smooth that the water
below me resembled the sky overhead . . . Once I
climbed Rinken Hill; shortly before the top, in a fern-
overgrown clearing with a single pine tree in the middle,
I found the place that every reader must have dreamed
of: close to the tree a patch of the soft grass locally
known as lady-hair, a bed of natural cushions, no bed
of vice but a throne of the spirit, which, I was confident,
would blow upon me from a book named *Fear and
Trembling*. But I didn't get beyond the first page or,

rather, the first sentence of it. My eyes were not opened to the sentences that followed until one afternoon in the school corridor, where I was sitting with other students who were doing their homework. And, along with the words, I took in the details of my surroundings, the grain of the wooden bench, the part in the hair of the boy in front of me, the lamp at the end of the corridor, and then at last I heard the wind in the pine tree, which had suddenly died down as I opened the book in the clearing. That place, all places, however pleasing, however inviting to the reader, disappeared as soon as I tried to settle into them; made illiterate by my father's grumbling, I crept away. To this day, I have known no settled reading place but that chest, long ago chopped up for firewood, on the balcony of my father's house. While looking for reading places, I learned only one thing; namely, that I could not withdraw into solitude, and especially not with a book.

And so, after the usual wanderings, I tried the station waiting room in its ring of chestnut trees, the graveyard, beside a tombstone with a falling airplane scratched into it, the stone bridge over the outlet of the lake. In the end, I studied my brother's copybook in my room at the inn with the grouse, dark, in the corner of one eye, and in the other, bright, the washstand with its bowl and pitcher. Before me, the tip of a spruce guided my gaze to a neighboring house with roof tiles running from left to right like the lines in the copybook.

Of course, I had looked at the book any number of times before that, but had been unable to make sense of it, because the classes in the agricultural school were conducted in Slovenian. What had interested me were the drawings, and above all the handwriting. It was clear and even; the long, narrow letters leaned slightly to the left and, as I leafed through the book, gave the impression of steadily falling, endless rain. As there were no curlicues or loops, no shortcuts or sloppiness, and never an unconnected letter, standing alone in the middle of a word, there had been no need to resort to block letters. Yet this script differed from the picturesque calligraphy of a nineteenth-century document by its smoothness, which also characterized the drawings that went with it. In looking at this writing, I had the impression that it did more than record something, that it moved hand in hand with its subject, each lined-up letter carrying its image, unerringly, toward a goal. And here in the Bohinj, it seemed to me that my brother's handwriting was right for this new country; the handwriting of a settler, of a man about to start on a journey, whose writing is an intrinsic part of this starting-out and not the mere record of a continued action.

In one of his letters he observes that a handwriting expert would find that "all our [the family's] scribblings have something in common." I have always seen pride and presumption in that sentence. His handwriting had never been childlike; even in his earliest school copybook, he had written like someone who takes a responsible part in an action, a leader, a discoverer.

Actually, the whole family was famous, even outside the village, for its, to quote the roadmender and sign painter, "masterful" handwriting ("The Kobals don't write just with their hands," he said, holding out his arm in a grandiose gesture), which, partly because there was no recognized "master" in the whole region, brought us the reputation of being a noble, self-confident family;

and this we showed by writing as we did—not "like painting," not "like printing," but precisely with the unmistakable "Kobal gesture." As I've said, my mother was much in demand as a letter writer and was regarded almost as an official. If I questioned one of our neighbors about my brother, he would usually, after telling a few anecdotes, talk about Gregor Kobal and his orchard, "as carefully, generously, and inventively laid out as his handwriting" (so the roadmender). Even my sister awoke from her confusion and sat very straight, a picture of authority, when she signed "Ursula Kobal" on the receipt for her early pension.

The only exceptions were the oldest and the youngest members of the family, my father and I. The one had too heavy, the other too uneven a hand. It was obvious that my father had had no proper schooling; in writing as in reading, he seemed to spell out the words. To the long letters my mother wrote me at the seminary, he added at the most one word, signature and greeting in one: "Father." For a while, after he was pensioned, he didn't know what to do with himself. I thought it might be a good idea to give him a copybook and encourage him to write the story of his life; for, when he tried to talk about it, he would falter time and again. Often after a long silence he would make a start, begin with a deep-voiced "And then . . . "—and finally break off, saying: "It can't be told. It's got to be written." But a few months later, when I looked at the copybook, I found not a single word, though he had had a whole winter's time, but only numbers, my brother's APO number, my laundry-mark number, our house number, and all our birth dates, gouged into the paper like cuneiform. (It was only with his carpenter's pencil that he could make light lines; before you knew it, he could draw a complete diagram on the wood he was going to work with.)

As for me, I often changed my handwriting; in the middle of a word my letters would get bigger, I'd push them back, then forward again. I'd begin every paragraph with the utmost care and then—as one can tell now by looking at the writing—start racing in my impatience to finish it. The worst of it was that I didn't really regard my handwriting as my own; today it has become regular, but it still strikes me as artificial, as an imitation; unlike my brother, I have never had a handwriting of my own, my present style was copied from him; the moment I stop concentrating, it loses its affected regularity and degenerates into a formless scribble that I myself am unable to read, a picture of harassed helplessness in place of the grandiose family gesture. It took the typewriter to teach me to write properly. Before that, the only writing that suited me was in the air, without any instrument, using my forefinger for a pencil. I couldn't see what I was writing, the movement of my finger sufficed and that was what gave me the feeling that I had a personal handwriting with a rhythm of its own. And besides, when I wrote in the air, I could be slow, pause, break off. But otherwise, convulsively clutching the foreign instrument, the mere sound of which threw me off, bent over the paper instead of sitting erect, I rushed from line to line, not knowing what I was doing, giving off sour, unproductive sweat, incapable of raising my head, with no eyes for my surroundings. It was only when I concentrated on my subject that my writing looked at all natural to me; then script and content seemed to take shape side by side.

And where, when writing, could I concentrate on my subject? In the dark, for one thing. There, stroke by stroke, pencil and fingers grew together and a writer's hand developed, beautifully heavy and deliberate, no idle scribble but a recording. Then, when I looked in the light at what I had written, I saw my thought framed in a script that seemed to combine my brother's fine inventive hand and my father's halting, self-educated one.

My brother's copybook dealt mostly with fruit growing. With the help of the dictionary, I managed to get the gist of it. Though the work of a man who was not yet twenty, it did not consist of lecture notes but was, rather, the record of a young scientist's independent research. A second section was a kind of treatise, made up of reflections on the subject, and the end a catalogue of rules and suggestions. The whole was a student's notes and a textbook in one.

Essentially, the book revolved around my brother's experience of planting and improving apple trees in his own orchard at home. He spoke of suitable soil ("loose and rich," "flat, slightly vaulted ground"), orientation ("east to west, but sheltered from the wind"), the best times for the various operations (often determined by the equinoxes or the rising of certain constellations, or by rural holidays).

I couldn't help reading my brother's observations on grafting and on transplanting young trees as in part a *Bildungsroman*. He had carried the young plants from the nursery to his garden "along with their earth" and arranged them in the same order as in the nursery, though much farther apart, because the branches of one tree should never touch those of another. He had woven the root branches into protective baskets before inserting them in their holes. The trees grown from seed on the spot had proved more resistant but also less fruitful than the transplants. Leafy crowns were advantageous, as they provided a roof under which more fruit would form. Branches that inclined toward the ground bore more fruit than those that soared skyward (though the fruit hanging higher up was less likely to rot). As for grafting, he used only branches pointing eastward. They were pencil-shaped and the cuts chamfered to let the rainwater run off. The cutting itself was done not with a blow but by pulling the knife through so the bark would remain intact. He had always chosen scions that had once borne fruit, "because otherwise we shall have worked not for a yield but for shade," and he had never inserted a scion in a fork between two other scions, for, if he did, it would draw nourishment away from them. Of pruning, he wrote that the earlier he did it, the more "wood" he obtained; the later, the more "fruit"; the wood just "shot up," while the fruit would "bow down."

At the beginning of the copybook he explained that originally there had been only one tree in his orchard; it had run wild and bore no fruit. He had driven a spike into the bark at the spot that was freest from lichen; from the festering wound had sprung a shoot with one promising eye after another. The spike, his own invention, had been more like an auger—instead of hole-plugging dust, it produced shavings that could be blown out. (Beside the description was a drawing of a "Kobal auger.")

But what made a deeper impression on me than

such incidental pedagogic metaphors, such allusive meanings, were the concrete details, the mere mention of things which up until then had been only a jumble to me. The bast my brother used to tie his scion to the branch, the wood splint (not round but square) that held it straight, the pebbles that moderated the temperature of the soil at the roots and protected them from the groundwater, took on a radiance that held my attention. Thus a light fell on the orchard, which has been neglected since then and run wild like the tree with which it began, and in the manuscript I caught sight of a blue-bordered enclosure, where, confronted with the rich diversity of "my thing" (as my brother called his orchard), I gazed around and around as though I stood in my brother's place at the center of it. "We shall not have worked for shade"—that was the battle cry which now, at the table beside the window, I shouted into the roaring of the torrent, as the black grouse in the corner of one eye and the white washbasin in the other swung across my field of vision like two intersecting pendulums.

Undoubtedly, the words owed some of their power to the fact that I did not immediately understand them but had to translate them, not from a foreign language into my own, but directly from an intimation—incomprehensible as much of the Slovene was to me, it seemed somehow familiar—into an image: into the orchard, a branch prop, a piece of wire. My brother referred to certain of his activities, such as removing sterile shoots, as "blind work." Possibly such translation transformed blind reading into sighted reading, an unseeing activity into intelligent work. It seemed to me that even my father, if he had come into the room, would have left his grumbling on the threshold and, at the sight of my sparkling translator's eyes, expressed his satisfaction with his son: "Yes, that is *his* game!"

Even where in the second part of his copybook my brother passed from his particular orchard to a general discussion of different varieties of apple, it was his own trees that appeared to me; where he was merely describing a method, I continued to read a story about a place and its hero; and it was also to them that the concluding remarks addressed to every fruit grower referred, to the effect that in a "thing" so closely akin to wisdom there could be neither professors nor students, and that what mattered most in fruit growing was "the master's presence."

What distinguished my brother's orchard from others was its situation outside the village, surrounded by fields and pastureland, bounded on one side by a small mixed forest, whereas most gardens and orchards began right behind the houses and, seen from the road, gave the impression of long rows of trees, ending, as one was bound to suppose, in fallow land, with Rinkenberg as an island of apples and pears at its edge. My brother's trees were small as in a plantation, and each tree, except for the usual plum and cider-pear trees at the entrance (intended, one might have thought, to mask the nature of the orchard), bore fruit of a different taste; on some trees, indeed, the variety changed from one tier of branches to the next. And most extraordinary of all: among the cider-pear trees there was one secret branch, known only to the family, that bore fruit which looked deceptively like that of the next branch but which, when you bit into it, did not—as we said in the family— "pucker your asshole" but opened your eyes.

The whole orchard, if you entered it from the side opposite the forest, had a more and more experimental arrangement, which had many advantages. After the first corner, marked by a lone poplar, which looked odd among the fruit trees, it spread out until at the edge of the forest it was several rows wide. Though unfenced like the village orchards, which thus had the air of public woodland, the area beyond the poplar was hidden. One reason for this was that, crossing the open fields, one suddenly, without having seen a single house, came across branches laden with the finest apples; and another was the hollow in which my brother had laid out his orchard. From flat ground one unexpectedly stepped down into the orchard and then at its end just as abruptly up into the little forest. The hollow was not deep; one became aware of it only at its edge, and only there did one glimpse the tops of the small fruit trees on a level with the tips of one's shoes; from far off, from the village or the road, one saw only the strange poplar, sometimes transformed into a torch by lightning, rising from treeless fields.

That depression—so the geography teacher had taught me—was formed by a prehistoric brook, an offshoot of the groundwater which in this particular plain does not stand still but flows down to the Drava in a regular, unbroken stream, hardly "the length of a walking stick" below the earth's surface. At the site of the present orchard, this stream of groundwater had welled up, carrying the soil with it, and washed out a bowl, whence it had dug a narrow ditch leading down to the river. Then the brook had seeped away—the ditch was locally known as the "still brook"—so that the bottom of the oval bowl formed by the spring was dry; the water was no longer a visible single stream but had sunk and joined the endless underground flow or, in the form of "sky water" (a literal translation of what my brother called rain in his copybook), carried the fertile decomposed soil from the walls to the bottom of the bowl. (The bowl, to be sure, had its vegetation-clogged outlet where the ditch began.)

Around the trees grew orchard grass, more sparse than meadow grass, and hardly any flowers. Where it arrived at the poplar tree, the sand track, which led across the fields to the edge of the hollow, acquired a middle strip of grass; on the way downhill, it narrowed and deep shining ruts made by braking cart wheels appeared; in among the rows of trees, it became a solid strip of grass, the "green track" (as we called it in the family), which ran straight as an arrow over the slightly vaulted bottom of the bowl to the farthermost tree of the orchard, not only distinctly lighter than the ground around it, but positively luminous beside it.

In its hollow, the orchard was sheltered from the wind; only the warm fall winds from the south touched its bottom. Thus, the trunks of the trees were perfectly straight, while the branches, most noticeably in the winter, grew evenly in all directions. The orchard was also sheltered from noise, from either the village or the road; apart from church bells and sirens, one heard only its own sounds, in particular the buzzing not so much of flies as of bees in the blossoms or of wasps in the fallen fruit. It had a smell of its own, heavy, cidery, which came more from the windfall fruit fermenting in the grass than from the trees; it was not until autumn, in the cellar, that the remaining apples became truly fragrant; before that, only if you held them up to your nose (but then the smell was something!). In the spring the blossoms were a solid white, but in the summer the orchard's color changed from tree to tree; the pale green of the early apples, to which passersby were free to help themselves, was the first to disappear.

Waiting for the different kinds of fruit to ripen was a part of childhood. Especially after a storm, I was eager to run out to the orchard, where at least one marvelous apple (or, under the improved cider branch, a pear) would be lying in the grass. Often there would be a race with my sister, who was long past childhood. We both knew in advance under which tree we'd be likely to find something, and each of us wanted to be first; it was not so much a matter of having and eating as of finding and holding in our hands. Autumn fruit picking was one of the few physical occupations in which I did not reach out blindly (and as often as not miss my aim). The trees were so small that one hardly needed the ladders generally associated with orchards. Our chief implement was a long pole, to the top of which a sack with stiff, jagged edges was attached. Even today, at this very moment, I can feel in my arms the jolt that occurred when an apple fell from its branch and rolled down to the other apples in the sack.

The crates being filled at the foot of the trees were also a part of my childhood, the lemon-yellow in one, and in the next the special wine-red, whose veins one could see extending from the peel through the flesh to the core of the fruit. Only the cider-pear trees could be shaken; then a loud rat-tat-tat resounded through the whole orchard. Instead of crates, there would be a ring of thick sacks around the pear trees.

Later came my deprived youth, my years at the seminary, during which I missed the fruit harvest; no more piled crates; at the most, a few apples would go into my suitcase before I left home and a few others in the course of the year, more and more shriveled as time went on.

Then my mother's illness, my father's stiffening limbs, my unlearning (yes, that is the word) of almost every kind of physical work which, after all, had contributed no less than my reading on the balcony to my childhood dreams—chopping wood, mending roofs, driving cattle, binding sheaves (for me at least, these activities never represented hard work, or, if they did, it never lasted more than a few hours).

Then came the decades of absence, during which the orchard was utterly neglected; only my sister kept going there for a time with a small basket and picking what apples she could reach with her bare hands; and then she, too, stopped going. Just one more dream about my brother's orchard: early apples lying pale yellow on the snow, and the family sitting at a table in the sun nearby.

In the years after my return, I visited the orchard now and then. There is still no house in the vicinity, and the old sand track leading to it, like the green track down in the hollow, has become solid grass. The trees are covered over with lichen.

The last time I was there, the rain had washed away what was left of the dam my brother had built of sticks, stones, and clay outside the hole leading to the ditch. It was a winter's day and the prevailing color in the orchard was the green of the lichen which completely covered every one of the trees and in places had destroyed the bark. The lichen seemed to weigh down the trees, and indeed there were broken branches, shaped like antlers, lying in the grass. The grass was no grass, it was moss; the few blades that pretended to be grass were colorless and as hard as bast, entangled with blackberry trailers that had crept in from the forest and the ditch. The most striking sight was the ash, an intruder from the forest, which had literally taken possession of one apple tree. Its seed must have taken root at the foot of the apple tree, and in growing, the young ash had half enfolded the old fruit tree. Through a slit in the living tree, one could see the dead one, from which the bark had been stripped. The graft scions, previously recognizable on the smooth, shining bark, had long been completely hidden by lichen; only at one point was their presence indicated by a square wooden splint fastened to a branch and lying on top of it. Over the years, a strange reversal had occurred; this branch, first the thinner of the two, had thickened and now carried the former splint wrapped in rusty wire on its back as a useless appendage.

The whole bowl was now shot through with gray; the only color in it, apart from the green track, was the very different green, the verdigris green of the clumps of mistletoe in the split crowns of the trees. The few shriveled apples on the branches were left over from previous years; those lying in the moss below burst like puffballs if one stepped on them.

Only one tree, leafless, was full of this year's apples that no one had picked; but time and again their yellow was blotted out by the gray and black of the starlings and blackbirds, which laid claim to every single apple and filled the orchard with their incessant pecking and beak-smacking. I was thankful for the train whistle in the distance, the crowing of a cock, the rat-tat-tat of a moped. Through the wild grapevines that covered the drain hole I seemed to hear, as though amplified by the narrow passage, the roar of the river far below.

I thought of running away from this world-forsaken hollow, but decided to stay. The shed on the slope leading up to the forest, formerly a shelter from the rain or midday sun, had vanished. Its remains at the edge of the green track, along with a pile of cast-off support poles, looked like something halfway between a pyre and a "hay harp." I stood there and waited, for nothing in particular.

It began to snow, just a few isolated flakes, which fell abruptly from the clouds, described great curves in the air, and disappeared. I remembered my father's habit of walking up and down the green track before every important decision, such as whether to make a will or to spend any considerable sum of money, and now I did likewise. I remembered one of the sayings that he used to direct at the corner where his missing son's picture hung: "The custodian of a run-down orchard—that's what I am."

Turning at the end of the track, I raised my head. In the pile of planks and poles I glimpsed a crucifix towering into the sky and knelt before it in thought. When I went closer, the crucifix turned into a sculpture, and in the same way the rows of trees became in my eyes, as I thought literally, a "monument to my noble ancestors."

The longer I stayed there, walked back and forth, changed direction, stood still, turned my head, the more distinctly the site, a moribund orchard, was transformed in my mind into a work, a form transmitting and honoring the human hand and offering the advantage of being translatable into another form by another hand, for example, into written characters on the side of that bowl, traversed by abandoned cow paths—white and still whiter lines, gradually making their appearance in the snow. Behind the ring of lichen and mistletoe, the eyes of the branches were rejuvenated; the dingy light on the roots was shot through with flint sparks; and from the frame at the center of the garden came a south wind, which later arose time and again in the closed rooms of the house.

Then, at the sight of the fungus shaped like a peaked cap on one of the tree trunks, I thought of one of my brother's letters, in which he mentioned just such a *goba* which he was carrying in the dusk of a Holy Saturday while walking around the Easter bonfire. That, he said, was the "holiest and merriest" part; after that "the feast was over, and not even the sausages could give me so much pleasure." And at the sight of the poles, I thought of the forked hazel branch on which my father, who was often cruel to animals, had once spitted a snake he had cut in two while mowing: and now the snake, which all that day and down through the years had waited on that hazel branch, a more lasting emblem of the place than any sun-drenched fruit, vanished. Then, turning to my forefathers in the emptiest corner of the garden and at the same time searching for the eyes of a child, diverted by the monotone of the lamentation for the dead and led out of the "eternal kingdom of separation" (my brother's words), I spoke in a tone of defeat rather than triumph. My exact words were: "Yes, I will tell you."

For each of the three years my brother spent at the agricultural school, there is one class photo. In the first, the young men all have open shirt collars, rolled-up sleeves, and dark, knee-length aprons; they are standing or sitting on a broad, sunny path bordered by fruit trees in such full bloom that not a single leaf can be seen. In the background, the vertical rows of a vineyard just beginning to put forth shoots lead upward to the chapel on the hill. The white of the flowering trees is repeated in the spring clouds. The shadows are short. It's during the midday break, my brother hasn't even found time to comb his hair, a strand of which is hanging down over his forehead; as soon as the picture is taken, they will all go back to work. The group is pressed close together; a few of the boys are resting one arm on the shoulder of a neighbor, who, however, never responds to this gesture; one, the youngest, is holding on to both his neighbors. Because of the sun, none of the boys' eyes can be seen. My brother is the one at the back, slightly taller than the others, or possibly it's only his thick mat of hair that makes him look taller; his face alone is cut off by the head in front of it; as though he had moved into that position at the last moment. An airily dressed woman is walking down the path behind the group.

The next picture shows much less of the surroundings but more of the class. The setting is a path flanked by a row of spruces with a lamppost in front of it and a tiled roof behind it. None of the group is without a jacket; some are even wearing ties with enormous knots, and some show watch chains extending from vest button down to vest pocket. In the foreground, a student is sitting cross-legged, with a small keg of wine on his lap and a tilted bottle in his hand. The faded flowers by the side of the path give the picture an autumnal look, corroborated by the boy with an ear of wheat in his breast pocket instead of a handkerchief or fountain pen. My brother, sitting in the front row, is among those with an open shirt collar; one oversized lapel of his jacket is visible, but neither breast pocket nor buttonhole. He alone is resting his hands, one on top of the other, on one knee. He is looking to one side of the picture, and though sitting erect, he seems relaxed; he is not posing, that is his natural self. These are no longer youngsters as they were last year, but young men; it's not just for the photographer that they've closed their mouths and that one has propped his hands on his hips.

In the last picture, the class is smaller; they are standing outside the school building, of which one sees only a wall and a bit of the windows. In the front, on round chairs, sit the teachers, who, except for the pale priest, look more like rich peasants, older relatives, or godparents than teachers. All the students are wearing ties; none has his arm around anyone's shoulder; they are grown men now; my brother, too, is twenty and holds his hands behind his back. Having learned the farmer's trade, he will now go back to a country where a different language from his own is spoken. He is looking southward, not to the north, where he belongs. All the young Slovene peasants of the class of '38 are looking straight ahead; not a single jutting chin, as though they embodied, perhaps not a state, but something else. My brother's face has filled out; his good eye has narrowed and, seen from the side, looks like a cleft; only the blind one protrudes round and white, as though it had always seen more than the other.

An odd thing about our family was that stories were seldom told about anyone's childhood but my father's.

Over and over again (though none of us had been present and it was all a matter of hearsay), we would tell one another how as a child the old man sitting there had walked in his sleep. One night he had got up and taken his blanket to the table where the others were still sitting. Leaving his blanket there, he had gone back to bed and started wailing that he was cold. Or how the child would roam around for days, remembering nothing. In the end, he found his way home, but, afraid to go in, started in the gray of dawn to sweep the yard as though in preparation for Sunday, to show that he was back. Or how, even as a small child, he had had such a temper that one day, when someone made him angry, he had run out of the house, come back with half a tree trunk that he could hardly drag through the doorway, and with it attacked whoever had aroused his anger; most frightening of all had been the gesture with which he threw the tree trunk down at the other's feet! Another strange thing was how much my father enjoyed hearing this family folklore about his childhood (usually told by his daughter); he would chuckle or tears would come to his eyes, or he'd clench his fists as though his rage were still with him; and in the end he would cast a triumphant look around: the winner!

Concerning my brother's childhood, on the other hand, I have retained only one anecdote. It seems that he once walked from end to end of the village with his sister, farting for her benefit the whole way. Apart from that, there was only the sad story of how he had lost his eye. He does not appear in an active role until the age of seventeen, when he set out for the agricultural school across the border. But then, on his very first vacation, he presented himself to the family as a discoverer, not only of new farming methods but, above all, of the Slovene language. Up until then, Slovene larded with German had been his dialect, the dialect of our region; now it became his written language, which he used in his notebooks and in letters and jottings. For these he always carried about with him a dictionary, a pencil, and slips of paper, in addition to the usual penknife and bits of string, and continued to do so later on, from one battlefield to the next. He wanted everyone else in the family to imitate him and at last show loyalty to their origins, whether in the city, in public offices, or on the train. My father, however, didn't want to; his wife couldn't; my sister was mute at the time, preoccupied with her broken heart; and I myself hadn't been born yet. Though our mother's Slovene was negligible, my brother calls it "our mother tongue" in his first letter from Maribor, and adds: "We are what we are, and no one can force us to be Germans." He was almost an adult when he left home, and unlike me, he went of his own free will. He saw nothing foreign in the foreign country; instead, he found "our most essential possession" (this in a letter)—namely, his language; after seventeen years of silence and farting, he had become a self-assured speaker; in fact, as some of his slips of paper showed, he had turned out to be a glib punster (which fits in with the photo of him standing in the middle of the village with his hat askew, supporting himself on one foot and holding the other far to one side). He was the first in the family who, at least during his school days in the south, did not suffer from homesickness. The school, not far from the "big city" of Maribor, was his second home. And it was he who returned from his travels through Slovenia with the

story of the executed peasant revolutionary Gregor
Kobal. Kobal was one of the most common names in
the Kobarid graveyard. He had looked it up in the local
baptismal registers, going further and further back,
until at the end of the seventeenth century he found
the record of the rebel's birth. Whereupon he appointed
Gregor Kobal our ancestor.

Yet my brother never actually became an insurrectionary; even during the war, later on, he never quite made
it. He was reputed to be the gentlest of the family, and
to judge by his letters, he was something else that I've
met with only in a few children: pious. He often used
the word "holy"; in his usage, however, it applied not
to the church, heaven, or any other place outside the
world, but *always* to everyday life—getting up in the
morning, going to work, meals, routine activities. "At
home, where everything is done in so lively and holy a
way," he wrote in a letter from the Russian front. Once
again, I'm reminded of his "holiest and merriest" walk
around the Easter bonfire—and Pentecost was for him
the feast day when "it's glorious to go out to the fields
bright and early to mow in the holy hours." A white
cloth spread on a table for a soldiers' Mass was "something to fortify my poor soul"; at home he sang the
Hallelujah aloud in chorus with the others, but at the
front he "mumbled it softly to myself." And in his last
letter he wrote: "I have seen and experienced the filth
of the world, and there is nothing more beautiful than
our faith." (According to him, to be sure, faith came
alive only in one's mother tongue; when after the end
of the First Republic one was allowed to pray and sing
only in German, to his ears that was no longer "holy,"
just a "caterwauling that I can't bear to hear.") Another

aspect of his piety was the fervid irony with which he spoke of home when he was far away. He refers to our few acres as our "lands," or as the "Kobal estate"; the rooms in the house, including kitchen, barn, and stable, became "apartments"; and he calls on his "revered family to gather around the table and study" his letters.

It was this irony that deterred him from active rebellion during the war; his indignation was expressed only in his letters. Hearing that a neighborhood family had been deported to Germany, he wrote that he had "but one wish . . . to tear *that man* limb from limb . . . but the thought of my parents, my brother and sister, holds back my rage." Thus, it was probably legend when my mother told us that, after a so-called farm leave, her son had deserted to join the partisans and become a fighter. My guess is that he simply disappeared, no one knows where. It is inconceivable that he would ever have joined in bellowing warlike partisan songs at the top of his lungs—but quite possible that he and a few others made their way to some hidden clearing, a secret patch of farmland, and that from there, looking over his shoulder, he addressed the following speech to the warlords: "I will now say to you the word that is often heard at the bowling alley at home, when the ball misses the tenpins!" That, in one of his letters from the front, is his euphemistic way of saying "Shit!" He was indeed a singer, but not a regimented one—you might have caught him singing with friends after a few drinks; he was a dancer too, but not a stamping, heavy-footed one, more a merry wag, dancing on one foot at the edge of the dance floor.

After his disappearance, the village thought him dead, and like all the village dead he was soon forgotten, except by a priest or two; few of the boys his own age who might have talked about him came home from the war, and the girl who was thought to be his fiancée married someone else and never spoke of him. He had left home too early to be remembered as a maypole climber or as a soloist in church, and soon after his return from school the young peasant with the apron became "the soldier Gregor Kobal," exchanging, as the saying went, "field blue-denim for field gray."

But at home he was honored. During my childhood he was so much talked of that it seems to me now as though he were there the whole time, as though I even heard an additional voice in every conversation, as though all heads kept turning toward the absent figure in the empty corner. It was chiefly my mother who brought him alive with her talk, while my father was the custodian of his belongings, not only of his orchard but also of his clothes and his two books. Only later did it occur to me that my parents' forehead-to-forehead whisperings in the sickroom may have been less an expression of married love than a union in mourning for their dearly beloved son and that their two foreheads may have been meant to form a bridge for his still-hoped-for return. It is certain that man and wife, each in his own way, worshipped their missing son as an "example"—these were the words of my godless mother—"of the son of man," and that at news of his coming she would immediately have prepared "his apartment," scrubbed the threshold, and hung a wreath over the front door, while my father would have borrowed the neighbor's white horse, harnessed it to the spit-and-polished barouche, and, with tears of joy running down his nose, driven to meet him.

Only my sister opposed this worship (because, or so my parents believed, she blamed him for the shipwreck of her love). She contended that he had definitely cast his one eye on women, but had had no luck with them because of his disfigurement; that he had complained incessantly when tilling the soil, especially in the heat on the steeper slopes ("stinking business"); that he had come home from agricultural school as a propagandist for the Slovenian language and sowed dissension in house and village; that, in particular, he had sinned against his beloved Holy Ghost by giving up hope long before the war, and refusing to marry (after the girl had literally proposed to him) on the ground that he was sure to die young.

It is true that my brother's letters and jottings over the years are outspoken in their despair. First because of machines—"It looks as if they will soon replace us all, and then there will be no need for me to come home"; then, at the beginning of the war, he expressed the belief that he would be "a soldier forever." His written curses become more and more frequent. On all-day marches in the fine spring weather he "hears no birdsong," "sees no flowers by the roadside," and fears that he is losing his voice: "In another year I won't be able to talk. Even now we are as shy as animals in the high mountains; we disappear when we hear someone coming. Our temperament needs harmony; without harmony, nothing can give us pleasure." Every day the same, no sign of any Sunday or holiday. He refuses to think about the past "and would like best to do everything in reverse." In the end, he curses not only the war but the world as well: "I curse the world!"

I for my part, whether as listener or as reader,

have never brought myself to believe in a brother who had lost hope. Haven't appearances ("Filip Kobal has a thing about appearances") always impressed me more than the most established fact? And what were these appearances? Didn't they include the way my sister paused, slowed down, and grew thoughtful when she spoke against her missing brother? She stopped making faces the moment her brother came up in the conversation, and her usual blinking, ordinarily so persistent and violent, became much less frequent. She seemed to wake up. A moment before, her speech had been muddled and cottony as though she'd been talking in her sleep, and now she drew a breath before opening her mouth, tilted her head slightly, and paid attention to every word she said.

Another such "appearance" was especially evident in Gregor's writing. Even when it dealt with the irrevocable past, it gave me, along with a plaint, a living image. Instead of saying something directly, like "When I was still happy . . . ," he would write (I translate literally): "When the birds still sang for me . . ." In speaking of springtime at home, he wrote: "When the bees were wearing trousers [of pollen]." Instead of saying "It's an ill wind . . ." he wrote: "Ugly mother, good food." Looking up his first name in the dictionary, he found the meaning "Skin on milk," which made him retch. And then his way of using colors, every one of which could depict a wide range of things and creatures: "How is Spotty getting along?" could refer to a pear, a cow, a goat, a chicken, or a variety of green pea.

But what seemed to me in reading to go beyond such images, and to transcend my own present, were sentences written in a particular tense, which my brother used with striking frequency, the so-called future perfect—because it doesn't exist in Slovene, he would switch to German whenever he wanted to use it: "We shall have walked on the green track." "The boundary stone will have been moved to the edge." "By the time the buckwheat is sowed, I shall have worked, sung, danced, and slept with a woman."

I realize, of course, that an appearance may have resulted from a twofold deficiency: my brother's papers are not complete, and I have no memory of him. His legacy is so fragmentary that I am in the position of a scholar dealing with the few fragments that have come down to us from the early Greek seekers after truth (this, at least, is how I visualize them—wringing their hands, stammering, and finally uttering their cry of joy). Two separate words taken out of context, such as "dancing" and "weeping," reveal a halo around them and irradiate the world; they derive their radiance from, among other things, not being shut up in a complete sentence or in an "explanation." And because, when I think about my missing brother, no picture of a living man, no smell, no tone of voice, no footfall, no particularity whatever intervenes, it has been possible for my brother to become a hero to me, an indestructible phantasm. True, after being appointed my godfather in his absence, he saw me once when home on leave; but I, barely two years old at the time, have no recollection of the meeting. "I shall have bent over my godchild," he wrote in his next letter from the front.

Through these words, so much more concrete than my memory, I felt my brother bend over me time and again. He was often a foil to my mother: whereas she would have liked best to veil her eyes from the future she foresaw for me, his good eye studies me with friendly attentiveness and enjoys the sunshine with me, while his blind eye—because it's blind—is none the wiser. The heaviness of my mother's face bent over me as opposed to my brother's airy radiance—that is my battle to this day. And that is why I call this person who has the same parents as I my "forebear"; yes, I have appointed Gregor Kobal—the peaceable descendant of an insurrectionary, a man who, as even his sister admitted, "never brandished a whip"—to be my ancestor, although I myself, in my thoughts at least, always keep a whip ready for one enemy or another. And indeed, precisely in certain crucial moments, a peace descended on me in which I not only saw my elective ancestor bent over me in kindness but myself embodied him. Of course I could not when threatened summon him to give me peace; it was the other way around: I found peace by myself, and he was present to bolster me; accordingly it was impossible to lean on my forebears (the only effective forebear, this much I know, is the sentence preceding the one I am writing now).

And yet, though it may be mere appearance, with an ancestor in me I am no longer alone; I sit more erect, walk in a different way; do and refrain from doing, say and leave unsaid what should be done or not done, said or left unsaid in a situation of danger. What are facts compared to such appearances? My brother writes in his last letter: "When I am able to project my thoughts into the distance, I picture the Kobal clan sitting at the table together, reading my scribblings." Long live appearances! Let them be my subject!

As I recall, it often rained in the Bohinj, and it can't be just the roaring of the torrent outside my window that

makes me think so. On a forest path, my feet sink into
the clayey mud. The plastic bags hung on the fruit trees
to frighten the birds away are plumped up with water.
I'm sitting with a family of vacationers under the roof
of a "hay harp," watching the road; a peasant woman
is leading a horse by the bridle, the horse is pulling a
hay wagon. The rain bounces back so violently from
the road that the woman seems to be moving without
legs, the horse without hooves, and the wagon without
wheels. The walls of the houses are aglow with the
lightning. Then the sun shines again; it has been shining
a long time, and along the shore of the otherwise quiet
lake the water sparkles with the drops falling from
overhanging branches.

In spite of the rain, I left the village every afternoon,
always with a definite goal, a kind of plateau which, like
the big pine forest at home in the Jaunfeld, is called
Dobrava (roughly, "place of the oak trees") but is bare
except for an isolated pine or oak here and there, and
hardly cultivated, presenting the appearance—strange
so near the bottom of the valley—of an upland pasture.

On this plateau I was all alone, but not outside the
world, for even more than at the inn with its roaring
torrent, one sensed that civilization was near: foresters'
tractors, hay turners, blowers in the lumber-drying
sheds; rising smoke and glinting windshields could be
seen on all sides, a single crowded rowboat on the lake
below. Not only the power lines but even the birds in
the air and the bees nearby indicated the presence of
unseen humans at the foot of the moraine. I had come
up here almost in spite of myself, guided by the pathways, at first an old road, no longer used by vehicles,
with meadow grass sprouting through cracks in the
asphalt, then uphill over what had formerly been the

bed of a brook but was now carpeted with short, soft grass. Here, too, I had as usual to find my place. As in the song: the hill was too high for me, the dale was too low, the sun was too hot, the shade too cool, the lee too sheltered, the open too windy, the boulder too eccentric, the tumbledown apiary too picturesque. In the end I sat down in the grass, leaning against the wooden wall of a field barn. It was the south wall, and when the sun was shining, it seemed to me that the weather-beaten wood gave off "just the right warmth." Indeed, the whole place was just right. The eaves had just enough overhang to enable me to stretch my legs without their getting wet, and the few drops that came my way reminded me of the balcony at home, where the corner I sat in, as here, was at the border between inside and outside—with the difference that there, because our outhouse was situated at one end of the balcony, with a chute leading down to the dung heap, the smells were not the same as here on the plateau.

And again I had a book with me, my brother's big dictionary; everything else had been removed from my waterproof sea bag. The orchard copybook had been suitable reading matter for the four walls of my hotel room; and now, here in the open, the dictionary released its arrows of meaning. Odd that a young man of twenty should spend whole afternoons in a foreign country leaning against a secluded barn, immersed in a dictionary—no, in a single page; no, a single word; that he should look up from that word, shake his head, laugh, drum his heels on the ground, clap his hands (scaring away the grasshoppers and butterflies), jump now and then to his feet and take a turn in the rain. When the people at the inn and in the village saw me start on my daily expedition with my sea bag, they took me for "a budding scientist" or "a young painter" (with its lake and solitary church the Bohinj had attracted droves of landscape painters in the nineteenth century); yet that young fellow sitting there hunched over his book, then suddenly starting to sing at the top of his voice, could only be an idiot.

And yet my senses—of sight as well as hearing—have never been so sharp as then, as I read those columns of unconnected words. Could you call it reading? Wasn't it more a discovering, and wasn't it the joy of discovery that made me shout the foreign words and phrases? (Out into the landscape with them!) But what was there to discover?

Foreign languages had fascinated me as a child. The one coffee tin in our house, with the curly-black-haired dancing girl on it, led me years later to study the dark beauty's language—Spanish; and I copied at least the first lessons of the Hungarian grammar I had brought home from the seminary, which attracted me first by its smell and then by the exotic look of its words. The Slovene language, on the other hand, which I heard every day in the village, had rather repelled me. Not so much because of its Slavic sound as because of the many German words that kept intruding; I heard the dialect of the villagers not as a language but as a ridiculous hodgepodge. My father would often humiliate his fellow cardplayers by imitating their manner of speaking—a mumbling, a gargling, a barbaric spitting out of gutturals—and following up with a sentence of his own pure, melodious Slovene (thus once again showing himself to be the master of the group). But even where the standard language was spoken, it usually sounded menacing to my ears, chiefly because the places where it was used suggested official announcements rather than communication. On the radio, the short daily broadcast in the foreign language was cut in like news of a disaster; in school, meaningless sentences served only to drum grammar into our heads; and in church, the priest, as he delivered his sermon, often switched in spite of himself to German, which seemed far better suited to his purpose, and continued quietly what in the Slavic language he had had to thunder out, sentence by sentence, in a tone of condemnation.

Only the litanies, even more than the hymns, made me prick up my ears. I joined with all my heart in entreating the Saviour to have mercy on us and the saints to pray for us. In the dark nave, filled with the now unrecognizable silhouettes of the villagers turned with their voices toward the altar, the Slovene syllables— those of the priest changing, those of the congregation unchanging—resounded with infinite fervor. It was as though we were all lying prostrate, addressing our supplication to a closed heaven. Those foreign sequences could never be long enough for me; I wanted them to go on and on, and when the litany came to an end, I experienced not a dying away but a breaking off.

I lost this feeling at the seminary, where the few Slovene-speakers aroused antagonism and suspicion in the others. Unlike the voices in school, on the radio, and in church, they spoke their language softly, hardly above a whisper, and this in a far corner of the study hall, so that the rest of us heard no more than an incomprehensible hissing. The rectangle of desks in which they stood as though entrenched, with their backs to the world, gave them a conspiratorial air, accentuated by the shouts coming from all sides. And what about me? Did I envy them their huddled heads? Did I begrudge them their evident solidarity? No, my feeling went deeper. It was abhorrence. At the sight of this conceited band of the elect, dissociating themselves from the rest of us, from the mob among which I—alone, jostled, jostling back, warmed only by the blue cavern of my desk and by sleep—had to count myself. I wanted these no-good Slovenes to shut up and crawl out of their entrenchment, I wanted every single one of them to feel as homeless in his assigned seat as I did, with some stinking, panting, scratching foreign body beside him. I wanted him to go out and exercise in silence, without the comforting whispers of his fellow conspirators in his ears, but only the splashing of the seminary fountain, to share the lot of Filip Kobal, who finds your clannish minority even more nauseating than the speechless, disunited, directionless majority standing around with hanging heads and clenched fists.

Not until much later did one of these Slovene-speakers tell me the truth: that they did not band together against the rest of us; meeting in their corner had been their only way of hearing their own language after a day of having to talk in a foreign tongue, for their language was frowned upon not only by the German-speaking pupils but by the prefects as well. If they spoke softly, it was for fear of giving offense, and they spoke only of indifferent matters, the weather, school, the packages of sausage and ham they received from home, though even such conversation had been a great comfort to them. The familiar sounds they offered one another were like "the bread and wine of Communion"; the few moments of the day when they could at last be among themselves with their persecuted language were for them "hallowed moments" even if they had deliberately spoken only of the most commonplace things. "Doesn't it make a difference," cried my informant, "if I can say *njiva* instead of field, or *jabolko* instead of apple?"

But for me as a growing child it was only the litanies and the thought of my missing brother, my hero, that deterred me from regarding the region's second language—for many their first—as a personal assault on me; and even now, toward the end of the century, the German majority, often in spite of themselves, feel the same way.

It was the old dictionary that first helped me over this prejudice. It was published in the last years of the past century, in 1895 to be exact, the year of my father's birth. Aiming at completeness, it was a collection of words and phrases from every part of Slovenia. Just as the sun inching over the darkened landscape opposite my desk helps me now to perceive the minutest objects and figures and the spaces between them—the bent arm of the girl sitting by the water, a bowed tree on the horizon, a boy at the end of the path with his face turned toward the girl—so then, under the eaves of the barn, words helped me to see the little things which up until then had almost always been lacking when I tried to visualize a childhood. The first thing that happened was that word by word—my brother had ticked many of them, so I was able to skip quite a lot—a people took shape before my eyes. Its members were an exact replica of the villagers at home, but they did not, as in the usual stories and anecdotes, shrivel into types, caricatures, and clichés; I saw only the glowing outlines of people and things. These words sprang from a rural people whose metaphors had their source in country life: "He uses his tongue the way a cow uses her tail." "You're as slow as fog on a windless day." "Your house is as cold as a burned-out barn." But cities didn't frighten them, they were waiting to be conquered. The country-folk would "rattle" to town in the wagon or "glide" there in the sleigh. The vocabulary of profanity was rich and varied; "he swore his last" was a way of saying "he died." These people had any number of terms for dying, but even more for the female sex organ. From one valley to the next, the names for varieties of apple and pear changed, they were as numerous as the stars in the sky (which were named after farm implements or called "reapers" or "mowers," or simply, like the Pleiades, the "Densely Sowed Ones"). As the Slovenes had never set up a government of their own, they had to resort to literal translations from the German or Latin of their overlords for everything connected with politics, public life, or, for that matter, conceptual thought—which seemed as stilted as if I were to say "far-writer" for telegraph; on the other hand, the language had familiar names, nicknames as it were, for all ordinary objects, and not just the useful ones. Everything indoors seemed to have been named by women, and everything outside by men. A kind of bread baked under hot ashes was called, to translate literally, "underash," and a variety of pear, "the little woman." It is typical of this language that the addition of a mere syllable, and not of another word, can transform words for large areas into diminutives, which serve as names for the things and creatures in these areas. The area becomes, as it were, a refuge and hiding place for the creatures that bear its name. A wood, for example, harbored "woodsies," a word that could designate not only a human inhabitant of the wood but equally well, wood rushes, a particular species of forest flower, a wild cherry tree, a wild apple tree, a wood nymph, and—the heart as it were of the forest— the coal titmouse. It was through finding unaccustomed names for things in the dictionary that I first acquired a feeling for them.

Thus I discovered a people as tender as they were crude, a people with many different ways of scoffing at those who were quick to think and slow to act; an industrious people ("When it comes to work, we Slovenes are miles ahead," my brother wrote in a letter) whose adult language is shot through with children's expressions; taciturn and almost mute in despair, voluble and almost eloquent in joy and yearning; without aristocracy, without military marches, without land (their land was leased), without kings, their only king being the legendary hero who wandered about in disguise, showing himself only briefly. But, on second thought, what words made me aware of was not specifically the Slovene people or a people at the turn of the century, but rather an indeterminate, timeless, extrahistorical people—or better still, a people living in an eternal present, regulated only by the seasons, in an immanent world obedient to the laws of weather, of sowing, reaping, and animal diseases, a world apart from, before, or alongside of history. (I am aware that my brother's tick marks contributed to this static image.) How could I help wanting to count myself among this

unknown people that has none but borrowed words for
war, authority, and triumphal processions, but devises
names for the humblest things—indoors for the space
under the windowsill, out of doors for the shiny trace
of a braked wagon wheel on a stone flag—and is at its
most creative when it comes to naming hiding places,
places for refuge and survival, such as only children
can think up—nests in the underbrush, the cave behind
the cave, the fertile field deep in the woods—yet never
feels obliged to call itself "the chosen people" and
distance itself from "the nations" (for, as their every
word shows, this people inhabits and cultivates its land)?

Just as my brother's copybook, without excursions through
another language, translated itself directly into his work,
his orchard, so now his dictionary led me beyond the
orchard into the whole landscape of childhood. Childhood? Was it my particular childhood? Was it my
personal places and things that I discovered through
names? Unquestionably, the scene of action was my
father's house. With the help of the word for the space
behind the stove, for the beam under the cider barrel
in the cellar, for the stone-rimmed watering trough in
the stable, for the last furrow in plowing, I visualized
the corresponding object in or around our own house.
It took only a word to evoke the broad end of "our"
scythe, or "our" cling peaches, or the blue mist on "our"
plums; and to lift even our subsoil—the layer of gravel
under the humus, the pit where we stored our fodder
beets—into a realm of light and air. And there were
many words that communicated images of things which
I had never seen but which must nevertheless have
related to our life at home. Our horse, for instance,

had never had an eelback, but once I had the word for
it, I saw a horse with just such dark stripes in the village
paddock. Nor had I ever heard the voice of the queen
bee, which now, thanks to the onomatopoeic verb,
resounded from within my father's abandoned apiary
and penetrated my innermost being, followed by the
sound, "as of boiling plum butter," of a whole swarm
of "our" bees. Yes, "one who produces whirring sounds
on a birchwood flute" was I myself, the reader of the
one word for all that, and likewise it was I who,
immersed in "the blade of grass on which strawberries
are strung," emerge forthwith from our community
forest beyond the Seven Mountains, holding that same
blade of grass in my hand.

At that point I thought of my teacher, the writer
of fairy tales, who precisely because he was absent had
been a kind of prop to me in the course of my journey.
There was never any plot in his fairy tales; they were
mere descriptions of objects, and each story dealt with
only one thing, a thing which, as accessory or scene of
action, must have been familiar to readers of folk tales.
The subject of one tale was a hut in the forest, but
without a witch, without lost children, without fire
(except at the most for a puff of chimney smoke, soon
carried away by the cold wind); and beyond the Seven
Mountains there was nothing but a brook, so clear that
its bed could be mistaken at first sight for a road—fish
could be seen swimming over its dark elongated paving
stones until at last the water, rushing over a round
protruding rock, gave forth an endless sound. The only
one of his fairy tales in which anything "happened" was
a description of a bramblebush (of course without a
struggling Jew tearing himself to pieces in it); this bush

is in the middle of an impenetrable wilderness but is surrounded by a large circle of sand where, in the final sentence, a first-person narrator suddenly turns up and throws a handful of sand, "and then another, and still another, and so forth and so on," into the brambles. According to the author, these "one-thing tales" were supposed to be "sun tales" and manage without the usual "moonlight of spooky additives"; "sun and subject," he thought, were fairy tale enough; they were the "situation." A single glance at a treetop, he held, sufficed to produce a fairy-tale atmosphere.

Seen as a collection of one-*word* fairy tales, the dictionary did the same thing for me: it gave me images of the world, even when, as in the case of the strawberries strung on their blade of grass, I had not actually experienced them. Around every word I came across in my ruminations, a world took shape, as much around "an empty chestnut husk" as around "the wet tobacco left at the bottom of a pipe" or even "a sunshower" or "the white weasel," which also means "a saucy beautiful girl." And just as certain passages in my brother's letters, comparable to the fragments from the Greek seekers after truth, had a kind of halo around them, so now isolated words traced circles that made me think of a prehistoric figure who lived in the hazy centuries before those early stammerers, namely, of the legendary Orpheus. Only a few of his idiosyncratic terms had survived; neither his poems nor his songs had been thought worth collecting, only his peculiar names for things: "woven chains" for the furrows in fields, "bent shuttles" for plows, "threads" for seed grains, "Aphrodite" for the sowing season, "the tears of Zeus" for rain.

On me, too, word circles had the effect of fairy

tales, for though the terrible, the repellent, and the evil were amply represented in them, they were only a component which took its place in the whole and, in the dictionary at least, could never win out. My teacher found fault with the stories I had been writing at the time, saying that I had a weakness for the macabre, that I was positively addicted to the gloomy and gruesome; the law of writing, by contrast, was to create, letter after letter, syllable after syllable, the brightest of brightnesses; even a last breath, he said, must be transformed into the breath of life. And now, immersed in the dictionary's "rain of blood," "rat turds," "spittle of disgust," "the fecal sausages of the earthworm," "shoes moldering in a corner," a beast named "understone" (a viper), a place called "land of moles" (the grave), I felt free from my addiction to the gruesome or even to the tragic and found in the contemplation of names a pattern in the world, a plan, which transformed country people and a village house into world people and a big-city house. Every word circle a world circle! The crux of the matter was that every circle emanated from a single foreign word. When people felt unable to communicate an experience, weren't they always wailing: "Oh, if there were only a word for it!" And in moments of recognition, weren't they much less likely to say "Yes, that's it!" than "Yes, that's the word!"

But wasn't I taking the side of a foreign language against my own? Wasn't I attributing this one-word magic exclusively to Slovene, at the expense of my native German? No, it was both languages together, the single words on the left and the circumlocutions on the right which—sign after sign—curved, inflected, measured, circumscribed, constructed space. How fortunate

was the existence of different languages, how meaning-
ful was the allegedly so destructive Babylonian confusion! Wasn't the Tower of Babel actually built, though
in secret, and didn't it, after all, reach up into the
heavens?

Day after day, I opened the book of wisdom more
excitedly. Is there any word for the adventures I was
experiencing? What can one say to express the simultaneous experience of childhood and landscape? There
is a word, a German word, and that word is *Kindschaft!**
I clap my hands in amazement!

Time and again in my afternoons on the plateau I
applauded the epic of words. And I laughed as well,
not the laughter of ridicule, but the laughter of recognition and complicity. Yes, there *is* a word for the bright
spot in a cloudy sky, a word for the way an ox runs
back and forth on a hot day when he's stung by a
horsefly, for flame suddenly bursting from a stove, for
the juice of stewed pears, for the star on a bull's
forehead, for a man on all fours extracting himself
from the snow, for a woman stocking up on summer
clothes, for the sloshing of liquid in a half-empty bucket,
for the trickling of seeds out of seedpods, for the
skipping of a flat stone over the surface of a pond, for
icicles hanging from a tree, for the raw spot in a boiled
potato, for a puddle in clayey ground. Yes, that's the
word!

But was my plan still valid? Wasn't the word for
"the sound of two alternating flails" obsolete, since the

---

* This brunch-word might be rendered as "childscape," except that
the word *Kindschaft* actually exists in the meaning of "filiation" or
"adoption," as in Romans 9:4, "the adoption, and the glory." [Trans.]

corresponding implements had for years been hanging inactive in the museums? Wasn't "the sound of a falling body" the meaning that survived? Didn't the term which in the past century designated only "emigration" lose its innocence when the events of the last war changed its meaning to forced "resettlement"? Didn't the old book suffer from the absence of resistance fighters, of partisans, for whom the "partisan," that obsolete, halberd-like weapon, was hardly a substitute? And even back at the time when the dictionary was compiled, were there not a striking number of designations for places where something *had* been but was no longer— for fallow land "where barley formerly grew," for the place "where the barn used to be," the stone surface "where bushes used to grow"? And even at that time, were footnotes not appended to certain particularly inventive designations, to the effect that they were no longer in use? And hadn't the scholars included in their book any number of words which even their source, the oldest inhabitant in the most remote valley, had stopped using except in word games? So, instead of saying that words had fairy-tale magic, wouldn't it be wiser to say that they performed the function of a questionnaire: What is my situation? What is our situation? What is the present situation?

Yet, at the same time, they *were* fairy tales; for in answer to every word that questioned me, even if I had never seen the thing it stood for and even if it had long departed this world, the thing invariably gave rise to an image, or more precisely, a radiance.

One afternoon on the plateau I came across the last word my brother had ticked. As in many other cases, the date and place were supplied: "At the front." In the early stages of the war he always carried the book with him; it was only at the end that he left it home, along with his jacket, "as a baptismal present." The rest of the dictionary, more than half of it, showed no further pencil marks and seemed never to have been opened; there were no prewar blades of grass or wartime flies pressed between the pages.

There I sat, contemplating the one word, leafing back to the others: was this a map of the areas of the earth or only of their memory—or perhaps even their obituary? Was it only the fault of the wars that human language in the time I was living in, in *my* time, was so inexpressive that we speakers always had to *emphasize* something? Why, at the age of twenty, did I feel tired at the mere thought that some interlocutor might open his mouth? Why did speech—even my own—often banish me to a muffled middle-class living room (where the windows might be "deaf" rather than "blind")? Why had words lost all meaning? Why was it only the rare *mot juste* that made me feel that I had a soul?

In the village, on my way to this spot, I always passed a house, one wall of which merged seamlessly with a boulder. Similarly, when I now looked up from the old words, I saw the upper edge of the book merging directly with the air. The book formed a ramp guiding my gaze to the foot of the southern chain of mountains (one Slovene name for which, in literal translation, was "underwing"). There I saw a bare declivity, somewhat veiled by distance, which, however, because of the spruce at the edge of my little plateau, seemed only a stone's throw away. The slope, overgrown with grass, was hatched to the very top with a dense pattern of

disused cow paths. These looked something like stair-
ways, which occupied the whole breadth of the slope
and crisscrossed to form nets. The large horizontal
pattern was broken by a smaller one of vertical grooves,
in which the clay-yellow water of the afternoon rain was
now flowing. Seen from a distance, the water moved so
slowly that I thought of oozing stalactites. The dead
sloping pasture made me think of the cows which had
climbed up and down it in the past, an image of slowness,
of hulking bodies, stopping now and then to pull up
grass, not jumping over any of the steps as sheep or
dogs might have done, their udders grazing the tips of
the grass, their hooves often getting stuck in the mud.
Sometimes they slipped from level to level, thus gouging
out channels for the rainwater. One beast jumped up
on the one ahead and was dragged a bit of the way on
its back. One raised its tail and urinated so violently
that I almost thought I heard it, followed by a plopping
of dung. And then I actually saw the steaming of urine
on the paths. So slow was the procession that it called
to mind the crossing of a great mountain range, the
baggage train of a migration that had been going on
since the beginning of time. And precisely the emptiness—the empty network, the deserted crisscrossing
paths, the empty, slightly irregular serpentines—reinforced my impression of animal clumsiness. Here, in
contrast to the terraces of a mine or gravel pit, there
were no helmeted men with machines moving busily
up and down the slope, but an aimless mass almost
marking time, with lowered heads, on all fours or
slithering on their hind parts, a caravan of carriers and
slaves, coming from nowhere and heading nowhere,
for which the slope was not even a stopping place,

except in the event of a broken leg or an emergency slaughtering.

I thought again of my teacher. As a historian, he took a special interest in peoples who had vanished from the face of the earth. He began his course almost ritually with an example taken from his study of the Maya (because of which the students had given him a related nickname). As a student he had explored the Yucatán for years: "As a geographer," he said, "I grew tan, and as a historian, pale—as pale as I am now." The Maya, he said, had never succeeded in building a state, because their peninsula "lacks a great river. Think of the Euphrates and the Tigris, or of the Nile." Nor had they known the wheel or the pulley or the windlass; the only form of Mayan wheel ever found had been part of a small toy. But what most impeded their political development was their inability to construct a supporting arch; they knew only "pseudo-arches," incapable of sustaining the roof of a room, let alone a hall. Their one element of cohesion had been religion. Instead of the wheel, they had had the roller, and with it they built roads, used only for processions to their sanctuaries in the jungle. But every peasant's hut was also regarded as a temple. All life was governed by the heavenly bodies, which were looked upon as sacred, because instructions for daily life could be read from them. The steles dedicated to the sun indicated the time to sow; the hieroglyphics engraved in the stone served as a clock. In these ancient inscriptions, ancestors were also honored; the popular religion demanded that every family should know its origin; the first man, the ancestor common to all, had been made of corn.

The decline of the Maya began when public religion gave way to private worship. "You see," the teacher went on, "the families were rather unsociable, each kept to itself; the only bond between them had been public worship. But then they began to build chapels of their own, each for itself, at a distance from the others; forgotten was the idea that the house as such was hallowed. The bond was broken. It was then that the hieroglyphics on the steles came to an abrupt end. In the year 900 of our era," said the teacher, "the last inscription was chiseled into a pillar not far from the grassy area which the Spaniards were to call the 'Savanna of Freedom.' Imagine the sparks in the flint, which was what most of the steles were made of." The end of this people is most strikingly symbolized by the stairs on one of the pyramids: step after step richly decorated with sacred reliefs and glyphs, the sign for the morning star, the sign for the tree that gives the villagers shade, the signs for sun and day, which taken together signify "time"—but on the topmost step only "a few muddled, scratchy chisel marks."

That stairway appeared to me in the empty sloping pasture. Much larger than the mound in our orchard at home, it actually had the shape of a pyramid and seemed with its hundred-odd steps, tapering toward the top, to reach the sky. I saw the words my brother had ticked climb the slope and then break off. Every line on the slope was an overturned hieroglyphic pillar, lying face down in the mud. The clayey brooks, welling up from scars in the earth, washed syllable after syllable away, until the whole place smoked like a field of ruins where not even the usual cherry trees had been spared. Seized with a need to mourn, I stood up, still holding my brother's book. Nothing more was moving on the empty steps, not even a blade of grass; even the water stood still; and hadn't being alive always meant simply being able to breathe with the flowing water, the waving grass, a rising branch? But what I wanted to mourn was not just a solitary death, it was something more: an annihilation. To annihilate means to do away not only with a particular human being but also with what gives the world its cohesion. To eliminate someone like my brother—who, unlike the great mass of those who speak and write, had the gift of bringing words and through them things to life, who never ceased to exercise that gift and to point out examples as he was doing now to me—was to kill language itself, the living tradition, the tradition of peace; it was the most unforgivable of crimes, the most barbarous of world wars.

But I was unable to mourn as I had wished. Instead, the phrase that had been the peasants' watchword in their earliest uprising—"Our old right!"—kept spinning around in my head. Yes, from time immemorial we had raised a claim that should not have been allowed to lapse. And it *had* lapsed, because we ceased to raise it. And why did we always demand our right of someone else, some of an emperor, others of a God? Why didn't we take it for ourselves, essential as it was for our self-preservation, letting no one else intervene? There at last was a game in which we wouldn't have had to measure ourselves against anyone, a lonely game, a wild game—Father, the great game!

Back from the empty cow paths to put my thoughts in order, back to the book. I had been sitting and standing barefoot, and barefoot I strode back and forth outside the barn. The last word my brother had ticked

had a double meaning. Translated, it meant both "to
fortify oneself" and "to sing psalms." (Immersing myself
in these words was the exact opposite of my usual
immersion in so-called breathtaking stories; time and
again the words made me raise my head and my eyes.)
I stopped and raised my head. By way of a ford marked
by a tree, I was carried back to the bluish cavern of my
seminary desk. Its back wall was the grooved mountain
slope. A sun shone on it, low in the sky as shortly before
setting and made brighter by the unlit spruce in front
of it. The steps were thick bars of shadow leading to
the summit, on which lay a thoroughly earthly glow.
The light pinpointed the smallest shapes on the slope—
a clump of grass, a half-overgrown hoof print, a
molehill, a line of birds along a rivulet, a wild hare
nearby—and connected them with one another by distinct interstices. I went on reading, my eyes at once in
the book and on the mountain. My staring became a
watching, as when in a strange crowd one knows that a
familiar face or two must be present. Here in the sun,
the resounding litany of the faithful which had begun
in the dark church was resumed in a silent litany of
words, with their many meanings. To breathe deeply
was to yearn was to tense the strongest muscle. Violent
anger was sobbing. Fireflies were June was a variety of
cherry. The mower was a sandpiper was the belt of
Orion. The grasshopper was the bridge of a violin was
the inner partition of a nut was the upper part of a
whip . . . A change of one letter transformed the word
for a slight breeze into the word for a powerful flow,
and another into a tempest, which was also the name
for flying sand . . . At last, silent invocations took on
human form, and I saw the absent ones appear on the

steps, silhouetted by the word-light: my mother as "the woman who had ceased to be a handmaiden"; my father as "the man who never ceased to be a servant"; my sister as "the madwoman," which, with a slight sound shift, became "the blessed"; my girlfriend as "the quiet one"; my teacher as "bitter sweetheart"; the village idiot as "he who stirs up wind while walking"; my enemy in the form of "a bruised heel"; and ahead of them all my brother "the pious," a word which also designated "the serene." And I?—I recognized myself, reader and on-looker in one, as the third party on whom everything hinged, without whom there could be no game, and who thus found in himself the salient features of the other players: my father's white, servant's feet and the torn corners of my brother's eyes.

Of course it was only for a moment that this picture writing shimmered on the mountain slope; then all was reliefless emptiness and the sun had set. But I knew I could bring the picture writing back, that unlike grief it could be willed; the empty forms both of the cow paths and of the blind windows could be relied on; they were the seal of our right. "Brother, you must have walked there in the gray blueness."

I shut my eyes. Only then did I notice that they were wet. But I was not weeping for myself or my family; no, the source of those tears was things and their words.

Behind my closed eyelids, the after-image of the cow paths: a stone-gray pattern. Now, a quarter of a century later, I see, there on the plateau, a man of indeterminate age. Barefoot, wearing an overcoat that's too big for him, he begins to wave his arms. His arm waving becomes a continuous movement which, if it were not done with the whole hand, including the fist, would be something like writing. Was this "he" or "I"? It is still I. I no longer write in the air as I did as a child; instead, like a scientist who is at the same time a manual laborer, I make hatch marks on a sheet of paper lying on the stone-gray steps. That is the movement I have chosen for my story. Letter for letter, word for word, as chiseled in stone long years ago, I want the inscription to appear on my paper; I want it to be handed down recognizably thanks to my light hatch marks. Yes, I want my soft pencil strokes to join with the hardness of the stone as did the language of my forebears, in which the term for "the monotonous note of the finch" is derived from the word for "a single letter." For, without the refuge of words, the earth, the black, red, greening earth, would be just one great desert, and I will no longer acknowledge any drama, any history other than the drama of the things and words of this beloved world—and I pray that the bomb which is threatening the cow-path pyramid will strike softly in the form of the word for "an elongated pear." I shall find a word for the dark interior of a white chestnut blossom, the yellow of clay under the wet snow, the bit of blossom that clings to the apple, and the sound of a river fish leaping out of the water.

I opened my eyes again, and again walked back and forth outside the barn, faster and faster as though taking a running leap. Again I stopped. Sensing that my chest had become an instrument, I shouted. Filip Kobal—whose voice was so soft that he could never make himself heard, whom the prefects at the seminary had scolded because his prayers didn't "carry"—shouted so loud that all who knew him would have looked at him with new eyes.

Something comparable had happened only once, at that same seminary. I had convinced myself that I was unable to sing, and then one day the teacher called on me to sing. With my heart in my mouth I had stood up and taken a deep breath. Then, in the midst of the sullenly brooding class, I had drawn from my innermost soul a strange and tender song, which had provoked first laughter, then awed embarrassment in my listeners, and which, it seemed to me, must always have been inside me. Now on the plateau, where I was alone, what came out of me was not singing, nor was it a bellowing or calling; it was a clear shout, imperiously demanding my right. With all my might I shouted the laconic or lyrical, monosyllabic or polysyllabic words of my brother's book. The words went out over the countryside, calling forth on the empty cow paths an echo whose other name was "world sound." And at every shout I saw the open ears of my forebears, the amused arching of their eyebrows, their joyful faces.

I propped up the book, touched it with my lips, and bowed down to the place. I cut a branch from the hazel bush near one corner of the barn, scratched the name of the place and the date into it: "Dobrava, Slovenija, Jugoslavija 1960," and declared it to be our stele, the record of a new and different family history. How little hope I had of a future at the age of twenty (never would my king appear), how firm were my expectations concerning the present; and how weak or cautious is my voice now as I repeat the young man's experience. Wasn't it drowned out long ago by shouts converging on the plateau from all directions, by shouts of command on drill grounds, by field-gray soldiers on firing ranges, by the scraping of shovels in the village graveyard? No, wherever I may be, the blind windows and empty cow paths strike me as the hallmarks of a kingdom of recurrence, where a locomotive whistle can become equally well the cry of a pigeon or the shriek of an Indian. I can still feel on my shoulder the cord of my sea bag with the book of words in it. Mother, your son is still walking under the open sky.

Then, flinging myself upon the ground, I discovered once and for all what the spirit is.

Three THE SAVANNA OF FREEDOM AND THE NINTH COUNTRY

THAT DAY I stayed on the plateau until the after-image of the sun left my retina. An axle seemed to be turning inside me, more and more slowly, bringing the things behind me into my field of vision. Beyond the northern mountains I saw a fiery cloud, which I situated exactly over the house of my parents. Heart, diamond, spade, and club shapes had been cut out of the west wall of the barn to let air in, and my father's centuries-old desolation came blowing out of the black holes.

I left the place, backing away; and later, while walking, I kept turning back toward it. A little bird rose high over the edge of the plateau—as though it had just slipped from the hand of the dwarf who had hoped with its help to win the stone-throwing contest with the giant—and plummeted to the ground as though shot. The lake at the end of the valley looked like jelly in the dying light, and I fancied it full of drowning bees, circling around with transparent wings.

Each time, I went there with head bowed and came back with head erect. A tablet was affixed to one of the houses at the entrance to this village. On such and such a day in the year 1941, it said, a meeting held here passed the first resolution on resistance to Fascism. (In every Slovene town or village I was to pass through, I found a house bearing the same inscription.) I, too,

wanted to put up resistance. I made my decision not in
a cellar but out on the street, without a meeting, all by
myself. "Form a sentence with 'fight' in it," I said to
myself. Only then did I realize that there already was
such a sentence and that it had as many meanings as
an oracle. Once, in such a mood, I went into a wooden
hut and brought the ax down on the chopping block
with all my might. An elderly woman came in and asked
me to split a pile of sawed logs. I struck so hard that
the pieces flew in all directions—I can still feel one
grazing my forehead. In one hour I earned an evening
meal and a few locutions such as "to split light" for "to
chop kindling." Another time, a soccer ball bounced
across my path and I kicked it so well that I was asked
to join the game (to this day, I sometimes dream that
I'm a forward on the national team). My shoes supported
my ankles, and my father's leather strap, no longer a
mere wristlet, strengthened my hand.

In the evenings, Filip Kobal had his corner place in the
Black Earth Hotel. No one, not even the militia on its
constant rounds, asked me my name; everyone called
me "the guest"; even the picture of Tito had been
turned away from me and was looking up at a squadron
of bombers. On the tables, instead of baskets piled high
with variously shaped Austrian rolls, which at times
could remind one of corpses thrown headlong into a
mass grave, there were simple stacks of sliced white
bread on the napkins that used to be called "bread
cloths." It was midsummer and sometimes warm enough
for serving meals outside. I was usually so overheated
when I got back that the breeze from the torrent made
me feel pleasantly fanned. There was a stool by the

open window of the dining room, and the waiter stood on it to take the dishes that the cook handed him. Next to the stool there was a concrete surface with deep grooves that looked something like piano keys: a bicycle stand, usually empty. This was where the lightning rod ended; the fact is that a day seldom passed without a storm, and the evenings in the open were brightened by the summer lightning, for which, as a secondary-school graduate, I knew the ancient Greek term "space eye." July came, and the fireflies which had just been flitting through the bushes crept into the grass and vanished.

The waiter was slightly younger than myself and may have come straight from trade school. Short, lean, with a brown, narrow, almost triangular face, he must, I felt sure, have come from a rocky, sparsely populated, inland region—one of a smallholder's many children, born on a farm surrounded by stone walls and growing up a shepherd or picker of wild fruit, which he knew exactly where to find. Other people had called my girlfriend beautiful; this waiter was the only person to whom I applied the word in my own thoughts. Apart from greeting, ordering, and thanking, I never spoke to him; he never chatted with the guests and said only what was strictly necessary. His beauty was not so much in his features as in his constant attentiveness, his friendly vigilance. One never had to call him or even to raise one's hand; standing in the farthermost corner of the dining room or garden—as he did when not busy—seemingly lost in some faraway dream, he kept an eye on his whole realm and anticipated the slightest flicker of an eyelid; in other words, he was a model of the courtesy and helpfulness lauded in books of etiquette. In the morning, he set the tables under the chestnut trees even if it was thundering, and had them cleared before the first drops began to fall. Sometimes, to my surprise, I'd see him alone in the dining room, putting each chair in its proper place, as though arranging for some festivity, a baptism or wedding, and allowing for the special quirks of every single guest. I also marveled at the care with which he handled the cheapest and shabbiest objects (there were no others in that hotel), at his way of lining up the tin knives and forks and wiping the plastic cap of the condiment bottle. Once in the late afternoon I saw him standing motionless in the bare, empty room, looking into space; then he stepped over to a far corner and gave a carafe an affectionate little turn that filled the whole house with an aura of hospitality. Another time, when the dining room was full, as it often was at dinner, he set down a cup of coffee on the bar before bringing it to the table and carefully aligned the handle; then with an elegant gesture he took hold of the tiny cup and carried it directly to the guest's table. I was also struck by the dead seriousness with which he gave a light to anyone, even to a drunk, always with a single, unbroken movement, and by the way his half-closed eyes would light up every time.

Alone during the day, in my room or out of doors, I thought about the waiter more than about my parents; as I now realize, it was a kind of love. I had no desire for contact, I wanted only to be near him, and I missed him on his day off. When he finally reappeared, his black-and-white attire brought life into the room and I acquired a sense of color. He always kept his distance, even when off duty, and that may have accounted for my affection. One day I ran into him in his street clothes at the bus-station buffet, now in the role of a guest, and there was no difference between the waiter at the hotel and the young man in the gray suit with a raincoat over his arm, resting one foot on the railing and slowly munching a sausage while watching the departing buses. And perhaps this aloofness in combination with his attentiveness and poise were the components of the beauty that so moved me. Even today, in a predicament, I think about that waiter's poise; it doesn't usually help much, but it brings back his image, and for the moment at least I regain my composure.

Toward midnight, on my last day in the Black Earth Hotel—all the guests and the cook, too, had left—I passed the open kitchen on my way to my room and saw the waiter sitting by a tub full of dishes, using a tablecloth to dry them. Later, when I looked out of my window, he was standing in his shirtsleeves on the bridge across the torrent, holding a pile of dishes under his right arm. With his left hand, he took one after another and with a smooth graceful movement sent them sailing into the water like so many Frisbees.

Young Filip Kobal's nights in his four-bed room at the Black Earth Hotel were almost entirely dreamless. Years before, penned into the dormitory at the seminary, nailed to his pillow by a persistent headache, he had often thought of lying alone in his bed under the open sky, in the midst of a raging snowstorm. His blanket, which he had pulled up to his ears, kept him warm, and only the dragon in his head had turned to ice. And now my wish was fulfilled in a different way by the thundering torrent, which pushed open the door of my room and took the place of dreams.

Only once did I dream of my father (who had

earned a pension as a flood-control worker) or perhaps only of the copybook in which I had wanted him to write the story of our family. It had turned into a genuine book, which did not as in reality consist of that one shaky line—my brother's APO number and my laundry mark—but was crammed full of text, not hand-written, but printed. The flood-control worker had become a peasant author, the updated successor to those Slovenian peasants at the turn of the century whose stories had been collected and who, because they usually told their stories in the evening, are known (in rough translation) as "evening people," a term which before they made their appearance may have referred to evening winds or moths and since then can only have applied to the evening papers. And the attentive reader of my father's book was the young waiter.

The morning wind was blowing when I stood with my blue sea bag and hazelwood stick on the platform of the Bohinjska Bistrica station. I was heading farther south. From where I stood, the tunnel through the mountain chain could be seen in the distance. As in Mittlern across the border, here, too, there were living quarters on the second floor of the building, and here, too, geranium petals came fluttering down on the roadbed from window boxes; in the meantime, I had come to like the smell. The small railroad stations of both countries had a good deal in common, even the inscription on the little enamel plaques indicating so and so many "feet above the Adriatic Sea"; they all displayed one and the same emblem: that of the old Austro–Hungarian Empire. A stone portal led to the toilet; the door was painted blue like the sky in the wayside shrines at home (but, inside, the only equipment

was an unadorned hole). Cow's horns as big as a buffalo's
were nailed to a wooden hut. The vegetable garden
belonging to the station ended in a triangular herb
garden surrounded by pole beans and dominated by
the feathery green of dillweed; at the tip of the triangle
a cherry tree, the ground below it dark with spots of
fruit. Swallows were screaming in the chestnut trees
outside the station, unseen except for a trembling in
the leaves. The floor of the waiting room was of black
polished wood, which along with the tall iron stove
repeated the bus station at home; unoccupied as usual,
it had windows on both sides, and the light inside it
suggested a living room. Near the entrance, half buried
in a layer of concrete, a footscraper of imperial cast
steel, resembling an upturned knife blade, was framed
left and right by richly ornamented miniature pillars.
The room as a whole seemed spacious and yet well
finished in every detail, and in it I sensed the breath of
a gentle spirit, the spirit of those who long ago, in the
days of the Empire, had designed it and made use of
it. And the man who was looking after it now was no
scoundrel either.

A group of soldiers were waiting there along with
me, dried sweat on their unshaven faces, their boots
caked with clay up to the ankles. From them I looked
up to the southern mountain range, the peaks of which
were already in the sunlight; for once, the sky over the
Bohinj was cloudless. In that moment, I decided to
cross the mountains on foot, and started off at once.
"No more tunnels," I said to myself, and: "I've got
plenty of time." With my decision a jolt passed through
the country, and with that the day seemed to begin.
Didn't "jolt" mean "fight" in the other language?

* * *

The only high mountain I had known up until then was Mount Petzen, which was a little higher than these mountains; sometimes even in the summer there were patches of snow in its shaded cirques. But I had always gone there with my father and, because of the slow climb, it seemed quite a distance. Halfway up, we would spend the night in a dusty hay barn, after which my eyes were too swollen to take in the view. If we came anywhere near a farm, a dog would come running, followed by its owner shouting and brandishing a stick— the mountain peasants had an ingrained distrust of the smallholders down in the plain, who trampled their pastures, frightened the cattle, and stripped the woods of mushrooms. They would calm down only when we came closer and one of the strangers proved to be the carpenter known throughout the region, who, as it happened, had raised the peasant's roof, after which we would be invited in for bacon, bread, and cider. One day on the crest dividing Austria from Yugoslavia, my father spread his legs, one foot on this side, one foot on the other, and made one of his short speeches: "See, this is what our name means, not *straddler* but *border person*. Your brother is a man of the interior; we two are border people. A Kobal is someone who crawls on all fours, and at the same time a light-footed climber. A border person is an extreme case, but that doesn't make him marginal."

On my way up I often turned around, as though in gratitude to the strange country where, so very differently from at home, no one was suspicious of me and the few questions I had been asked were not designed to trap me. The rest of the time I kept my head down, gazed at the summery meadow passing by in silent flight, and thought of my brother, who, while marching to war, had heard no birds and had ceased to see "what flowered by the roadside." I felt that the steady climb was strengthening my body for the events of the autumn, whether military service or study, and for my encounter with my next enemy. The lizards rolled away like round stones or swished into the bushes like birds. The last sign of human life I was to see for some time was the dark wet bundle of washing outside the end house of a mountain village (the Slovene language, I reflected, has a special word for someone living in such an "end house"). After that, I followed traces in the grass, which often turned out to be animal tracks leading into impenetrable tangles, and all I heard was a monotonous buzzing of insects that made me think of a population gradually receding into the distance. At my back the valley had vanished, but on the horizon before me I could see the Julian Alps and in the midst of them the Triglav, the highest mountain in Yugoslavia; ahead of me and behind me, only wilderness.

Again I attempted a shortcut, supposedly a straight line, where the workings of the water made a straight line impossible. I had started out cautiously, but now I rushed headlong through underbrush and over rocky debris. At the tree line, the bare crest seemed to be coming closer, and the grass, which up until then had been knee-high, became short and stubbly. Suddenly I saw ahead of me an utterly motionless cloud, and at the same moment the first flash of lightning darted out of it. I was not untroubled; to tell the truth, I was terrified— only the day before, there had been talk at the hotel about someone being killed by lightning. Yet I kept on climbing. Since then, I have often run straight into danger as though hypnotized by it, not the least bit cheerful, let alone happy about it, panic-stricken in fact, humming some hit song or counting out numbers. That day, I was so terrified that I even heard the flapping of my trousers as thunder. What from a distance I had taken for a stone hut on the summit turned out, when I got there, to be the remains of a fort; the windows proved to be embrasures. Even so, the ruin provided shelter. A jolt, and equanimity took over; calmly, I looked down on a distant field that was white with hailstones when everywhere else it was raining. So great was my exhaustion that my eyes forgot their perspective and saw the white patch as a sheet spread out to bleach. Sitting there, I toppled over. In a letter written after a forced march, my brother speaks of a faint as "involuntary sleep."

Night was falling when I came to; most of the embrasures were aimed at the southern valley, and looking out, I saw the lights of a few houses. I walked up and down in the rain outside and then decided to stay; in the dying day the honeycomb cells of the fort seemed positively inviting, like small hotel rooms. The mists coming up over the ridge were clouds—I had never been in a cloud before. When I looked down at the grass, the little mountain flowers would vanish in the mist and reappear a moment later; the motionless wings of a falcon drifting with the clouds looked frayed. Inside the fort, reclining on a bed of old newspapers, I ate some of the food I had brought with me. Nothing more could happen to me, not that day at least; I thought of the story about the goblin who, safe in his rocky niche, stuck out his tongue at the elements; but then, his attention diverted by a malignant human, he was struck by lightning.

Night was long in coming; the twilight outlines of

things merely dissolved into a more and more formless brightness, the only contour in it being my blue sea bag. "Sea bag on the mountain ridge," I caught myself mumbling as I was falling asleep. Then I swam for hours in the Arctic Ocean, which froze solid around me. Suddenly I felt fingertips on my face, no contact could have been warmer or more real, and a familiar voice said to me: "My dearest!" But when I opened my eyes in the darkness, no one was there; only a crackling that grew louder and louder, closer and closer; then a crash, but the wild beast proved to be my sea bag, which had tipped over.

I got up before first light and made my way along the ridge, step by step. That's how I wanted it; I wanted at last, like the barefoot child on the path beside my father at the border between night and day, to pick out every detail signifying the start of day and everything else besides; I wanted at last to repeat the adventure of "existence." But it didn't work. In my childhood, the primordial world had imprinted itself on my mind along with the separate drops of early-morning rain, which dug tiny craters in the dust of the path; but now everything was the primordial world—the rain gushing out of the dark sky as it had been falling since the world began, the smoke rising from the black earth as though from clefts in lava, the gray-on-gray of the wet, cold rock, the creepers catching at my feet, the absent wind— thus, nothing could take the form of that pattern in the dust. Perhaps the hand-in-hand-with-my-father was lacking or the closeness to the ground, something the present narrator can sense but not so the child's successor up there on the mountain ridge; in that case, might it not be possible to renew an experience not so much by imitating or aping it as by retracing and actively reliving it? Instead of the glow rising from the dust craters, as though the sun itself were rising right here on the planet, I perceived nothing on my solitary march but a dismal dawning in which all shapes, even those of the night, dissolved, and no feeling of a sun, however distant, was born; and now, stumbling over rocks and roots in the gray of dawn, freezing and sweating at once, soaked to the skin, my wet, lumpy sea bag growing heavier and heavier on my back, I found myself re- peating, not my childhood walks with my father, but my soldier-brother's plodding through a wasteland into a battle that was lost in advance; instead of a path through fields, a military highway. Though I was sure of going westward, I thought with anger that I was being sent to the east like my brother years ago, and though I was heading exactly for my desired destination, I was plagued by the thought that every step was carrying me farther away from the place that was my one and all. Was the first warning cry of the marmot addressed not to its fellows but to me? Wasn't the albino- pale mountain hare, darting out of the clouds and passing me by with a squeak, a symbol of catastrophic flight?

Such were my angry, oppressive thoughts, yet nothing could deflect me from my path. At daybreak the rain let up and I started the descent into the still-hidden Isonzo Valley. There was no discernible trail, but I would make one. And, to be sure, I discovered in myself the light-footedness of my father's speech on the moun- tain crest, a quick, steady leaping from boulder to boulder, without halt or hesitation. It even gave me pleasure, a pleasure which increased in one place where a bit of rock climbing became necessary. There, Father, I was on all fours, but erect; I felt a simultaneous pull in my fingertips and the balls of my feet, as I never did in the physical labors you gave me to do. I reached the foot of the little wall alive, and plunged into the light of the sun, which actually appeared at that moment.

That brought me to the southern tree line. I still had a long, but easy, hike ahead of me. As I went on, I was overcome with something different from fear of lightning or wild beasts or falling. In telling me about his solitary expeditions as a young geographer, my teacher said that he hadn't felt free until he left "the last signs of hunters" behind him. I, on the contrary, far from any settlement, in a spot where I could be almost certain that no one else would turn up (and no one knew I was there), fell a prey to anxiety, to fear of a monster—and I myself was the monster. Vanished was every contact with a world; instead, a pallid light, through which, harried by the bloodhound that had suddenly erupted within me, the monster named Alone wandered blindly. And then another jolt, which was at the same time recollection. Had I given myself that jolt, or did it just happen? It happened, and it was I who gave it to my wandering self. Sometimes, as a boy, I had encountered myself in that way, usually on waking, and always at times when I felt threatened. My anxiety turned to terror, as if the end had come, and my terror into a dread with which, reduced to a tumor, I waited— unable to stir a muscle—for the tumor to be removed. But it wasn't. Instead, an utter stranger appeared and that stranger was I. It was "I," written with a capital letter, because it wasn't just anybody; gigantic and space-filling it stood over me, paralyzing my tongue and my limbs; it was my written name. My dread became amazement (to which for once the word "boundless" applied), the evil spirit became a good one, the tumor became a creature, toward which in my imagination, instead of the ominous one finger, a whole kindly hand pointed—and with the appearance of this "I," it was as though I had just been created: wide-open eyes, ears that were pure listening. (Today, alas, my wonderment at that incomprehensible "total I" refuses to reappear; it seems to have departed from me forever, and this may have something to do with the guilt which has become a part of me at the age of forty-five, and leaves me alone with my often depressing reason, whereas I see my twenty-year-old "I" in a state of grace, in the madness of innocence. Madness? There in the wilderness it was madness that cured me of my fear.)

Reassured, I went my way, with myself on my back, not as a burden, but as protection. I had no sooner reached the forest than I heard a crashing behind me, and a boulder came hurtling between the trees. In the moss a buzzing, as if a swarm of flies had been shooed away from a dung heap—that was a moss-green snake rearing its head and hissing at me. I brought myself to admire it. The skeleton under the pile of brushwood was a roebuck's; it had horns on its head; I took head and horns with me for a while, then I threw them away. While crossing a pathless clearing covered with chest-high ferns, I took time to listen to the humming of the invisible and otherwise soundless birds in the ferns at my feet. It was not inconsistent with my carefree mood that I was glad to catch sight of an overgrown path, which in descending widened into an old road, and was even happier to see the first fresh wagon tracks and the

groove made by the brake claw—it was that steep—in
the middle strip of grass. At the sight of this groove, of
the clods of mud ripped up by the brake, the oily water
in the deep black, glistening wheel ruts, the horseshoe
marks, the boot prints of the driver walking beside the
wagon (the writing on the soles had left a clear imprint),
it even seemed to me that a whole orchestra was starting
to play, and this most delicate of all melodies has remained to this day my ideal of music. Then came the
first cheeping of sparrows and the barking of dogs.
Though it was beginning to rain again, I sat down by
the roadside and ate a few blackberries, which here on
the southern slope were beginning to ripen. I took off
my shoes and let the "sky water" wash my aching feet.
I was so hot that the sweat was steaming off me. The
shiny handle of my flashlight showed me a face plastered
with pine needles. Since the berries failed to quench
my thirst, I drank of the warm rainwater as I walked.
The elder bush at the entrance to the village was already
sprinkled black; next to it, bearing fruit that seemed to
grow straight out of its branches, an adventure: my first
fig tree. At the foot of the village terrace a desert of
white stone, with a bright green stripe twining through
it—the Soča, or Isonzo.

I had been roaming about for two days, and now
in security I thought, as I often did later on "arriving
safely," that I hadn't wandered nearly long enough.
Security? In my whole life, I have never once felt myself
in security.

I spent only a night and a day in the Upper Isonzo
Valley. I slept in Tolmin, the largest town in the valley;
its coat-of-arms shows the river's meanders, crisscrossed
by the pitchforks of the peasant uprising. I found shelter

in the basement of a private house, where there were rooms for rent. There were spiders on the ceiling, and after midnight the cellar smell was fortified by the stench of vomit. In the next room a man retched loudly, wordlessly, and uninterruptedly until dawn. When I got up, there was no one in the kitchen-living room but a mute child with a cat on his lap; his parents had already gone out to work. I put the money on the table, took breakfast at the inn, and breathed deeply at the sight of the bread.

An old road leads along the terrace where the villages are situated. I headed up the river for Kobarid, or Karfreit; at first the Isonzo lay far below me, then it came closer; on the far side of it I saw pastureland, with windowless and chimneyless huts for hay. At a place where the road touched the meandering river, I went down to the bank, took my clothes off in the rain, and let myself down from an overhanging rock into the current, which from a distance had looked so furious but wasn't so bad once I was in it. Up ahead of me, the river split in two. The water was up to my shoulders; having just come down from the mountains, it was ice-cold; for a moment it stabbed me in the pit of my stomach. I swam against the stream with all my might and noticed after a hundred counted strokes that I was still on a level with the stone where I had left my clothes. I stood up and with my head barely above water surveyed the countryside, which, seen in that perspective, became part of a strange continent, a single shimmering flow from all sides, subdivided only by tongue-shaped gravel banks, surmounted by swaths of mist and fringed by mountains dark with conifers and veiled in rain, the ever-active watershed for these nameless streams. Soča? Isonzo? The desolation that extended from the tip of my chin to a bow-shaped peak lit by a distant sun, nothing but cold river water and warm rain, made me think of a primeval world that doesn't want to be named but only to stand alone for itself. But then in the middle of the river I sighted, one after another, three fellow swimmers, evidently—to judge by the outline of their undershirts on their otherwise brown arms—workers taking a midday break. They were swimming fast and shouting, one louder than the next; they soon disappeared from view (I saw them later on the road in a file of gravel trucks). Soča or Isonzo? Which suited the river better, the feminine Slovene or the masculine Italian name? For me, I thought, masculine would be better; for the three workers, feminine. As I resumed my march on the road, I felt a warming hand between my shoulder blades, and my shoes became slowly gliding dugout canoes.

Later on, when for the first time I heard the name Kobarid pronounced by a native, it sounded to me as if a child had said it. Yes, time and again, names have rejuvenated the world. When I got there, it was different from anything I had ever seen at home. This was no village; all of a sudden I was surrounded by a fragment of a metropolis; a forest jutted into the center with its bookstore and flower shop, and there were wet cows right next to the factory on the periphery. Though in the foothills of the Alps, Kobarid, or Karfreit, struck me then as the embodiment of the south, with its oleander bushes at the entrances to houses, laurel trees outside the church, stone buildings, and streets of multicolored cobbles (which, to be sure, led after a few steps into the evergreen forests of Central Europe).

The people spoke a jumble of Slovene and Italian,

just as the houses were a jumble of wood, stone, and marble; all that together had a spark of daring about it. At my inn, which like the others was named after a mountain, two men were playing cards; at the end of the game, one showed his opponent his winning card with a quick smile. A woman on a curved balcony snipped the faded flowers from the geraniums that ran the whole length of the house, and then put a gleaming red flowerpot down beside the other pots. "This place is my source." That was my decree.

The bus from the north that I was waiting for came around the corner. But it wasn't the right one; unlike Yugoslavian buses, it gleamed with enamel in which, when it stopped, the lanceolate leaves of the oleanders were reflected; when I looked up, I saw the whole population of my home village, in window after window a familiar profile. Involuntarily I moved away, looking for a place where I wouldn't be seen. Were the villagers really perched up so high? Weren't they, rather, huddling or crouching? And when they rose to their feet, weren't they actually picking themselves up off the floor? Painfully, as though crippled, they crawled out of the bus, and the driver had to help several of them down from the doorstep. Outside, gathered together in the bend of the street, they sought one another with their eyes, as though afraid of getting lost. Though it was a weekday, they were festively dressed, they had even put on their peasant costumes; only the priest shepherding the tour was wearing his traveling habit and a white collar. The men were wearing hats and under their brown suits velvet vests with metal buttons; the women, in fringed rainbow-colored shawls, all had enormous handbags, all of the same shape. Even the oldest among the women had braided their hair and wound the braids around their heads like wreaths. I was sitting half in shadow at a distance, on a chopping block under an outside staircase. A few of them glanced in my direction, but none of these people knew me; only the priest had a moment's pause, and it seemed to me that the sight of this stranger may have put him in mind of Kobal, Filip, apostate and fugitive from the seminary. Where, I wonder, could that fellow be now?

Then one by one they stepped into the inn and stayed a long while. I decided to wait for them; there would be a later bus to the Karst, which was probably where my search for my brother's traces would end. Beside me, there was a woodpile with a pyramidal tunnel at the bottom resembling a kennel; on the wall above it, the remains of a Latin inscription: UNCERTAIN THE HOUR. It seemed to me that I could tell by the look of the villagers that my mother was well; just the sight of those familiar handbags reassured me.

I was left undisturbed in my place; the fact that I so obviously had time seemed identification enough. When the Rinkenbergers came out into the open, the old men had flushed cheeks. They were not drunk but were all seized with a strangely awkward exhilaration. From them I heard the language of the land, for the first time spoken purely, with clear voices, without the garble and swallowing of syllables usual in our village. Before getting into their bus, they all, as though on command, turned back toward the wall of the house, which, windowless at that point, was only a large yellow surface with horizontal grooves. The dark backs of the villagers stood out clearly against it, and I saw some of the women, regardless of age, holding one another by the hand, while some of the men threw their arms over one another's shoulders. They all sagged at the knees, and it occurred to me that not only we, the Kobals, were exiles, but all the smallholders, and that the whole village of Rinkenberg had always been a village of exile, all its inhabitants equally servile, equally wretched, equally out of place; here with the others even the priest struck me, not as a man of the cloth, but as a close-cropped convict. Most likely they stopped to look at the house because they had been served so well and cheaply there, but in my eyes they were looking up at the grooves of a wailing wall, and at the same time they were pilgrims (Pelegrin was a common name in the village), and that fitted in with the solemnity of the hairdos and costumes. For the first time I saw meaning in these costumes (as I would on a future occasion in the picture of an old woman standing with half-closed eyes outside her stone hut, holding her black-and-white shroud, her old wedding dress, over her arm). The group included a child, who now jumped nimbly up onto the window ledge, then, clinging to the grooves with his fingers and toes, climbed halfway up the wall and, applauded by the grownups, dropped to the ground: end of trip, signal for return.

When the excursion bus, after describing a loop, drove away to the north, in the direction of the so-called Alpine Republic, it grew smaller, as though seen by tired eyes, began to buzz, and turned into a toy bus, in which the servile villagers, on their way from their mother country to their place of banishment, disappeared forever. How fine, how distinguished the lost band had seemed (even the veins on their hands a noble design), and how crude and profane, for all their southern verve, were the native Yugoslavs with their incessant cigar puffing, phlegm spitting, and scratching of private parts.

Crossing the empty square to the wall, I, too, began to look at it. Seen from the outside as I followed the grooves and leaned back to study the overhang of the roof, I was someone examining a building of the Imperial Age. But seen from inside myself, I raised both arms skyward and felt them to be stumps. Thoughts of cursing and spitting. Nothing that led upward; the wailing wall was imaginary; there was only a structure of horizontal parallels, no guidelines, only concave forms smudged with street dust, and spiderwebs on both corners of the house, both north and south, bordered by nothing. "My source?" Let the wall, seen from close up as a yellow flickering, crumble and cave in—on me, for all I cared. But is the southern flame-shaped cypress on one side, brightened by its cones, filled with the piping of the ubiquitous sparrows—ogling one another in their hiding places—are the oleander blossoms with their vanilla smell, nothing? "Oleander," "cypress," "laurel"—these are not my words—I didn't grow up with them—I've never lived near the things they signify—laurel, or bay, is known to our people only as a dried leaf in soup. And once again description only makes matters worse: if I wanted to describe a palm tree that meant something to me when I stood looking at it, the foreign word "palm" would get in the way; the tree itself with its scaly trunk and rattling fans would vanish. Over and over again I can name the snow, for instance, which at this moment is flying past my north and south windows; I can name the wind, the grass, the spruces, the firs (my father's lumber), geraniums, dill; but as soon as I, who grew up inland, try to evoke the sea, of which I have had such varied experience in the meantime, it escapes me along with the word "sea," which does not belong to me. It still makes me uneasy to speak of things that were mere names to me as a child. Having spent my whole childhood in the country, I even have difficulty in adjusting my lips or hand to things connected with the city, things such as a boulevard, streetcar, park, or high-rise building. Even to tell a story involving the tree I have come to love, whose bright-splotched trunk and dangling seed capsules have so often cheered me, shaken me out of my villager's lethargy, which to my mind embodies south and city in one, the plane tree, I have to shake myself to down a feeling of presumption—and the same goes for the cypress, which meant "nothing" to me and yet spoke to me, just as the apparent wailing wall with the sky above it gave me the command that I now give myself: "It must mean something. These things in a foreign country belong to me as much as the wayside shrines and the box trees at home."

Being able to think this over calmly meant that my plea was answered; as though it were only in the calm that inevitably followed my cursing that I could make myself heard. But what an absurd expedition to rediscover the law governing the naming of every object of experience. God bless you believers! Damned border person! Hasn't the other language a word for "one who wanders endlessly on the face of the earth," and the corresponding adage: "Strangers will slam their doors in your face"?

The afternoon bus had become a night bus long before it reached the Vipava Plain after the last pass and before the coastal highland of the Karst. Shining in through the window in the roof, the moon hardly moved; at last, the road was straight. With all the curves and detours, I had lost my sense of direction, which returned only at the sight of an inn sign at one of the stops, painted with a still life of fishes and grapes. Then, shining out of the darkness like a landmark, the first vine, immediately followed by the shimmering bottom rows of the great vineyards. The bus was full and all the passengers were talking at once; the driver was talking too, with the man beside him on a folding seat, the conductor (strange idea in a long-distance bus). At the same time a radio program blared from loudspeakers, folk music in time with the speeding bus, interrupted now and then by the news. Most noticeable among the passengers were the soldiers, jammed into the middle aisle and sitting on one another's lap in the rear seats. A horde would burst in at one stop, surge out at the next, and vanish instantly behind a stone wall. In the course of the long trip, not an hour passed without a rest stop. The driver would halt outside a restaurant or bar and announce the length of the stay: "Five minutes"; "Ten minutes." Each time, I got out and sipped the wine, which the natives drained at one gulp. I soon felt that I belonged now and forever to this squeaking night bus with its ripped seats and lidless chewing-gum-plastered ashtrays, in which all was speed and at the same time unhurried ease, and to these chattering, incurious, nondescript passengers, and as if I had found my itinerary for life. Haven't I now and then felt myself in security, after all?

When we piled back in after the last rest stop, a new soldier was with us, in uniform but without a cap. He was carrying a packaged rifle, which during the trip he held upright between his knees. He sat separate from the other soldiers, in the row ahead of me. The moment I looked at him, not at his rifle but at his profile, I knew that something was going to happen. To us? To the soldier? To me? All attention, I looked at the irregular crown of his head and in it saw myself from behind. Bristling close-cropped hair that yielded a double image of a young soldier and of a No one the same age. At last this No one would find out who he was. (Described by third parties, he had always known himself to be under- or overestimated, he had never trusted his own self-image—when he succeeded in forming one—and yet the question "Who am I?" had often become as urgent as a cry for help.) At last I had before me that protagonist of my childhood, my double, who, somewhere in the world, of this I was quite certain, had grown up along with me, and would someday turn up and be my true friend, who, instead of seeing through me as even my own parents did, would understand me without a word and acquit me, just as I would acquit him with a look of recognition or a mere sigh of relief. At last I was looking into an infallible mirror!

Anyone would have taken to that soldier's looks. He was quite inconspicuous, hardly distinguishable from other young men of his age. Still, he differed from the others by keeping to himself, though without rebuffing anyone. Nothing in his surroundings escaped him, yet he paid attention only to the things that interested him. Never a side glance, throughout the trip his head pointed straight ahead. He sat perfectly still, and his half-closed eyes with their rarely blinking lids suggested contemplative alertness. His thoughts could be far away, yet without a break in his fantasy he would calmly catch the parcel which, unnoticed by anyone else, had fallen from the baggage net just over his neighbor's head; before anyone knew it, he would put it back in the net and, as if nothing had happened, carry on with his peculiar blinking, which may have been connected with a mountain in Antarctica. It was chiefly his ears that expressed the young man's ability to keep track of the present along with the absent. While registering every sound in the moving bus, they were equally aware of the glacier that was calving at the same time, of the blind feeling their way in the cities of every continent, or of the brook flowing now as always through his native village. They had no distinguishing feature except that, thin, transparent, glassy, they protruded a little; nor did they move; my impression that they were unceasingly active, more active in fact than anything else far and wide, a reservoir of internal and external impulses, that this man was literally all ears, resulted no doubt largely from his statuelike posture, preserved throughout the trip, the posture of one who was waiting, and who was prepared for anything. Whatever happened, he would be ready for it; it might affect him, but it would not take him by surprise.

That was the trip. Of course, arrival in the garrison town dissipated the statue; all that remained was shifting images, different with every glance. In later years I have often been in Vipava, and have learned to know the village, the city, the "domain" at the foot of the "holy" Slovene Mount Nanos (a white limestone ridge, the hiker's companion on his way, turning and changing its shape, food for the soul, but also the trademark of numerous profane local products), along with the like-named body of water (several contiguous springs, seeping soundlessly from fissures in the rock, gather as soundlessly in pits, then suddenly merge into one roaring stream, which thunders amid stone houses and

rushes under one stone bridge after another, carries off
the branches of wild fig trees like a whirlwind, spreads
out foaming into the broad valley and there soon calms
itself). I have come to know it and the wine named
after it (white, grassy, almost bitter) as a place I would
like to see as often and as long as possible, as a means
of remembering that I can become the world and owe
it both to myself and to the world to do so. But on my
first visit I had eyes only for the soldier, whom, agitated
but at the same time cool and on my guard like a
detective, I could not have helped shadowing until *it*
happened. I have had various experiences since, but
none so amazing as this encounter with my double. Still,
there was no need for caution; I could have kicked the
heels off his shoes and he would still have gone straight
ahead without looking around. He still held his rifle in
his left hand, but now I attached even greater significance to his free right hand, the thumb and forefinger
of which formed a circle. First I followed him to the
movies, where for a time he was one of the laughing
crowd, then to a bar named Partizan, where the waiter
and myself were the only civilians. What did I represent
myself as? No one asked this question but me; the
soldiers ignored me.

The soldier sat down at a table with the others—a
mere listener. Then the images began to change. Sometimes when half asleep I see a face that changes its
expression as fast as a tenth-of-a-second clock face. That
is what my double, whom I didn't take my eyes off for
a moment, did now. Seriousness changed to merriment,
merriment to mockery, mockery to contempt, contempt
to pity, pity to indifference, indifference to desolation,
desolation to despair, despair to gloom, gloom to beatitude, beatitude to carefreeness, carefreeness to levity.

Sometimes he didn't listen at all, and allowed himself to be distracted by a fly or by the Ping-Pong players out in the corridor, or transported by the jukebox thundering through the room. But when he did listen, he became the supreme authority; soldiers came to consult him, and when one group turned away, others took their places. Even when he sat alone for a time, his comrades kept eyeing him as though waiting either for a sign from him, or, better, for a weak spot. Yes, he struck me as vulnerable, as a man whom the others were always watching, because he was many things in one but nothing permanently, because, one way or another, they were eager to measure themselves against him. Of this he was aware, as he had not been in the bus, and little by little he lost what had most distinguished him, his composure. After that, nothing came natural to him, and most unnatural of all was himself. Not only did his expression change constantly, but his posture as well; he would cross his legs, stretch them out, tuck them under his chair, experiment with resting his bent right leg negligently on his left knee, but not for long. Gone was the pleasing conjunction of presence and absence, which left the beholder with an impression of equanimity, attentiveness, gentleness, and above all of purity; instead, a disfiguring, repellent jumble of rigid eyes, red ears, crooked shoulders, and a clenched fist, which reached for a glass and knocked it over. Was I like that? Last stop, end of dream? My question changed to horror, horror to disgust, disgust to recognition of disgust (with oneself, with others, with existence) as the disease of our clan; the recognition turned to amazement, and there the process stopped. Who, then, was this double? A friend such as I had hoped for as a child? An enemy, the most terrible of enemies,

my companion from now to the end of my life? Even
the answer yielded a multiple-aspect picture: friend-
enemy, friendenemy-enemyfriend . . .

It was getting on to midnight and the bar was
emptying. The archaic Wurlitzer along the back wall
was surmounted by a glass dome in which, steeped in
a garish light, hoisted by a gripping arm, upright as a
wagon wheel, a black disk was turning; a sight so
overpowering that the music, whatever it happened to
be, could only be its accompaniment. The soldier and
I looked in the same direction, across the large, somber
room, and along with the circling wheel at the other
end—grooves shining in the light—I again saw the part
in the soldier's hair, as many-fingered as a delta.

We both left the bar, I once again following; we
stood on the deserted square, the far side of which was
bordered by a delegation of diminutive stone figures
dating back to the Empire, looked at the asphalt, our
ground; up at the moon, our domestic animal; to one
side, where there was nothing. O Slovene language
which (what other living language can show anything
of the kind?) has a special form for what two people do
or omit to do, the dual, there, too, dying out of late
and used only in writing.

On our way to the barracks we detoured along the
river, the distance between us steadily increasing. On a
sandbank I found not the soldier but only the imprint
of his rubber-soled shoes, stamped every which way,
often one print over another, all blurred, and spattered
mud around the edges, as though a fight to the death
had just taken place there.

I saw him next at one of the barracks windows. He
was in darkness, but I recognized him by his silhouette.

He was holding a spherical object that could have been an apple and could have been a stone all ready to be thrown. When he drew on his cigarette, his face, as familiar as it was uncanny, stood out for a moment, and again, as in the bus, I saw his searching eyes. But I thought of the eyes of a researcher who doesn't want to discover anything but wants, rather, to make something unknown, to pace off and enlarge the realm of the unknown.

It was a warm, quiet night. I crept into a parked bus that I found open. I stretched out on the back seat, which extended the whole width of the bus, again using my sea bag as a pillow; after initial discomfort, this was my place.

Still, I could not fall asleep. The bus creaked as if it were about to drive off, and the moon shone into my closed eyes, as glaring as a searchlight. I thought of the autumn and of my military service, which then for the first time became imaginable. All the strenuous things I had done in my life I had done alone; once I caught my breath, it was as though nothing had happened, for there is no satisfaction in solitary experience. But, it seemed to me, when soldiers had crossed a mountain range or built a bridge together, they assured one another of what they had done simply by stretching out by the roadside together, all equally exhausted. I wanted to wear myself out over and over again; exhaustion could be my only justification for not remaining a villager and not becoming a laborer.

But then I remembered the speech that a physical-training officer from headquarters had made to the country boys after our medical. Bouncing on one heel

and banging the desk with his fist, he had stared into
the distance and felt the icy tundra wind blowing over
the heroes' graves, filled his lungs with it, and bellowed
an interminable harangue at the weaklings and cowards
at his feet. After a last blood-curdling blast from his
iron lungs—"No finer death than death in the field!"—
all of us together had sung (often stumped for the
words) the national anthem, whereupon, clicking his
heels and touching the edge of his hand to his brow,
he had dropped through a trapdoor and disappeared
into his hell. For Filip Kobal this was his first encounter
with a dangerous lunatic, while for the other boys of
his age it was a natural phenomenon, under which, as
then in the "multipurpose" auditorium of the district
capital, they may be cringing to this day. But didn't the
experience of loneliness also give forth a liberating
light?

Reclining in the bus, I finally saw a road along the
seashore, and war had been declared. No one was left
in the world but two sentries, one on either side of the
bay, both far out in the water on small disks rocking in
the waves. And I heard a voice saying that it would
soon be made known why wars were the only reality in
the world.

When I awoke, I didn't know where I was. No fear,
only enchantment. The bus was standing still, but in a
strange, differently colored region; the moon, which
had been so bright, had become a pale daytime moon,
a cloud, the only cloud in the sky, small and round,
exactly opposite a small round sun. I had no idea how
I had got from one place to the other; all I remembered
was a frequent shifting of gears and bushes brushing

against the windows. The folding door was open, and outside I found the driver, who calmly—whatever happened now could only have a fairy-tale quality—bade me good morning and, as if I were an old friend, offered to share his breakfast with me.

The bus was on the open road, but from there a dirt track led to a village such as I had never seen before; that was where the passengers came from, all at once, apparently from the same house; this must have been the terminus. They moved in a body and were dressed for their working day in some other place, among them a gendarme whose uniform made him look like the Marshal. Once these people disappeared inside the bus, the village seemed uninhabited as it had been when I first saw it, a light-gray stone monument, one with the empty, windy country around it. But coming closer, I heard a radio, smelled gasoline, and met a dispiritingly ugly woman, who threw a letter into the usual yellow mailbox. Why did she greet me as "the son of the late blacksmith, returned home at last," invite me to sit on the bench in a courtyard sheltered from the wind by high walls, bring me a basin of water to wash in, sew the missing buttons on my jacket and darn my socks—unlike my brother, I'd never been capable of taking care of my clothes; the very first time I put it on I had torn a shirt that was as good as new after he had worn it for ten years—show me a picture of her daughter, and offer to put me up in her house? As though complying with the fairy-tale rules, I asked no questions, asked the name neither of the village nor of this airy, free country, whose border I had crossed in my sleep—a transition resembling none before or after—and where, for the first time on my journey, nothing looked familiar to me; even so, I knew I was in the Karst.

My anguished wonderment at being in a fairy tale soon gave way at the sight of the oilcloth-covered kitchen table, of a newspaper headline (no longer rendered obscure by the different language), of the cistern with a plaque on it saying that resistance fighters had used it as a clandestine radio transmitter during the World War. Nevertheless, the Karst, along with my missing brother, is my motive for writing this story. But is it possible to tell a story about a region?

Even in my childhood, the attraction of the Karst began with a mistake. I had always thought of the bowl-shaped depression in which my brother's orchard was located as a dolina, the most conspicuous feature of the Karst. This alone was what made our unimpressive Jaunfeld Plain interesting; the few bomb craters in the Dobrawa Forest were hardly big enough for garbage pits, and the Drava was so deeply hidden in its trough-shaped valley, navigated neither by ships nor by small boats (though perhaps at night by partisans in washtubs), that hardly anyone in the village of Rinkenberg was conscious of living near a real and important river. The hollow in the plain was the only "sight" in our part of the country, not so much because of its conformation as because it was the only one of its kind. Here, I thought with pride as a schoolboy, so far north of the Karst, an underground cave had collapsed, earth had slid in from above and created this fertile bowl. Where something had once happened, such was my childlike belief, something would happen in the future, something entirely different, and I looked into the supposed dolina with expectant awe.

Later on, by the time my history and geography teacher enlightened me, my years-long belief had done its work, and if my wanderlust had a goal, it was the Karst. Yet I formed no picture of it, except as naked rock interspersed with enormous numbers of dolina craters with red earth at the bottom. Once, when I was sitting at home on the window seat, I burst into tears at the thought of the unknown coastal plateau beyond all the mountains. Much more violent than the usual child's weeping jag, my outburst had the force of a shout. Those tears, it is now clear to me, were the first statement I had ever made unasked, the first that was strictly my own.

It is that same teacher's method that I am now adopting in my attempt to give my Karst story a beginning (though there is a voice within me which, in keeping with my tears that day on the window seat, would rather content itself with exclaiming "O Inspired Rock!"). True, he would introduce his favorite story, that of the Maya, with an exclamation, but he would go on to ground it not in any historical event but in the nature of the subsoil. This history of a people, so he said, was predetermined by the nature of the soil and could only be told properly if the soil played a part in every phase; every true historian, he contended, must also be a geographer, and he was firmly convinced that, given the geological configuration of a country, he could calculate its historical cycle and determine whether its inhabitants would even be able to form cycles or a nation. The Yucatán Peninsula, he went on, the land of the Maya, was also a karst, a hollowed-out limestone plateau, but differed from *the* Karst, from "Mother Karst," the high plateau above the Gulf of Trieste, from which all comparable phenomena in the world take their name, in being its mirror image. The concave craters of the European Karst became in the tropics convex towers and cones; while in Europe not only the scant rainfall but also the rivers flowing down from the interior are absorbed on the spot by the fissured limestone, the torrential Central American rain is spewed from holes in the stone and even produces fountains of fresh water offshore in the salty Atlantic (the Maya, in their day, would row out to gather it in their water jugs).

Thus, according to the teacher's theory, the people in the "Ur-Karst" must have been the mirror image of the Maya. Instead of climbing up to terraces when going to work the fields, they went down to the dolinas; instead of hiding in the jungle, their temples showed themselves plainly on bare hilltops; their grottoes served as refuges, whereas the Maya performed human sacrifices in theirs; all buildings, the huts as well as the temples of the Ur-Karst, chicken coop as well as mansion, threshold as well as roof, were built not of wood and corn husks but of solid rock.

Nevertheless, the people going to the bus stop on the dirt road, even the fat woman who took me in, and all who followed her, became in my memory a procession of Indians. Were they a people? Whether they were Italians or Slovenes struck me as of secondary importance. But the Karst had too few inhabitants to form a nation of their own despite the size of their territory and their many villages. Or perhaps they were not so few: in any case, I have never seen more than one, two, or three people at a time; anything resembling a crowd only at church, in the bus or train, or at the movies. There'd be one person in the graveyard; one or two (usually man and wife) hoeing down in their dolina;

three (usually war veterans) playing cards in the stone tavern. I've never seen them in a group or club, gathered for a common purpose; I have to admit, there was no lack of portraits of Tito, but I had the impression that, up there on the plateau, state power and political system had only a formal existence; so rare and small were the patches of fertile ground in that barren country that collective farming was out of the question. The field no larger than the shadow of an apple tree at the bottom of a dolina far outside the village could only be the property of an individual. Why, then, had the peasant uprising of Tolmin spread to the Karst, where the peasants had fought not only for the "old right" but "to be free at last," proclaiming: "We don't want rights, we want war, and the whole country will join us." Why in the years that followed were more schools built here than anywhere else? Why do I imagine that if the waiter from the Bohinj and the soldier from Vipava were to pass each other in a faceless crowd, they would recognize each other at a glance as displaced persons from their native high plateau, where the earth is still seen not as a modern globe but as a disk? Nevertheless: I have in the Karst encountered not a separate people (with a historical cycle) but a population for whom everything in all directions is either "below" or "outside," having a sense of community and place worthy of a metropolis, with differences between villages as between neighborhoods in a big city (in my brother's dictionary, the Karst was cited as the source of more words than any other part of Slovenia), except that every neighborhood is isolated in a no-man's-land an hour's walk from the next, and none is known as a slum or as a middle- or upper-class neighborhood. The roads (few of them named) leading to the villages all run uphill; on the

southern edge of the city you're likely to find a cedar
outside the church instead of the chestnut tree on the
northern edge, and on the western rim perhaps one
more Italian name on the monument to the war dead.
A poorhouse and a villa are equally inconceivable; the
only castle (erected by the Venetians, who, like the
Romans before them, deforested the region to build
their ships, so completing the work of making this a
region of water-swallowing stone) stands ruined and
forsaken on its rocky dome, the curved battlements of
the Venetian Republic incongruous ornaments in a
monotonous rectilinear landscape.

As for the "people," so designated and so fetishized
by my countrymen, I didn't miss them in the Karst, nor
did I find any banished king to feel sorry for; and here
there was no need to look, as I do in my home surroundings, for the marks of the defunct Empire, for
empty cow paths and blind windows; here the houses
can get along without pedestals and volutes. And looking
northward to where my Central European cloudbank
has piled up beyond Mount Nanos, I say: They not
only can but *should*!

Where, with my very first look around, did that sense
of freedom come from? How can a countryside mean
"freedom" or anything of the kind? In the last quarter
century I have many times carried knapsacks across the
Karst (where I've never seen anyone else carrying such
a thing), or satchels or suitcases. Why is it that I've
always felt as if my arms and hands were free? And
why is it that my very first day there I felt as if the sea
bag that I carried with me wherever I went had vanished
from my shoulders?

The only answer that occurs to me offhand is the

Karst wind (and perhaps the sun as well). It comes from the southwest, rises up from the Adriatic, and in blowing over the plateau becomes a steady breeze that one barely notices when sitting or standing. In this breeze one gains an intimation of the sea, which can be glimpsed only from a few almost secret spots in the Karst, a powerful, never-ebbing intimation, far more reliable and more effective than if one were actually on the shore or sailing along on the open sea. Undoubtedly, the feel of salt on one's face is imaginary, but not so the wild herbs by the roadside, the sage and thyme and rosemary (all smaller, hardier, more primitive—every leaf or needle the very essence of the spice—than in our kitchen gardens), the concentrated, almost African fragrance of the gnarled mint, the labiate blossoms of the flowering ash, the spruce resin dripping from the trees, the juniper berries that put one in mind of a strong drink (without threatening drunkenness). This is an upwind, not only because it rises from the sea but because it takes hold of you, ever so gently, under the armpits, so that walking, even in the opposite direction, you feel buoyed by it. Are there not, especially in the south, old coastal peoples whose most festive holiday it is to withdraw at certain times to the deserted high plateaus, where they worship the wind in secret and let it initiate them into the law of the world?

Time and again, the Karst wind has given me such an initiation—but into what law? Or was it a law? Once my mother told me about the moment of my birth: though her last child, after my brother and my sister, I had been overdue and had stopped moving inside her; then finally I was delivered into the daylight; after a first whimpering, I let out a scream, which the midwife called a victory fanfare. My mother may have wanted to please me with this story, but I was as horrified as if she had been talking about my death rather than my birth. Instead of my first moments, she had described my last; my throat tightened as though that fanfare were the signal to drag me to my execution. The fact is, I had often reproached my mother for bringing me into the world. I said this without thinking, it just popped out of me, not so much a curse as a reflex, first when my enemy was persecuting me, sometimes when suffering from chilblains or a mere hangnail, sometimes when I was just looking out the window. My mother took my plaint to heart and burst into tears, but I never really meant it; my moods of disgust and anger were opposed by something constant in my makeup, a sense of anticipation, which, however, found no expression because it had no object. The Karst landscape now provided me with such an object, and though it may have been too late, I could have said to my mother: I have no objection to being born. And what of the Karst wind? I have no qualms about saying: It baptized me then (as it repeatedly baptizes me now) to the tips of my hair. However, the baptismal wind gave names, not to me—wasn't "nameless" implicit in "joy"?—but to the strip of grass in the middle of the wagon track, to the sounds of the various trees (each called something different), to the bird feather floating on a puddle, to the perforated stone, the dolina of corn, the dolina of clover, the dolina with the three sunflowers, to everything in the vicinity. From that gently fanning wind I learned more than from the ablest of teachers: sharpening all my senses at once, it showed me, amid the apparent confusion of desert wilderness, form after form, each distinct from the last, complementing the last; it taught me the value of the most useless thing in the world and enabled me to give names to all things; without the Karst wind, I would not have been able to speak of the rather windless Carinthian village as I do; there would be no running inscription on my stele. Doesn't that amount to a law?

But what of the contrary wind, the ill-famed *burja* or bora from the north, an incessant frosty roaring over the high plateau; on such days, all fragrance was gone and one was completely stupefied. If you were out of doors on such days, you could go down into the dolinas, where you were sheltered from the wind and where, without fear of one another, the beasts of the Karst could assemble, a stocky little roe deer along with a hare and a herd of wild pigs; at the top of the bowl all the trees were bent at the same angle, while at the bottom the stubbly grass hardly trembled, the bean or potato plants hardly swayed. But even if you were out in the storm without the protection of a dolina, you had only to sit down behind one of the numerous stone walls, and from one minute to the next you had escaped from the icy blast into a quiet warm bath. In such shelters I had time either to think of the ancient battle in which the bora carried the arrows and spears of one army over the heads of the other, and stopped those of the other army in midflight; or else, as in the gentle west wind, I acquired a feeling for the things of nature and eyes for the works of man, stone walls as well as the little latticework gates leading through them, a pattern of parallel sticks cut from the bushes nearby, so thin, so bent, with such ample interstices that the prototype of a door, a gate, a portal could be discerned in them. Just as nature needs interstices in which to form crystals, so does the searching eye need them for the perception of prototypes. Even the path, which proceeded to lose itself in steppe grass and desert rock (the whole Karst was traversed by promising trails of this sort), was not just any path, it was *the* path, manmade, for, at least up to the level of the tilled fields, the oasis, and the dolina, it revealed a distinct triad of boundary walls, beaten roadways, and vaulted middle strip.

These visions, isolated in the wasteland—for there was no desert inn on the plateau—coalesced in the villages. The bora drove people together, showing that self-defense and beauty can be one. The north façades, stone dovetailed with stone, broken only by an occasional tiny gap, though many were as long as the nave of a church, curving gently away from the storm wind and thus elegantly evading it, and the farmyard walls, higher than many of the fig trees behind them, rounded at the top, with marble portals as wide as a princely coach (complete with the appropriate white edgestones and the monogram IHS at the top), enclose a square courtyard which, half blinded and deafened by the storm, one entered as one might enter a showroom, a bazaar full of precious objects, where the sawhorse harmonized with the vines, the faggots with the corncob wall and the piles of pumpkins, the wicker cart with the wooden balustrade, the tent of bean poles with the logs (put your hazel rod and the cloth with the mushrooms on the bench along with the rest, they will fit into the picture). The houses of the Karst, fortified castles seen from the outside, one interlocking with the next, surmounted by chimneys that are houses in themselves, were often all the more gracefully furnished inside; they need no barrel vaulting; it suffices that their outer walls are slightly curved to resist the wind.

In none of the houses there did I see what is called

a work of art. How, then, did it happen that almost every time I looked into a farmhouse—even when I merely passed by—my heart leapt up as at the sight of the most magnificent paintings, and that a stool, barely big enough for a small child's behind, positively invited me to sit down? One cannot fail to see how much of what the Karst people make reproduces the most essential feature of the landscape, the dolina or bowl; that all the slender baskets, basket-shaped carts, rounded stools, hay rakes with an arc at the end, seemed to celebrate the one fruitful thing in the country, Mother Dolina, and the belly of the wooden medieval Madonna in one of the churches shows the same rounding.

Without the furniture and implements of the Karst I would never have learned to appreciate the heritage of my forebears, neither my brother's orchard nor my father's roofs and cupboards. Up until then, I had always wanted to see our house adorned not only with a blind window but also with a statue in the blind window and perhaps beside the statue a fragment of a centuries-old fresco, and inside the house an ornamental carpet or a remnant of a Roman mosaic; my brother's accordion, in a corner with its mother-of-pearl keys, was in itself a magnificent adornment, and it was an event when every few years a paint roller impressed a fresh pattern on the walls. The inhabitants of our plain were reputed to be sober-minded, concerned only with utility and the greatest possible simplicity. But in this utilitarian simplicity I now recognized the effect I had felt so much in need of and which I had hoped to obtain from additions and embellishments: my father's table and chairs, crossed window bars and doorframe not only made the room inhabitable but radiated warmth and good taste; they not only bore witness to a careful hand but communicated something which the man, often brusque, irascible, unfeeling, could impart only in this way, and which alone was the whole man; embarrassed and intimidated by his person, I breathed easy in the presence of the things he made, and acquired an eye for proportion. The letters IHS over portals in the Karst became connected in my mind with the date my father had sawed into the gable of the wooden barn to provide air holes for the hay. I had always seen this pattern, which seemed burned into the weather-beaten, light-gray wooden triangle, as something unique, such as only a work of art can be, and after that I needed no other ornament in the house. Short as it was, the green track in my brother's orchard culminated in the Karst middle strip, which encompassed all the roads of the north and led straight as an arrow to the ocean horizon, just as the stone dam at the entrance to the orchard, which my brother had once built to preserve the topsoil but which had since then been reduced to a ruin, was now extended in the unbroken, even, curved boundary walls of the Karst—as though it had simply sunk into the earth up there in its alpine land and reemerged here not far from the sea, intact as on the first day, bedecked by the southern sun as though for a roof raising, nobler than before, thus making it manifest that our continent is traversed by the European counterpart of the Great Wall of China.

But could the objects in a countryside and the works of its inhabitants be relied on for any length of time? What of those windless days which occurred in the Karst at every time of year, worldless days without sun or cloud formation, without contour or sound or shimmering color on this disk of earth, when all life seemed to have died out overnight and I myself was the last creature that still breathed; and this forlornness was not as in other places confined to the moment of waking, was not dispelled by the crowing of cocks or the bells of high noon, all equally tinny, converging from the hundred sectors of the city (the television sets blaring in abandoned houses, the empty roaring buses, black rattletraps with drivers looking as if they'd been burned to a crisp long ago and were held together only by their uniforms). No dead satellite could be more lifeless on such days than a Karst that seemed covered by bone ash, the so-called karren fields where innumerable knife-sharp bones protruded and wouldn't allow you to tread on them. But that, too, taught me something which only a metropolis can teach a visitor; namely, a way of walking.

At home in the village, walking was just a way of going from one place to another as directly as possible, alert to every shortcut, every detour a mistake. Only unhappy, desperate people walked aimlessly. As though in a fit, they would suddenly rush out across the fields, blindly into the woods, through the creeper-clogged ditch, somehow down to the river. When somebody rushed off like that, it was to be feared that he wouldn't come back alive. When my mother was told of her illness, her first impulse was to run out of the village; we had to lock her up in the house, and she almost tore off the door handle. The sauntering step of the idler and the resolute stride of the hiker were also alien to the villagers, who wouldn't have dreamed of climbing mountains or stalking game for sport; a hunter always came from somewhere else. You walked to work or to church, with a possible stop at the bar, and you came home; the legs, by and large, were a mere means of locomotion; the body sat stiffly on top of them, and it was only in dancing that its parts worked together. Except in a cripple or an idiot, a conspicuous gait struck the people of Rinkenberg as pretentious; in their Slovene dialect they called it "stirring up wind while walking."

Thus, walking, too, stirred up wind in the Karst when there was none, and with it all brooding ceased. That great thought, more liberating than anything else in the world—"Friend, you have time"—turned me outward again. And it was having time that taught me my particular gait, a way of walking which, with every rise of the shoulders, every swing of the arms and turn of the head, was designed, not to catch the eye of any particular person, but to carry me deeper into the country (just as sometimes the peculiar gaze of a person or animal can make one look around to see what amazing thing this other may be gazing at, which, to judge by his elated expression, must be something pleasant). One feature of walking in this way is that from time to time the walker himself, involuntarily but quite consciously, turned around, not for fear of a pursuer, but out of pure delight in moving about, the more aimlessly the better, with the certainty of discovering a form behind him, if only a crack in the pavement. Yes, the certainty of finding a way of walking, of being all walker and thus becoming a discoverer, set the Karst apart from the few other free regions I have known. True, the impulse to "get up and go" has proved itself elsewhere, in dried streambeds as on roads leading out of big cities, in bright daylight and (even more effectively) in pitch darkness—but I have never set out for the Karst without the conviction that there I would not only fill my lungs with air but also encounter something new. So firm is my trust in the power of the Karst wind to bring someone who has time for it an archetype, a primordial form, the essence of some thing, that I am not far from speaking of piety; the baptismal wind blows as on the first day, and the walker, caught up in it, still feels himself to be a child of the world. Obviously, he won't barge ahead like a tourist; he will slacken his pace, turn around in circles, pause, bend down: discoveries are usually to be found below eye level. No need to drive himself; before he knows it, landscape and wind have given him his due. Conscious of having time, I never hurried in the Karst; I ran only when I was getting tired, and then it was a slow run.

But didn't my finds relate to a time long past, weren't they the last remnants, leftovers, shards of something irretrievably lost, which no artifice could put together again, and which took on a radiance only in the imagination of a childish finder? Was it not the same with these elementary particles as with the dripstones which in their grotto, in the flickering candlelight, give promise of a treasure, but, once broken off and exposed to the daylight, are nothing more in the hands of the thief than grayish stone potatoes worth less than any plastic glass? No. Because these finds could not be carried away; these were not things you could stuff into your pockets, but rather their prototypes, which impressed themselves upon their discoverer's inner self by letting him know where, unlike the dripstones, they could flower and bear fruit, telling him that they could be removed to any country whatever, most enduringly to the land of storytelling. Yes, if, in the Karst, nature and the works of men were archaic, they were so in the sense, not of "Once upon a time," but of a beginning. Just as I've never thought "medieval" when looking at a stone roof-gutter but, as never in the presence of a modern building in either country: "Now!" (heavenly thought), so at the sight of a dolina I never thought of the prehistoric moment when the earth suddenly settled, but time and again saw something future rising from the empty bowl, swath by swath, a primal form that merely had to be held fast. Nowhere, up until now, have I found a country which with all its divers components (not excluding a few tractors, factories, and supermarkets) struck me, like the Karst, as a possible model for the future.

One day I got lost—as I often did on purpose, impelled by curiosity, thirst for knowledge—on a pathless steppe interspersed with thickets and loose rock. Before long, I had no idea where I was; there were no detailed maps (apart from secret military ones) of this frontier region. As usual once you take a few steps across country, the wind brought no sign of life from any of the hundred villages, no barking of dogs or children's screams (which carry the farthest). For hours I struggled on, obstinately, zigzagging around dolina after dolina, which lay fallow, their red-earth bottoms strewn with pale boulders, between which here and there great trees shot up, their tops level with my feet. Here I could speak of wilderness and here I learned that this whole waterless country was an immense desert, merely pretending, by putting forth vegetation, to be fertile, a land in whose gentle breeze many an inexperienced traveler had doubtless died of thirst, possibly hearing to the last the soft sound of flowering ash trees, while—supreme irony—a clear mountain stream may have been flowing not far away. For a long time I had heard no sound of a bird (actually, even on the fringe of the villages, one seldom heard a peep); I hadn't even seen a lizard or a snake. After struggling through a dense thicket, I found myself hopelessly lost in the waning afternoon, at the edge of an immense dolina, as big as a football stadium, barred at the top by a tall, dense palisade of virgin timber, which I noticed only at the moment when I had forced my way through to it. The dolina seemed uncommonly deep, partly because of the walled terrace ledges that divided the evenly gentle slopes; on every level a different green, varying with the crop grown on it, the most intense green shining from the uncultivated empty ring of ground at the bottom, more magical than the floodlit grass of an Olympic stadium. Of all the dolinas I had seen thus far, only one or two were in use. Here, to my amazement, I was confronted by a whole population. On every one of the terraces from top to bottom, there were small fields or gardens, all with several people working on them. They worked with consummate slowness, there was charm even in the way they bent over or squatted with legs spread. From the whole wide circle arose, softly and evenly, what has remained in my ears as the pervasive sound of the Karst: the sound of hoeing. On the vineyard terrace I saw only standing persons, half hidden by a roof of foliage, tying vine shoots to strikingly crooked posts or spraying them, while in the tiny olive field only hands were visible. On every level I saw at least one tree, on every level a different variety, among them, though it seemed almost inconceivable so far from any running water, such meadow trees as elders and willows (of which I once heard an inhabitant of the Alps say, "They're no trees, just junk; now take a spruce or an oak, *that's* a tree"). I distinguished so many different greens that I could have given each a different name; all of them together, dear Pindar, would have added up to a new Olympian Ode. The last light seemed to gather in the dolina as in a lens, which sharply outlined and magnified the details. This enabled me to notice that no wall was like any other; one consisted of two tiers of stones, the next had a layer of earth between the two, while what looked like a boulder at the edge of the bottom circle was a conical hut, built of stone blocks growing smaller toward the top, with a keystone in the shape of an animal's skull and a roof gutter, from which a long pipe led down to a rain barrel; the hole in the ground was no accident, it was the entrance to the "casita" and had a lintel the length of an eagle's wing with a sundial scratched into it.

Now a stooped figure is coming out, a boy with a book in his hand; he straightens up to become a man, and I am again immersed in the wood smell and summer warmth of my father's shed; I've gone directly to the fields from school, and I'm sitting there at the table with my homework, barefoot; in one corner I see a napkin-covered basket with bacon and bread in it and a jug of cider; in the other the dead nettle plant from which, though there isn't a breath of air in the room, cloud after cloud of pollen puffs trace on the floor the pattern of sunlight formed by the cracks and knotholes in the boards. I hear the voices of my parents as they work toward each other from the two ends of the field (monosyllabic greeting, followed by an exchange of words—Father cursing, Mother laughing at him—all leading up to their afternoon snack together in the field); I play solitaire, listen to the rumbling of the thunder, stretch out on the bench, dream, am awakened by the droning of a hornet as a whole squadron of bombers comes shooting out of the mist, eat an apple, the skin of which shows the bright image of the leaf that shaded it, and on the stem the shriveled blossom, go outside, straighten up in my turn into a grownup, a man, take a deep breath, and recognize the hut as the center of the world, where the storyteller sits in a cave no larger than a wayside shrine and tells his story.

So friendly was the room into which I now looked down, and such power rose up from it that even the Big Bang, so it seemed to me, would be powerless to harm this dolina; both blast and radiation would pass over it. And looking ahead, I saw the people at work in that fertile bowl at my feet as the remnant of mankind after the catastrophe, starting to farm again. Yes, this place tucked away in the dead desert struck me as a self-sufficient farm where the earth still fed its inhabitants. And no thing in the world had been lost; true, abundance was a thing of the past, but there was at least one viable exemplar of every basic substance and of every basic form. And since every necessity was both on hand and a rarity, it showed the beauty of the beginning. And precious was not only what was at hand but also everything that could be seen, the grain in the fields as well as the shadow on the stone—and in this imagining I was reinforced by the people of the Karst, for, living in want and menaced by the void since time immemorial, had they not a hundred names for a corncob, an ear of wheat, a bunch of grapes, and just as many for every one of their few birds, all sounding like nicknames (though neither "throttler" nor "mocking-bird," neither "wolf's milk" nor "kitchen bell"* was among them), as though the many names were intended to fence the thing in and preserve it. The image of this plantation sunk into the Karst earth, protected from any enemy incursion, secure from atom bombs, under the open sky, as a goal to strive for is still with me, nor have I forgotten the tootling of the transistor in the stone hut—its prize song. Image? Chimera? Fata morgana? No, image, because it is still in force.

Although my time in the Karst was entirely made up of walking, stopping, and going on, I never had my usual guilty conscience about being a good-for-nothing idler. My sense of freedom every time I arrived some-where was not the consequence of a release. I had no feeling of detachment; on the contrary, I knew that I had at last become *attached*. Didn't I secretly say to myself immediately after crossing the threshold of the plateau: "Now *we* are here!"; didn't I see my solitary self in the plural? Just as my father's daily chores, plugging a hole, unwinding a rope, chopping kindling, were for a time rituals designed to make my mother get well, so I imagined that by investigating the Karst I was serving a cause, and not only a good cause but a great and glorious one. Many motives were at work together: to prove myself in my own way worthy of my forebears and to save what they stood for; the desire to

---

* "Throttler" = shrike; "wolf's milk" = spurge; "kitchen bell" = pasqueflower. [Trans.]

be the disciple—his only one, no doubt—my teacher so
longed for; an irresistible feint in my duel—a strange
obsession—with my enemy; to earn the love of the most
lovable of women precisely by going into the desert and
enduring all manner of hardships—but transcending
all this there was something that I call the desire or
appetite for an orgy. What sort of orgy? I have always
believed in dreams, so I shall answer with the story of
a dream. In a glass cage, intercity bus and funicular in
one, the same passengers kept meeting time and time
again for a group trip to the Empire of the Karst. Not
a single word was spoken. The crossing was marked by
a shimmering, towering Indian mountain, which any
child could have climbed, under the bluest of skies. This
was the last stopping place. Our group was now complete. From here on, nothing could be seen of the
country; there was only the vehicle, moving as quietly
as if it were standing still, and with it the passengers all
at a distance from one another, no two together. True,
this one and that one were known to me from the street;
the man at the ticket window, "my shoemaker," a
shopgirl; ordinarily we greeted one another, but once
we boarded this vehicle, none of us gave any sign of
recognition. Instead of exchanging glances, we sat motionless, united in expectation. The more often we set
out on this trip, always from a busy station accessible to
all, the more festive became the light in the cage.
Rapture awaited us at the end of our journey, in the
heart of the Empire, the greatest joy a human being
could know; the bliss of being gathered into nothing-
ness. Of course it never happened, we never even came
near it. On the last journey, however, one of my traveling companions smiled at me, so giving himself to be

recognized and at the same time recognizing me. An orgy of recognition: instead of rapture and confluence, shock and oneness, with the verb corresponding to "orgy" translated as "to yearn steadfastly," and the place name *Orgas* as "Land of Demeter" or "Meadow" or "Fruitland."

In reality, the Karst is a land of want and the crossing is not marked by a strange Indian mountain. It's long after the border before you notice, to your surprise, that you are climbing and that something has changed. First the wind, then the flowing brooks are gone, there's not even a trickle of water; dark pines have replaced light-colored deciduous trees; conversely, the brown clay and gray-black stone, so long the companions of your journey, have abruptly given way to a massive chalk-white, covered by only the scantest of sod; stubbly pasture has taken the place of succulent meadows. Though the plain down below is still near, the towns and rivers still clearly visible—you can even see an airfield with a steeply rising jet plane and a drill ground with hopping soldiers—the plateau is as quiet as if you were far out on the open sea. At first you had sparrows flying ahead of you; now it's butterflies. It's so still that you hear the sound when a butterfly chasing a falling leaf grazes the ground with its wings. You hear last year's dry pinecones crackling, one high overhead, the next at eye level, and so on, a graduated sequence, a constant chirping until sunset, while from this year's fresh pinecones the resin drips steadily—dark spots in the dust of the path, getting larger and larger.

Stick to the path; even so, you won't meet anyone; the dark men escorting you to the left and right, fanning out now and then into the pale savanna, are juniper bushes. Hours, days, years later, you will be standing at the foot of a white-flowering wild cherry tree, with a honeybee in one blossom, a bumblebee in another, in the third a fly, in the fourth a beetle, in the sixth a butterfly. What glitters like a water hole on the path up ahead is a silvery snakeskin. You pass long rows of woodpiles, which on closer scrutiny prove to be camouflaged ammunition dumps; you pass round heaps of stones, which turn out to be the entrances to underground storehouses; if you touch them with your foot, the rock is cardboard. At every step, grasshoppers will squirt up at you from the middle strip of grass. A dead black-and-yellow salamander moves almost imperceptibly along the wagon rut. When you bend over, you discover that it's being carried by a procession of dung beetles. After all these tiny creatures, the first animal of any size, a white-faced fox, a dormouse wrapped around a branch, will look to you like a brother. That breeze in the solitary tree over there—a moment later you feel it on your face. Your resting place is a cave; to explore it you won't need a lamp, because daylight shines in from the far end and through a few holes in the roof. Water will drip on your overheated forehead, and in a niche there are quail's eggs, not bullets but stone balls, rounder and lighter in color than in any mountain stream. As you go your way, you shake them in your hand, and their smell, quite unlike the stinking heaps of bat's dung, will bring the widely ramified clay chambers of the Karst caves into your room as long as you live.

Now you can go naked; the wild sow, one enormous black-brown hump, which bursts grunting and panting out of the underbrush on your right, followed by two piglets no bigger than hares, and crashes on into the underbrush on your left, has no eyes for you. Your feet stamp the ground, your shoulders soar, and your eyeballs touch the sky.

At your next resting place, you hear a long-drawn-out croaking of frogs in the stillness; a delicate monotone in the desert. You will go toward it and come to a puddle that takes up a long stretch of the path. The water is clear, a single feather is floating on it. The deep-red bottom shows a hexagonal crack, the hoof prints of two deer, any number of arrow-shaped bird tracks pointing in all directions, a cuneiform inscription that asks to be deciphered. You find its counterpart in the sky where a patch of azure blue the size of your big toe appears in the middle of honeycomb clouds— speaking of cirrus clouds, the Karst people say: "The sky is blossoming," just as they say: "The ocean is cascading," where we would speak of a rough sea. The feather will blow away, the wind will raise a swell in the long puddle. Stretch out on the bank, using your bundle of clothes as a pillow. You'll fall asleep. One of your hands will pass between your knees and take root in the earth, you will hold the other to one ear (the torn corners of our eyes, brother, come from listening). In your dream you will hear the pond spoken of as a lake, and see a boat with your hazel stick as a rudder in the rushes by the shore; a dolphin will spring up from nowhere, its back bent into a dolina by the weight of the fruit it is carrying. Your sleep will be short but refreshing, and you will be roused by raindrops on your ear—there can be no gentler awakener. You will get up and dress. You will not have been out of the world, but for once wholly in it. And sure enough, a duck from the savanna will come flying low, land gently on the puddle, and swim back and forth in front of you; and a cow that has lost its way will stop and drink. You will let the rain fall on you. It will make you so calm that butterflies will alight on you, one on your knee, another on the back on your hand, while a third will shade your brow.

As you continue on your way through the Karst, the sky will turn blue again (only the usual black pileup to the north, beyond Mount Nanos, will give you a feeling of "weather"); the trees will sough clockwise, each with its own music, and you will understand why, when the rustling of the oak trees was especially loud and penetrating, the ancients heard it as the voice of the oracle. You will take notes, and the scraping of your pen will be one of the most peaceful sounds under the sun. It will lead you back to the hundred villages and city quarters (the Karst movie house, the Karst dance hall, the Karst Wurlitzer), which, when night falls and the sky is again overcast, will be recognizable in the soundless wilderness by the circular glow here and there on the cloud cover. There you will be regaled with white bread, Karst wine, and that special ham that will give you an aftertaste of your walk with all its smells, from the rosemary of the middle strip to the thyme at the foot of boundary walls and the juniper berries of the savanna. You will need no more for the present. And one day in the course of your years, you will come to the place where the sunlit patch of fog on the horizon far below you will be the Adriatic; and knowing the region as you do, you will be able to distinguish the freighters and sailboats in the Gulf of Trieste from the cranes in the shipyards of Monfalcone, the castles of

Miramar and Duino, and the domes of the basilica of
San Giovanni di Timavo. And then, at the bottom of
the dolina at your feet, between two boulders, you will
discover the ultra-real, many-seated, half-rotted boat,
rudder and all, and involuntarily, taking the part for
the whole (you will then be free enough), name it ARK
OF THE COVENANT.

A time will come of course when walking, even walking
in the heartland, will no longer be possible, or no longer
effective. But then the story will be here and reenact
the walking.

On that first trip, I was in the Karst for barely two
weeks, on just about every day of which I was someone
else. I was not only a seeker after traces but also a day
laborer, a bridegroom, a drunk, a village scribe, a
member of a wake. In Gabrovica I saw the bell that had
fallen out of the church tower; it had dug deep into
the ground and children were playing on top of it; in
Skopo, emerging from the wilderness, I frightened the
solitary old woman hoeing in the dolina; in Pliskovica I
went into the only church that was unlocked on week-
days, and sketched the black-and-yellow hornet that was
crawling over the altar cloth; in Hruševica, brookless
like every other village in the Karst, I marveled at the
stone statue of St. John of Nepomuk, who as a rule is
found only on bridges; in Komen I stepped out of the
movies into a moonlit night, brighter and more silent
than the Mojave Desert, through which Richard Wid-
mark had just fought his way; got lost in the chestnut
forests of Kostanjevica, home of the only tall trees in
the Karst, where the ankle-deep rustling of past years'
leaves and the crunching of nutshells underfoot can be

compared to no other sound in the world; strode through the freestanding portal of Temnica, which from the edge of the footpath leads out into the steppe and wilderness; bowed my head in Tomaj before the house where died the Slovene poet Srečko Kosovel, who when hardly more than a child celebrated the curative properties of his region's pine trees, stones, and quiet paths, and—at the end of the war, when the alien monarchy ended and Yugoslavia began—entered ("clanked into") his capital city of Ljubljana, where he, the brother of my waiter and my soldier, made himself the herald of the new era and, perhaps in the long run not brazen enough for that sort of thing, too much affected by the "stillness" (*tišina*, his favorite word) of the Karst—see his conspicuous jug-ear—was not long for this world.

An Indian squaw took me in, mistaking me for the son of the dead blacksmith in the next village. I never disabused her. She spoke with such certainty that I was glad to be taken for someone else, and in the end I was playing with conviction the role of a man who had returned to his home country after a long absence. When I spoke of incidents in my Karst childhood, the old woman shook her head and nodded by turns, a reaction that could only signify amazement at a story both incredible and credible. As I soon noticed, I took pleasure in my fabrications, all of which, to be sure, had some basis in fact and had to be both consistent and imaginative. Such invention was a part of my joy at being for once free; invention and freedom were one.

Yet this woman was the first person by whom I felt appreciated as well as recognized. In the eyes of my parents, I was always "too serious" (my mother) or "too dreamy" (my father); my sister, it is true, regarded me as the secret ally of her craziness; my girlfriend's gaze when we met was often rigid with an embarrassment that melted only when at last—and I didn't always succeed—I smiled at her from deep inside me; and even my teacher, who understood everything, once said—when in the course of a class excursion I had suddenly run off across the fields and into a thicket, just to get away! to be alone!—well, when I came back, he said with an undertone of irrevocable judgment: "Filip, you're not right in the head." The squaw of the Karst, on the other hand, gave me, heartwarmingly, the trust at first sight which, after a few days in her house, became an expectation, a wordless refutation of my constant self-disparagement ("I'll never amount to anything"); an acquittal as surprising as it was reasonable; encouraging and protective; and so it has remained. And it was she who, before I had even opened my mouth, gave me credit for a sense of humor. At home I had often forbidden my mother to laugh, because her laugh reminded me of the way women guffawed when men were telling dirty jokes, and my school friends thought I was a killjoy, because when someone was telling a joke I'd point out a scratch in the tabletop or a loose button on his jacket just as he was coming to the punch line. Only my girlfriend, when we had been alone for a while, would sometimes manage—addressing me in the third person as in eighteenth-century dialogues—to cry out in astonishment: "Why, he *is* an amusing fellow!" But whereas she had reacted to some little random remark of mine, my way of looking and listening was enough for my present hostess, and whatever she showed me or told me, she did it with the joyful gusto that an actor absorbs from an alert audience—so perhaps the so-called sense of humor is nothing other than a happy alertness. Though once, toward the end of my stay—the two of us were sitting at the kitchen table and I was just looking silently out into the yard—she said something different. Something contradictory? Or complementary? She said that I had inside me a great, silent, passionate tearfulness; it wasn't just there, it was raging to get out, and that was my strength. She went on to tell me that once in Lipa, when it was almost dark in the church, a man had stood there alone and erect, and sung the Psalms in a firm yet delicate voice. What had struck her most was that he had held his eyes shut with the fingers of one hand. She stood up to act out the scene for me, and we both burst into tears over that absent man.

Now and then I helped her with her work. Together we hoed the little family dolina, dug the first potatoes out of the red earth, sawed firewood for the winter. I drafted her daily letters to her daughter in Germany and whitewashed the daughter's room (as though she were ever going to come back). At the bottom of the dolinas, as I found out, there is no breeze to dry the salty sweat. It was the same as at home, all physical exertion cost me an enormous effort; once started, to be sure, I often warmed to the task, but even then the thought of getting it over with was never far from my mind. I can't say that I showed more skill than in the past, but since the old woman, quite unlike my father, left me alone, she opened my eyes to my mistakes; in the main she showed me what I was like and how I moved when I anticipated having to start working.

She taught me to recognize that I had seldom been at hand when there was work to do, and had almost always had to be called from some distant hiding place. But my seeming laziness was in reality a fear of failure. I was afraid not only of being no help but, worse, of getting in the way and making things harder for the person I was supposed to be helping, afraid that a false move of mine might ruin the work of a day or even of a whole summer. (How often my father would summon me to his workshop with loud oaths, and then after my very first hammerblow send me away without a word.) When I was supposed to fit things together, I forced them; when I was supposed to take them apart, I wrenched them; when I was supposed to put things into a box, I stuffed them; regardless of who might be holding the other end of the saw, I couldn't adjust to his rhythm; if someone handed me a roofing tile, I dropped it; and the moment I turned my back, my woodpile would start sliding. Even when there was no need for haste, I hurried frantically. I might seem to be moving fast, but my partner, with one slow movement following from the last, was always done before me. Because I tried to do everything at once, there was no coordination. In short, I was a bungler. If I was expert at anything, it was at making mistakes; where another needed one blow of the hammer, I missed my aim so often that whatever I was working on would be either damaged or broken; if I'd been a burglar, I'd have left dozens of fingerprints on the smallest object. I realize now that the moment I was expected to make myself useful I would go into a daze and have eyes for nothing more, least of all for my work. I would blindly shake, tug, kick, rummage, until, often enough, both work and tool were in pieces.

I was deafened by what I took to be other people at work, the gentle swishing of the scythe or the soft sound of potatoes tumbling from a crate into a cart; I ceased to be receptive—though I must have heard it— to the sound I loved best, the rustling of the trees, different from one variety to another. A chore could be ever so easy—"Take the milk cans down to the stand," "Help me fold the sheets"—and before I knew it, I'd be out of breath and red in the face, my tongue would be hanging out. Suddenly, regardless of whether I was walking, reading, studying, or just sitting there, my body ceased to be all of a piece, my torso lost its connection with my abdomen; bending over to gather mushrooms or to pick up an apple, for instance, became a marionette-like jerking instead of a smooth movement.

Most of all, I came to understand while working with the Karst squaw that my problem began the moment I was asked to help, even if I had plenty of time to prepare myself. Instead of getting ready, I would brace my fingers and arms against my body as though in self-defense, and even arch my toes in my shoes. Perhaps, I thought, my horror of physical labor came from the look of my parents' bodies. Even as a child, I had been ashamed of my father's flat chest and sagging knees, and of my mother's heavy buttocks, and during my last two school years the poise and elegance shown by lawyers, doctors, architects, and their wives, even when asking one another how their children were getting along, made me still more ashamed of my parents.

And now my recognition of what was wrong with my way of working helped me to control my body, so that with each passing day I enjoyed my daily labor more. Watching the old woman, I learned to pause in my movements; the transitions, at first forced and spasmodic, became easy and natural, and my working place, the red earth or the white wall, appeared to me in full color. Once when I started home with a handful of *terra rossa*, I even found a fragrance in it. Command to myself: Get away from your father.

One day my hostess took me through the wilderness outside the village to a field that was not in a dolina, a rarity in the Karst. Enclosed by a low wall, it was overgrown with weeds, but the light-red earth shone through and furrows were still discernible. Access was barred by a wooden stile, beside which there were stone steps leading over the wall. At the bottom of the wall there was a square opening, through which rainwater could drain from the path into the field. Here the woman stretched out her arm and said: *"To je vaša njiva"* ("This is your field").

I climbed over the wall and bent down to the earth, which was loose, as if it had been plowed not too long before. The field was narrow and slightly vaulted in the middle, ending in a row of fruit trees, each of a different sort. Had the old woman simply made a mistake, or was she pulling my leg? Or, as I had asked myself when I first laid eyes on her, was she mad? When I turned around to her, she was laughing all over her broad face, with the little delighted sounds of a very young girl—a laugh deserving of the name.

Not only the squaw, everyone in the hundred villages treated me like an old friend or the son of an old friend; I had to be something of the kind, because strangers never came to the Karst. And just as Odysseus was often full of wine, so I, his son, in the course of my search for him, once lay on the ground dead-drunk. At home, we never drank anything stronger than cider, and that only when thirsty; and I had always steered clear of my roistering classmates, especially after one of them, on our class trip to Vienna, after groaning and retching for hours in his upper bunk, had spewed a great flood of sour vomit down on me. The mere smell of liquor, the peculiar glug-glug, and worst of all its devastating effect on the drinker's behavior, repelled me. Up until then, I had barely tasted wine; but here in the Karst, in the open air, in the sun, in the spicy wind, I began to—what was the word again?—to savor it. I drank swallow after swallow, putting down my glass after each one. Often after the very first swallow I felt at one with the world and at the same time, as though the two pans of the scales were at last evenly balanced, experienced a sense of justice. Afterward, I saw more clearly, dreamed astutely, perceived connections, took pleasure in precisely staggered intervals, which composed a well-ordered globe, rotating clockwise; I had no need to rotate with it. Incredible that anyone should slander wine as "liquor."

That's the way it was when I drank by myself. But in company—remember that companions flocked to Telemachus—I usually lost all sense of proportion. I didn't guzzle, I didn't drain my glass at one gulp as the others often did, but I did down my wine without tasting it, and I especially liked to stay on until everyone else had gone home. One night—a cock was already crowing, my companions had all drifted away—I got up from the table and noticed that for the first time in my life I was drunk. I took a few steps and collapsed. I lay face down in the grass, unable to stir a finger. I had never felt so close to the earth; I smelled it, felt it on my cheek, I heard the roar of the underground river, the Timavo, and laughed to myself as though I had accomplished something. Later, when they lifted me up by my arms and legs and carried me home, I was able to give my accomplishment a name: at last I, who had all my life set so much store by independence, was making a display of my helplessness; at last I, who had always made a secret of my indignation that no one came to my assistance, had allowed myself, unresisting, to be helped—a deliverance, in a way.

The next day I was told that my drunkenness hadn't even been noticed; I had only been "very stiff and proud"; my eyes had "sparkled"; I had "told them all off"; and in the end I had made a speech about grammar, especially the "suffering form" (the passive voice), which did not exist in the Slovene language, for which reason the Slovenes should stop feeling sorry for themselves and calling themselves "the people of suffering."

In the course of those weeks, I saw someone die for the first time in my life. On my way through a village, I was almost knocked down by a woman who came running out of a house. She threw herself down in the street, writhing, screaming, and hugging her knees as though in labor. They laid her on a bench, where she stretched out, letting her head dangle. I have never heard such deep, agonizing sounds as her last breaths. For a time, her lower lip moved as though to suck in air; it slowed and stopped; it seemed to me in the deafening silence that her lip had written something, and that her writing had now run its course. I felt as if I had known her, and her family took it for granted that I should watch through the night with them, though with all their mumbling of rosaries I could hardly keep awake. The corpse's face was smooth; but all her suffering was still written in her distorted, shriveled eyelids. Strange what veneration I felt for this unknown dead woman; strange my vow to be worthy of her.

It was such a promise of fidelity that I then, as a twenty-year-old in the Karst, celebrated as my "wedding." This happened on a Sunday after Mass, in the walled-in yard of an inn, under a broad-leafed mulberry tree. I was sitting there over a glass of wine when a small mixed group in holiday dress came through the gate—in a festive mood, as though still enfolded by the blessing of the "Go in peace." The children ran or hopped about in a ring, the grownups kept turning to one another, a one-legged man and a dwarf woman completed the round. After greeting me, the stranger, with a natural grace, the men by lifting their hats, the women with a smile, they sat down at a long table requiring several tablecloths, which billowed in the Karst wind and reddened with the hours, not only from spilled wine but also from the soft fallen mulberries. In this company—they talked a good deal, though none raised his voice or held forth—I noticed a young woman who remained silent the whole time, a mere listener, her eyes almost unblinking in their attentiveness. At last, she turned her head slightly and looked at me. Her face revealed a gravity as the listener became a speaker, and it was I she spoke to. No smile, no crinkling of the lips, only two eyes, looking at me and saying: "It's you." I was so startled that I almost turned aside, but I stood up to her gaze, recovered my composure, and fought through to a seriousness that came as a kind of shock, as though I had for two decades been leading an unworthy life, without soul or consciousness, and had just now, thanks to my meeting with these eyes, come to myself and the world. Yes, that was a world-shattering event; this was the face of my wife! And to this woman I was now wedded, in a meticulous, gradual, solemn, exalting— *Sursum corda!*—ceremony, presided over by the Karst sun and the sea wind and perceptible only to the two of us. Without a word or gesture, keeping a diffident distance, joined in the look of our eyes, without a witness, with no other document than this story. Eye to eye, in intermittent jolts, we came closer, until you were I and I you, adorable woman under the mulberry tree. From no other woman has a secret voice come to me saying: I am yours.

Twice during that time, I glimpsed my brother. My night in the railroad tunnel had taught me that the essence of a place is often best perceived through another, neighboring place—that of the torture tunnel through the tunnel I pioneered. Thus, I deliberately avoided the Karst villages mentioned in my brother's letters, in the belief that I would be able to get a clearer idea of them by studying the neighboring villages. Places whose names I heard day after day in my childhood, places which I approached but never got to, had much more of an aura than those that I actually knew. On the eastern edge of the Jaunfeld, for instance, there was the hamlet of Sankta Luzia, consisting of little more than a church; my parents often mentioned it because that was where they were married. I was never there, but I circled it on all sides, and because my perception of it amounted to no more than the edge of a field seen from the woods, church bells in the evening, or the crowing of a cock, I have a feeling to this day that there, hardly an hour's walk from home, a new world began. And so it was that in a sunny hour, once again outside an inn, in just such a neighboring village, I saw my brother stepping through the door to the yard. He appeared to me in a crowd, because the parish was celebrating its saint's day and people had come from the whole Karst plateau. Did he really come in? No, he just stood in the doorway, and despite the constant coming and going, an empty space formed around him which, as it seemed to me then, brought back his time, the years preceding the World War. My brother was younger than I, his twenty-year-old descendant, and this was the last holiday of his youth. He was wearing the jacket with the wide lapels, which since then had been handed down to me, and his deep-sunken eyes—both had their sight—projected an infinite dream. Though I remained seated with my companions, I also had the impression that I got up to make sure it was he. His eyes were the blackest black, the black of the elderberries that had ripened all about during those summer days, and shone with their living light. Neither of us moved; we stood facing each other for an eternity, at a distance, beyond reach, unapproachable, united in grief and serenity, merriment and forlornness. I felt the sun and wind on the bones of my forehead, saw the festive bustle on both sides of the dark passage with my brother's image in it, and knew we were in midyear. Holy forebear, youthful martyr, dear child.

The other time, it was an empty bed that spoke to me of Gregor. I often took the train in the Karst, and sometimes I just hung around one of the extraordinary stations. Most of these were in the wilds, far from the villages, and could be reached only by paths without signposts. Some of them, at night, were plunged in total darkness; the only way to find them was to feel your way slowly, if possible under the guidance of a native. But then, just before the train pulled in (even if I, as happened often enough, was the only prospective passenger), the whole area lit up, revealing a large, diversified building, as big as a factory and as majestic as a manor house: light-colored gravel, fountains under a cedar tree, resplendent façades covered by clusters of fragrant, light-blue wisteria, heraldic blind windows. Here again, the upper floor was inhabited, and while the stationmaster sat in his office downstairs at the brightly lighted switchboard as in a space capsule, his wife upstairs passed window after window on her way from room to room. Time and again, the telephone bell jangled in the desert stillness. And then at last came the imperious signal that a train was coming. Since the tracks were encased in the Karst rock as in a canyon, the rattling and rumbling of approaching trains reverberated as in a subway tunnel. As often as not, the station bell began to ring immediately after the great clatter in the wilderness, as though the train would instantly shoot out of its grotto; but then it would lose itself in one of the countless looping ravines and much later, when I was beginning to think my ears had deceived me, I'd hear it again from an unexpected direction, accompanied by the repeated melodious tooting of a departing overseas steamer, and then at last

the thundering organ of the Karst would come bursting
out of the pitch darkness, whistling, roaring, trilling,
booming in every register, recognizable by the triangle
of eyes at the front of the locomotive, the one in the
forehead going out as it came closer. Almost more
fantastic were the freight trains passing through, with
their massive, unlit cars, sometimes of varying length,
among them a string of empty undercarriages with
jutting rods, an apparently endless procession, with a
powerful pounding, hammering, knocking, and drum-
ming, leaving behind it in the void a wake compounded
of metallic smell, buzzing and singing, as though the
world of men were unconquerable.

On such a night I was waiting in one of the Karst
stations for the last passenger train. As I still had a long
time to wait, I sat in the grass by the cedar tree, walked
up and down on the gravel, sketched the grain of the
table in the waiting room with my stick lying on top of
it, looked at the green-painted cast-iron stove, the pipe
of which was missing. Outside, under the stars, the
shadows of bats. A warm night as usual; the smell of
the wisteria, more delicate than that of any lilac. I still
remembered the plan drawn up under the Empire to
build the Slovenian stretch of the Vienna–Trieste line
underground, cutting through the caves of the Karst.
As I was pacing back and forth, I passed a lighted
basement window that I hadn't noticed before. I bent
over and looked down into a big room, comfortably
furnished with bookshelves all along one wall, and a
bed. The bed was made up and the coverlet turned
down, as though ready for someone to get into it; the
bedside lamp cast a circle of light on the pillow. So that
was where my deserter brother was hiding. I stepped

back and saw a woman's silhouette in one of the tall windows of the upper story. She cared for him; he was happy in her house.

I saw myself at a goal. My purpose had been not to find my brother but to tell a story about him. And another memory took hold of me: in one of his letters from the front, Gregor speaks of the legendary country, which in the language of our Slovene forebears is called the "Ninth Country," as the goal of our collective longings. "May we all meet again someday," he wrote, "in the festive Easter vigil carriage on its way to the wedding of the Ninth King in the Ninth Country. Hear, O Lord, my prayer!" I now saw a possible fulfillment of his pious wish: in writing. Just as I would transpose the empty bed from the basement of the station, so also would I move the thermometer on the outer wall of the station, fashioned by a Vienna instrument maker at the turn of the century, the three-legged stool next to it, the vine pattern of the waiting room, and the chirping of the crickets to our family home. Thus, my train approached, meandering through the wasteland, roaring, fading, welling up, headlights shining from the gullies and ranging far ahead, then itself coming into sight, the locomotive halting at last, chinks and joints traced by all the lights inside it, a crackling, fabulous monster, bursting with power, and the cars full of people returning home from the cities, from the sea, from abroad, snoring, working crossword puzzles, knitting.

As bright as were my waking moments, by night as by day, so dark were my dreams. They banished me from my supposed paradise and flung me into a hell where, without other company, I was the damned and the tormentor in one. I was afraid of falling asleep, because my guilt at not being at home with my people figured in every dream. I kept seeing our home but never a human being in it. And the house was a ruin, the roof had caved in, the garden was all weeds and jumping snakes; not a sign of my family, only their plaintive, receding voices, or a few spots in the dust, as of melted ice cubes. From time to time I woke up, an outcast. In time even the sun, the baptismal wind, my walking, the piles of onions drying under my window (they reminded me of fishermen's nets) lost their power, and I decided from one minute to the next to escape homeward.

Not until I was on my way did I regain the calm needed for the last station on my Yugoslavian journey. I went to Maribor (or Marburg) to look for my brother's school. But there was no need to look for it; from the train window I saw the hill with the chapel on it, familiar to me from the prewar photo. Even when I came closer, nothing seemed to have changed in the last quarter of a century; nothing had been destroyed, and nothing new had been built. Only the big painted apiary had fallen into disrepair; in its place there were bright-colored little boxes on the grass among the fruit trees. I walked around the spacious, airy grounds, looked at the palm tree outside the main building, the Virginia creeper twining in and out of the clefts in a poplar, the initials that had grown immoderately with the smooth bark of a hornbeam, the many steps leading up to the door of one of the smaller buildings ("there he sat in the evening with the others"), and wished when I was done that this activity, this plantation, this admirable country had been my seminary. Time and again, as I climbed to the top of the vineyard—the clay under my feet became thicker and thicker—I felt the need to bend down, to reach into the earth, to collect, to take something with me. Keep it, keep it, keep it! Bits of coal were encrusted in the slate. I dug them out and today, a quarter of a century later, I am drawing quavering black lines on my white paper with them: You have earned your keep.

The chapel was on the top of a rocky hill. It was as devastated as the agricultural school down below— the treetops, the shimmering leaves of an olive grove, the brown tile roofs, each patterned like a secret script— was unscathed. It was like entering the roofless, deserted house of my nightmares. The altar stone was shattered, the frescoes smeared with the names of peak stormers (the barest vestige of the celestial wayside-shrine blue); on the floor, buried under rubble and boards, the statue of a Christ fallen from the cross, lying headless, his crown of thorns replaced by barbed wire; the threshold cracked by tree roots. I wasn't alone for long; a young man came and stood beside me; he folded his hands, and after that I heard only his breathing; later, a group passed by, part of a factory excursion, I thought. Rather randomly they turned aside to the chapel, stood with legs spread in front of it, considered the ruin and the young man at prayer with an utterly uncomprehending, unbelieving look, which as they went on became a frozen collective grin, not so much of mockery as of surprise and embarrassment. Only then was I jolted out of my timeless dream and given a clear picture of history, the history at least of this country, and what I wanted was not "no history" but a different history, and the one worshipper struck me as its embodiment, its nation, erect, alert, radiant, composed, undaunted, unconquerable, childlike, vindicated.

Outside, on the façade, I found my brother's name. In capital letters, in his finest handwriting, he had scratched it into the plaster, so high that he must have been standing on the ledge: GREGOR KOBAL. That had been the day before he left the school to go back to his hostile country, where he was awaited not by a loved one but by a foreign language and a war, in which he would be fighting against the boys who had become his friends over the years. I was surrounded by silence; in the grass a crackling of rain, produced by the wings of a pair of dragonflies.

Late in the afternoon, I was in the town below, standing on the big bridge across the Drava. Less than a hundred kilometers east of my native village, it had become a different river. At home, sunk in its trough-like valley, hidden by rank growth, its banks almost inaccessible, its flow almost soundless, it emerged here in Maribor as the glittering artery of the plain, visible from far off, flowing swiftly, with a wind of its own and sandy coves here and there, which offered a foretaste of the Black Sea. Looking at it through my brother's eyes, I thought it regal, as though adorned with innumerable pennants, and its ruffled waters seemed to repeat the empty cow paths, just as the shadows of the railroad cars on the parallel railroad bridge seemed to repeat the blind windows of the hidden kingdom. The rafts of prewar times drifted downstream, one after another. Close-of-business bustle on the bridge, more and more people, all in a hurry, their eyes widened by the wind. The globes of the lamps glowed white. The bridge had those lateral salients which at that time I looked for in all bridges. The endless flow behind me shook the ground under my feet; I clutched the railing in both hands, until I had transposed the bridge, the wind, the night, the lamps, and the passersby to myself. And I thought: "No, we are not homeless."

The next day, in the homeward-bound train, a sudden storming of the compartments as though this were the last possibility of flight. (And yet only the pilot trains had been canceled.) Wedged between strange bodies, as though armless and legless, even my chin dislocated for fear of contact with other chins, I felt more and more cheerful as time went on. In this crowd I was at home. Even my cramped position gave me a certain sense of well-being. And I wasn't the only one. One man, for instance, though no better off than I, found room to read a book; one woman was knitting; and a child was eating an apple. Then, as we neared the border, I had the whole car almost to myself. A dreary luxury.

It made me happy to see Austria again. I realized that even in the Karst I had missed the Central European green; it was in my blood. It did me good to see Mount Petzen, "our mountain," again from the familiar side. And the mere thought that, after struggling for weeks to get my tongue around a foreign language (especially when tired), I was again in the midst of my familiar German made me feel sheltered. In the sunset sky on the way from the border station to the town of Bleiburg, I saw a second, deeper sky, wreathed in many-colored clouds and as resplendent as a glory. And as I walked,

I vowed to be friendly while demanding nothing and expecting nothing, as befitted someone who was a stranger even in the land of his birth. The crowns of the trees broadened my shoulders. No sooner in the small town than I found myself in the hustle and bustle of local society, which, so it seemed to me, had been going the rounds during my absence, on the lookout for a victim. And now the unconscionable enemy was back again. Even on my way into town, they overtook me in their cars and informed others of my arrival. The commando was waiting for me, disguised as evening strollers. The leashes dangling from their necks were really rifle slings, their whistling and shouting at every street corner were only a stratagem to surround me. But that day they were powerless against their adversary. I looked them in the eye as though telling them about a country so remote that they either greeted me in spite of themselves or looked the other way, at the Plague Column, for instance, and when they turned around to see what their dogs were up to, it was mainly out of fear, as much for themselves as for their four-footed friends. And indeed, with every step through the town, my hatred and disgust redoubled, until, instead of a heart in my breast, I felt only a boiling and bubbling. I wanted to spew fire at them as they marched, swaggered, minced, crept, shuffled, as they grinned at one another from the protection of their cars, as their voices (beside which the creaking of a branch, the scraping of a woodworm was delightful), malicious, whining, sancti-monious, wiped the blue from the sky and the green from the earth, and every word they said was a cliché, one more hateful than the next, from "remove from circulation" to "a poem or something." These people were neat and clean, well barbered, fashionably dressed, they had gleaming badges on their lapels, they were scented with this and that, excellently manicured, shoes shined to a high polish (the first thing I noticed was that their welcoming glances were aimed at my dusty shoes), and yet the whole procession had a guilty, hangdog ugliness and formlessness. That, it seemed to me, was because of their colorless eyes; the colors had been washed away by their stubborn malignance. I asked myself if that couldn't be my imagination and in that same moment I was struck by a sidelong glance which, helpless with rage at being unable to kill the first comer, shifted to the next. And then it occurred to me that not a few members of this crowd were descended from people who had tortured and murdered, or at least laughed approvingly, and whose descendants would carry on the tradition faithfully and without a qualm. Now the revanchist losers were marching along, sulking because peace had been going on too long. They had probably been busy all day, but their work had given them no joy—at best, they had enjoyed sending someone to jail or giving someone something to remember them by; so they hated themselves and were at war with the times. I thirsted for a Christian glance to which I could have responded. Idiots, cripples, madmen: breathe life into this procession of ghosts, you alone are the bards of the homeland. But it took an animal, appearing to me as the symbol of all the small-town persecuted, to comfort me and show me, the villager, a vast country with steppe, seacoast, and sea beyond this petty state. Suddenly, in the dusk, a hare appeared at the edge of the town, ran straight across the main square, zigzagging between cars and pedestrians, and vanished, unnoticed by anyone. Hare, heraldic animal of the harried and persecuted.

I followed the hare and came to a bar. Up until then I'd known it only from hearsay as a meeting place for drunks. At that bar I came across members of the philistine procession. Sitting among the derelicts and misfits, they were transformed. As if they had finally changed to civvies, they radiated friendliness and trust. They were burning to tell stories, and not only about war. In my memory I hear them give vent to a strangely gentle lament and song of thanksgiving about the sweetness of childhood and their stolen youth, and I see them as isolated fugitives and exiles. They had suffered at being involved with the philistines; they dreamed of being accepted, not by some high-class club, but by this noisy gathering. Noisy? Maybe they all talked at once, but it seemed to me that I understood every word. My dominant impression of this smoky cavern was one of transparent order, regulated by the inter-action between individual exuberance and an urgent collective seriousness. When the waitress appeared, a path was made for her, and the cook's hand with a plate in it would pop out of the mist as from a cloud. The sound of cards being shuffled suggested the flapping of dogs' ears and the whirring of birds' wings, and rolling dice supplied the music. Whenever the telephone rang, everyone looked up, hoping it was for him. The pro-prietress behind the bar had eyes that nothing could surprise. A peasant woman came in, incongruous in those surroundings, put a bundle down beside her son, who had slumped over the table—his washing that she had just done—ordered a glass of schnapps for herself, and proceeded to drink it very slowly. The man beside me asked me who I was and I told him. We were standing shoulder to shoulder. At the back, one looked out on a vegetable garden, and in front on the street. Cars sped by and a dark bus overtook a lighted one as in a free and nameless metropolis.

Homeward across the deserted plain, under a starry, moonless sky. As always when I approached my village after being absent for any length of time, I was excited. My mood was positively festive. I was drawn to my village as by a magnet, but I commanded my heart to beat slowly. The night was unusually mild for that part of the country, and the only sound was the barking of dogs here and there, which put me in mind of a big estate, though big estates were a thing of the past. There were so many stars (even the spiral galaxies were clearly visible) that the constellations merged, suggesting a cosmic city girdling the earth. The Milky Way was its main thoroughfare, and the stars on the edge of the city bordered the runway of its airport; the whole city was getting ready for a reception. I thought of the mountain on Mars, almost twice as high as Mount Everest, with the suburbs of the heavenly city on its slopes.

Back to earth. In the distance, the few lighted windows of the village of Rinkenberg seemed embedded in Rinken Hill, as though the hill were a prehistoric formation converted into a modern housing complex. At the crossroads with the milk stand, which marked the village boundary, I was glad to be weighed down by my sea bag with the heavy books in it, for without it I might have flown away. The roofs of the houses, especially those made of weather-beaten shingles, had a silvery sheen that made them look like pagodas. The

roadmender was a silhouette standing in the doorway
of his porter's lodge; his greeting to me, in a quavering
voice that seemed to come from a great distance and
didn't wait for an answer, had the liturgical sound of a
muezzin's exhortations high up on his minaret. Outside
a house at the end of an avenue of fruit trees far from
the road, a whole family of villagers were sitting on a
bench, knee to knee, plunged in a consensual silence,
as though the essence of a summer night had been
translated into human terms. I made a detour to the
graveyard: no fresh graves (until my subsequent homecomings, but then more and more of them). On the
way to our house, a neighbor woman passed me, mute,
with arms half upraised; a poignant sign of helplessness.
I couldn't tell whether the buzzing in my ears came
from the ventilator at the inn or from my blood.

There was light in our house, in every room. My
sister was sitting by herself on the bench outside. Her
eyes recognized me but gave me no greeting. In her
face I saw a sorrow so pure that at first I mistook it for
sublime happiness. But it came to me later on that she
was sorrowing not so much for her dying mother as for
her lost love, decades old, undying. "Grieving dancer."
Never had I seen a more beautiful woman. I wanted to
kiss the sorrow away from my sister's face, and—
overwhelming event!—I was aroused by compassion;
but she was untouchable.

Under the espaliered tree, the pears were lying in
piles, unharvested, rotting. I went to the window and
saw my parents lying on the bed. Side by side, holding
each other tight; his leg on her hip. They rolled this
way and that; I kept seeing first one face, then the
other. For once, I saw my hard father softened by
weakness, at last holding his wife in his arms. Over his

shoulders he was wearing the purple robe beneath which he had stretched out on the church floor during those Easter vigils; my mother's eyes were wide with the fear of death; she wanted her husband's embrace to keep her alive. —Years later, where the bed had been, I found a thriving rubber plant in the warm sunlight; it was then that I remembered that scene of suffering most keenly and foresaw a time when the rubber plant would again give way to a human being in pain.

A hundred times I walked back and forth in the night outside the house before I was able to go in to those two people whom, grateful to have been born, I loved. And to this day I have no image of what followed, but only something hot and huge—my empty hands in which to gather, now and forever, the looks of my parents' eyes.

I have often mentioned numbers in this story, numbers of years, kilometers, people and things, and it has cost me a struggle every time, as though numbers were incompatible with the spirit of my story. For this reason I shall speak once again of my fairy-tale-writing teacher. He is now retired and I go to see him now and then. He has set up a garden outside the town with a hut in it, where he sometimes spends the night. The pale historian's face has again become the sunburned face of the geographer. His mother is still living, but she is very old and, as often as I've been there, I've never once laid eyes on her; I hear her talking to her only son through some doors, no longer in words as before, but with tapped signals, which he interprets by counting them. He has given up writing fairy tales; their place has been taken by counting. Even in childhood, he was always counting to himself, often unconsciously. In those days he had thought it an ailment. But then, on his solitary expeditions in the jungle of the Yucatán, he had discovered that counting, now consciously, his steps and breaths could be a means of survival; it had often helped him in danger, a more powerful "medicine" than any fairy tale, and more effective than any prayer. Now in his old age he felt increasingly allergic to the public notices and posters that were taking over, and more at ease with numbers, even price tags and the luminous figures in gas stations. Hadn't the archaic poet said that number was more powerful than any ruse. Counting, he said, moderated him, slowed him down, regulated him, and cared for him; in counting he recovered from the world of headlines. His sacred numbers were those of the Maya: 9 and 13. Nine times he scraped his shoes before coming into the house; he would not start work until thirteen birds had flown across the garden; now and then he needed a nine-minute breather; and he walked around in a circle nine times thirteen times before going to bed.

So much for the old man. At the end of this story, however, though I may die before the day is out, I find myself in middle life; I look at the spring sun on my blank paper, think back on the autumn and winter, and write: Storytelling, there is nothing more worldly than you, nothing more just, my holy of holies. Storytelling, patron saint of long-range combat, my lady. Storytelling, most spacious of all vehicles, heavenly chariot. Eye of my story, reflect me, for you alone know me and appreciate me. Blue of heaven, descend into the plain, thanks to my storytelling. Storytelling, music of sympathy, forgive us, forgive and dedicate us. Story, give the letters another shake, blow through the word sequences, order yourself into script, and give us, through your particular pattern, our common pattern. Story, repeat, that is, renew, postpone, again and again, a decision that must not be. Blind windows and empty cow paths, be the incentive and hallmark of my story. Long live my storytelling! It must go on. May the sun of my storytelling stand forever over the Ninth Country, which can perish only with the last breath of life. Exiles from the land of storytelling, come back from dismal Pontus. Descendant, when I am here no longer, you will reach me in the land of storytelling, the Ninth Country. Storyteller in your misshapen hut, you with the sense of locality, fall silent if you will, silent down through the centuries, harkening to the outside, delving into your own soul, but then, King, Child, get hold of yourself, sit up straight, prop yourself on your elbows, smile all around you, take a deep breath, and start all over again with your all-appeasing "And then . . ."

About the Author

PETER HANDKE was born in Griffen, Austria, in 1942. After graduating from a Catholic seminary in 1959 he studied law at the University of Graz. Handke first attracted public notice in 1966 when he delivered an unprecedented attack on contemporary German writing at a seminar at Princeton University. That same year saw the publication of his first novel, *The Hornets*, and his first stage success, *Offending the Audience*. With Wim Wenders, he wrote the screenplay for the film *Wings of Desire*, released last year. His other works include *Weight of the World* (1984), *The Left-Handed Woman* (1978), and *A Moment of True Feeling* (1977)—all of which are forthcoming from Collier Fiction—as well as *Across* (1986), *Slow Homecoming* (1985), and *3 × Handke* (1972 and 1974), which are now available from Collier Fiction. He is widely regarded as the most important postmodern writer since Beckett. Peter Handke lives in Salzburg, Austria.

*Available from your local bookstore, or from Macmillan Publishing Company,
100K Brown Street, Riverside, New Jersey 08370*